DARK OF THE CURL

BOOK TWO IN THE SURF MYSTIC SERIES

PEYTON DOUGLAS

CASTLE BRIDGE MEDIA
DENVER, COLORADO, USA

SURF MYSTIC:

DARK OF THE CURL

© 2022 Jason Henderson

All rights reserved.

ISBN: 979-8-9859702-2-7

CASTLE BRIDGE MEDIA

Denver, Colorado, USA

castlebridgemedia.com

Cover photo by Sesha Reddy Kovvuri/Unsplash

PROLOGUE

1968 —Vietnam

THE ROAR OF THE SURF OUTSIDE Frannie Cohn's hooch was so loud that it blotted out the rest of the world and permeated her dreams. It was so loud that at first, she didn't even hear the helicopter. But there was a tiny piece of her brain that was accustomed to the sound of the whirlybirds, that listened for it even when her bones were so tired that she slept like the dead, dead, dead.

A helicopter was close. She awoke and immediately felt the coolness of the concrete through her blanket against her hip. As she turned slightly, listening, her shoulder grazed the bottom of her cot. She slept under her cot because it was darker there, shielding against the bright lights of the compound outside... and because errant rockets were a problem in Danang.

For a moment, as she looked across at the wall, there was still just the sound of surf. Her roommate, Truly Turner, turned over and looked at her in the dark, a pair of glimmering eyes in dark skin.

Just surf. Just waves. She held a silencing hand up off the concrete.

1

Her body didn't relax. It never did anymore.

Then, rotors. Not loud yet. The PA system blared, and Frannie rolled out from beneath her cot as Truly did the same.

"What time is it?" Truly asked as she pulled on a pair of green cotton pants.

"I don't know," Frannie said as she moved to the sideboard by the front flap of the shelter. She snatched up her watch, read it as she clasped it. "Three-forty-five." Truly groaned and Frannie agreed.

The walls of the thatched hut swayed with the wind, though in Frannie's mind the swaying was caused by the helicopter, reminding her that it was almost here. She wasn't moving fast enough. She pulled on her khaki uniform pants and zipped them, leaving the belt unclasped. She skipped the socks and stuffed her tiny feet into her boots, then stuffed her pants down the sides, looping the laces twice around the outside of the boots and tying them off.

No time. Every second was blood that flowed. Every second was awaiting death. She grabbed her hat off her cot.

As Truly and Frannie ran out of the hooch, Frannie was pulling her uniform blouse on and left it open over her t-shirt.

The PA blared again as they stepped out onto the concrete expanse dimly lit by swaying, dangling electric lights.

—TRAUMA SURGEONS TO THE OPERATING TENT INCOMING TRAUMA SURGEONS TO THE OPERATING TENT INCOMING—

Across the yard was the operating tent, which was bursting with light. Between them and it, an array of other officer's quarters, supply tents and all manner of Army crap lined the concrete. Giant palm trees swayed over the green walls and directly behind Frannie and Truly, beyond a line of trees, was the beach. It occupied Frannie's ears and mind all the time. That was where the helicopter pad was. They surfed sometimes, and sometimes she could pretend the helicopter pad didn't exist.

"Three-forty-five," Frannie said as she scanned the dark blue sky. "It's gonna be a long morning."

She spotted a couple of surgeons running madcap to the OT but Frannie and Truly had another stop first. The nurses ran for a nearby supply tent as the rotors got louder. Truly tore open the doors and they each grabbed a gurney and turned around.

Frannie began running with the gurney towards the beach. For a moment, with the light rack bouncing on her hip as she ran for the water, she was in another place.

Her hat nearly flew off her head as she and Truly reached the edge of the pad because the chopper was coming down, a UH-1 "Iroquois" Medevac. The waves beyond the craft were glistening blue in moonlight. The side of the chopper was open, and she could see men inside: it always reminded Frannie of one of the windows in the abdomen she'd seen in nursing school, in old books. Researchers had built glass windows into the bodies of some subjects so they could see the organs working inside. It was so unnatural and exposed. There was nothing natural here, either. Everything had bloody insides and she could see them all.

When the helicopter had settled, Frannie slapped her gurney sideways into the bed of the chopper. Two medics moved fast, hauling a soldier onto the rack, and hopping out to spin the gurney towards Frannie. One of the medics grabbed the front of the gurney, shouting a few words to Frannie that she didn't hear over the rotors, but that amounted to you take the end. As the guy started to run, the gurney with the soldier on it bounced forward and the four-eleven nurse caught the end and started running with it, she and the medic humping back through the trees.

Frannie took the time now to look at the wounded soldier. He was unconscious, pale skin specked with blood. She saw a mass of blood on his chest and the blanket over his lower body was soaked. And it was obvious that he was missing a left foot, but she couldn't tell how high the damage went. She was itching to pull the blanket back to see how much of a leg there was. "What am I looking at?" she shouted.

The medic looked back. They were reaching the compound. "GSW through the shoulder."

"And the leg, above the knee?"

"Yes, above the knee."

"You do the tourniquet?"

"Yes," the medic said.

The soldier on the gurney groaned and Frannie looked at his face. He was probably eight or nine years younger than her, probably just out of high school. His eyes were still closed. He would be drugged up and completely disoriented. His name tag said CLANCY.

"Hey Clancy, we got you," she said, although of course he couldn't hear her yet.

Just out of high school. She couldn't hear the waves, but she did hear them in her mind. Why was she thinking about it so much?

They got the kid to the operating tent. Truly came in right after with her own gurney and her own accompanying medic and they got the busted kids onto the operating tables and said goodbye to the medics.

They watched the medics hustle back towards the chopper and the insanity that would bring them right back again.

Frannie turned and hurried back to the operating table where the kid Clancy was lying, the blanket gone now. He was in terrible shape. The surgeons started moving around her and in between her own rapid reports and the setting up of intravenous lines, she leaned forward. She put her hand on the kid's shoulder, blood welling up over her skin.

He stared into her eyes, and she said what she always said.

"Hey. My name is Frannie and you're in an American hospital."

"No," the kid groaned, "No no, I'm far, I'm far."

"No," she said again. "You're in an American hospital. And we're going to take care of you."

They took care of him for hours. And Clancy did not die, although it was one of those mornings where it could have gone any which way. There were more choppers all day and it got a lot worse, and at some point, Frannie became an automaton of efficiency and blood.

About four in the afternoon, it was suddenly quiet, and she stepped onto the baking hot concrete expanse. She picked a tree to sit under on the periphery and slid down like a dead thing. As she breathed, she struggled to get a pack of cigarettes out of her blouse. Her hands had started shaking from exhaustion.

She barely had the pack out when one of their Vietnamese attendants ran up. Frannie peered up at her from beneath her cap.

"Lt. Cohn!" The woman—Americans tended to call them mama-sans—was tinier even than Frannie, and she bowed as she stopped.

"What's up?"

"He back," she said, pointing towards the beach. "You say tell you if he back."

Frannie sat forward and got up. She started walking down the path to the beach.

Her senses were tingling now, the shake gone, but she was still bone tired, and sometimes she thought she would never feel rested again.

He back. She had been hearing word of a figure ever since she had gotten to the hospital at Danang. And she told the mama-sans, "tell me if you see it again." A tall figure. A strange figure. A figure from a dream or a nightmare, she could no longer remember the difference.

When she reached the beach, she could hear distant choppers and see hundreds of miles of jungle—but what caught her eye was beyond the waves. She took off her hat to shield her eyes with her hand.

Almost at the horizon, a sailboat, and on it, an impossible figure. Frannie's body dropped to its knees in the sand, and she wasn't sure whether she would laugh or cry. Instead, she reached outward with her mind, her will, to the sailor.

I've been wondering when you were going to show up.

CHAPTER 1

Summer 1959

CHARLOTTE NAGLE AND HER YELLOW sheltie dog Lucy followed her boyfriend Tom across the slippery stones. She was hoping Tom knew where he was going, but he was usually good for that. The sun was going down however, making it a little more of a challenge to see where to place each foot. Luckily, the shore would never plunge into true blackness—the moon and stars reflecting off the waves cast the sand, rocks, and cliffside in a shiny blue glow.

"Look, there it is!" Tom stopped and faltered a little, reaching back for Charlotte. She grabbed his hand and came to stand beside him. Lucy danced around her feet, jumping here and there out of the way as water splashed up occasionally against them. "There's the pirate tower," he said, pointing a little way up the beach next to the cliff. "Against the sky."

She adjusted her glasses with her free hand and looked where he was pointing. Her blue canvas beach bag swung at her hip, and she caught it as she righted herself.

"It really is a pirate tower," she laughed. She could see it more clearly as her eyes adjusted: a sixty-foot-tall brick turret with a pointy top just like in the movies.

Tom said, "I think what it really is, is just a very nice staircase for some rich guy up there." He pointed up to the top of the cliff. "There's a mansion up there."

They approached the tower steadily, Tom goofing off as he jumped from stone to stone in his sneakers. Finally, they reached the bottom of the tower. It looked like the entrance of a dungeon in a Robin Hood movie. There was a rounded entrance of brick and peeling plaster, and paint that faded beyond any color but gray. The door was an iron gate, red and rusted. The boy and girl pressed together and looked through the iron bars. Inside the staircase wound its way out of sight. "It looks like a King Arthur movie," Tom said, which was very similar to what she had thought.

"We used to come here when we were kids," he added. Tom had actually grown up here in Laguna Beach, while Charlotte still lived fifty miles inland. But now that she was sixteen, her parents let her go on dates all over, including Tom's home of Laguna. They had met when Charlotte was on a family outing to Pacific Park in Santa Monica and had been together every opportunity they could get for six months.

Tom put his hands on the bars and started to pull. He tried several times, his chest muscles rippling, until finally the iron gate started to creak loudly, and slid out, scraping the stone floor of the entrance. When he got it open a couple of feet, he stood back with satisfaction. "Come on!"

They went inside the tower and were enveloped in echo. Charlotte looked down as Lucy tried the steps gingerly with her paws, until finally the dog was satisfied with their height and started darting up them. Occasionally Lucy would turn around to look back down and yap at them. The wind howled all around and whistled through the tower, which was not much wider than the Charlotte and Tom. Tom gave her a kiss, his blonde hair brushing against her glasses. And then they began to climb.

The place smelled damp and musty as her shoes scraped against the grit on the stones.

About halfway up, they reached a landing and stopped, sitting down next to a tall, narrow window that looked out to the sea. They snuggled together with the dog rubbing up against Charlotte's hip. Tom put his hand on the bars looking out the window. "It never ever changes," he said. Charlotte was slightly chilly in her light wool sweatshirt, and when she shivered, Tom put his arm around her and rubbed her shoulder. He was looking out at the waves.

She had no idea what was on his mind. "What are you thinking about?"

He took a moment and said, "I'm wondering if I'm going to meet Elvis."

"Well..." She thought for a moment. "Where's Elvis?"

Tom splayed out his fingers, thinking. "He went in the army last year. To Fort Dix, which is where I'm going."

She hadn't wanted to think about it and moaned into his shoulder, "When are you going?"

"Two weeks," he said. "Anyway, I don't know... I think Elvis is in Germany now. What are the odds of meeting one soldier, even Elvis?" Then suddenly he kissed her, and his hand went under her sweater and brushed her stomach, which was typically about as much as she would allow him to get away with. She looked out on the swell of the waves as she pulled away. "Do you ever surf?"

"No, I never learned," he said. "Anyway, nobody surfs at night." His voice echoed up and down the tower.

It felt like there was nothing for miles around, like they were in the crumbling remains of an ancient civilization. There was no sound except for their voices and the waves, glistening with moonlight and roaring through the tower. They kissed again, this time with a little bit of tongue.

Something caught Charlotte's eye out there on the waves. It was a small round shape, like a melon or volleyball, floating and poking just barely out of the water.

"What is that?" she asked. Tom was kissing her neck and she gently pushed him away. "Tom, wait, what is that?"

He looked out the window. "What is what?"

"That shape, that round… thing, what do you think it is?" The moonlight sparkled on the wet surface as it rolled forward.

It took him a while and then he said, "Huh."

The shape was moving along at a strange, steady pace, moving in too straight a line to be something swimming. Charlotte tried to sense of the shape, but it was impossible to see, between the darkness and the ripple of moonglow across the waves.

Finally, it came to her: "A turtle, perhaps?" Because she had heard that sometimes turtles would actually come onto shore to lay eggs. She had no idea if it was the time of year for turtles.

But now that she looked at it, the object was too odd and smooth to be a turtle. It looked like wood or plastic.

Tom shook his head. "Looks like a flotation device. Like—maybe something that broke off of a fishing barge or something? Maybe part of a net?"

He obviously wasn't really interested in the mystery, though, because he kissed her again and this time his hand crept up to her breast. Her skin tingled and she thought maybe she would allow that this time, because after all he was going to go into the army, and he might not get to meet Elvis.

Something in her couldn't help looking out the window again. Maybe it was all those Nancy Drew novels she read. "Wait." She pulled away, because now the wooden shape which really did look wooden, because it had clear, dark grain through its smooth surface, was still moving shoreward. And it had risen a little, so now it looked like the top of a post bobbing along towards the shore. "What in the world is that?"

"I don't know," he said with irritation.

And then, just as she was thinking of it as a post, the ball of wood rose a little bit more and looked out across the ocean with glowing eyes.

Eyes and the top of a nose, like a drowned man marching towards shore. She was thinking of ghost pirates, maybe because she was in a place that reminded her of pirate movies. There were pirates coming to take the tower. But that was crazy. That couldn't be. But whatever it was, it was getting closer to the shore and the tower now. As the face came into view, the wooden head might have been white and might have been grey. It was impossible to tell as it glistened with water and the green blaze of its eyes.

There was a wooden man walking towards the shore. The water gave way as the mouth and neck and shoulders became clear. A mouth that was carved and opened on tiny hinges. Shoulders that were jointed like a puppet lengthening down into arms and elbows and finely detailed hands.

Like Charlie McCarthy— she suddenly had an image of the ventriloquist Edgar Bergen with his top-hat-wearing dummy sitting on his knee. She knew that Edgar had a little string that he could pull in the back, which made Charlie's hinged jaw open and close. Charlotte's brother loved Edgar Bergen so much that he'd asked for and received a ventriloquist dummy for his birthday. The sound of the dummy's wooden mouth opening and closing was inescapable every time it spoke: it went clack clack. This mouth was coming towards her now—with a clack clack.

As the wooden man came out of the water, she saw the patterns on its chest, a suggestion of a painted-on tie and vest. The head moved back and forth with the mouth clacking almost idly, the eyes appearing to sweep along the shoreline.

"I don't like this," she said.

Tom got up and held out his hand. "Boy, I don't either."

They got up and started to run down the stairs. After a few steps, Tom was moving too fast, and his feet flew right out from under him. He fell back and Charlotte winced as he saw him land on his tailbone. As he scrambled up, she took a moment to look out the window they were passing. The wooden man was closer now, the water lapping at a hinged, marionette-like wooden waist. Tom rose and soon they were at the entrance to the tower.

As they looked out the iron gate at the entrance, they could see that the water was down to the knees of the wooden man now. She was struck again by the peeling paint on the arms which swiveled and moved in time with the legs, which were not yet visible. "That's a mannequin," Tom said.

He pushed the gate entrance open, and the metal groaned loudly. The mannequin swiveled its wooden head toward the pair.

For a moment, Charlotte thought that they should run back up the tower. But there was no time, and besides, what would happen? They'd trap themselves at the top of a tower. There was a mansion up there, Tom had said, but that meant there was probably a locked door at the top.

No. "We gotta run," she said. She and Tom could make it down the beach, they could run until the beach opened up and they were closer to the highway stairs and the Riviera.

But Tom wasn't yet sold on running. He was staring at the wooden man.

Now Lucy yapped angrily, and the little dog scampered past Tom out onto the rocks, barking at the mannequin as they kept walking. The waves sloshing around them, their fused fingers solid and swiveling on the ends of wooden wrists. As it finally reached the rocks, Lucy ran towards it with a growl, and it kicked her away.

The dog's yelp echoed along the cliffs.

"Lucy, let's go!" Charlotte shouted.

"Yeah." Tom agreed. Lucy meanwhile disappeared beneath the waves and came up, growling and yapping at the wooden feet while Charlotte and Tom moved along the rocks.

But she had misjudged how quickly the invading mannequin was moving. As she moved along the slippery stones, the mannequin seemed to suddenly appear in front of her, reaching out its glistening, weed bedecked arms. Tom tried to get between it and her, and then he yelped like a dog as the mannequin responded by grabbing him in a bear hug. It squeezed and Tom shouted and pummeled its arms with his fists. He was kicking wildly as the mannequin lifted him up from behind like a parent picks up a child. The jaws of the wooden man clacked, its eyes swiveling as it turned and walked back towards the water.

Charlotte scrambled, trying to get distance, all thought draining from her mind. She began to run, but the cold dry sand fought her every attempt for speed, and she did no better than a desperate scramble. She dropped the bag, screaming for Lucy and for Tom. Tom who would never hear her, or Elvis, again. She turned to look for him and saw his body tumbling over and over in the surf, the wet wooden man disengaging itself. Then it turned for her.

"No....no!"

Sobbing for breath and in fear, she dug her feet deeper into the sand. Lucy was running along the surf toward freedom, too far to hear Charlotte's cries. A loose stone under the sand betrayed her, the ball of her foot glancing off it and wrenching her knee and ankle. Charlotte fell to her hands and knees, screaming as she heard the soft and strange footfall of wood on sand. These things happened all the time to Nancy Drew, and in the stories, it was thrilling. In reality, it was terrifying and painful, leaving her groaning and panting in desperation. What would her heroine do?

When the mannequin came to pick her up, she turned in its arms to fight. She tried to scratch at the glowing eyes, but they burned her fingers. She saw her hands blistering and bleeding, and she choked on her own voice in the darkness.

"Oh my God, what are you, what are you, WHAT ARE YOU!?"

As she beat on its face, the mouth snapped down on her fingers and she tore her hand away, screaming in agony as her pinky nail wrenched free. She couldn't get away. The eyes blazed as she screamed, leading her out to sea. She beat on its shoulders and neck and chest with her bloody hands. The water began to drench her sweater as the creature's wooden legs pumped. Over its shoulders, past its glowing eyes, sat the pirate tower and the cliff.

Its jaws closed and opened, clack clack, as Charlotte looked up at the lights of the mansion at the top of the tower. The water was up to her arms and then her chin. The last thing she saw was the wooden man's glowing eyes, as the water closed all around.

Lucy the dog snuffled and whined, confused and afraid. But nothing came back out of the water.

Not that night.

CHAPTER 2

FRANNIE COHN TOOLED HER PARENTS' Studebaker away from the house with the all-important envelope burning a hole in her pocket.

She was trying, to no immediate avail, to understand what she felt now that she had graduated from high school. It was the day after graduation day, and she knew that she was supposed to feel some kind of relief, but it hadn't come. When she had walked across the stage in her gown and looked out at all the parents sitting politely on wooden folding chairs under the sun, she'd felt only a dull ache. Her English teacher had slipped the word 'ennui' into their last vocabulary test, as though Mrs. Cipriano had known that Frannie would need it.

Ennui. She had felt it before, when Noreen Swail had been killed in the cycling accident last spring that had almost taken Frannie as well. She had felt ripples of it returning when Noreen's name was ceremonially called in alphabetical order, her diploma and cap left on a chair draped in black crepe. Frannie had joined the school in her junior year and had never really felt completely at home, though she'd found friendship and companionship in the cycling club with Noreen and a few other girls. The rest of the club, to their credit, had made a commendable show of supporting Frannie after the accident, as much as teenage girls with no real experience of tragedy could. Unfortunately, the accident had only increased Frannie's 'otherness.' It was already enough to be a relocated Bronx Jew dropped into the sun and surf world of southern California, a world away from everything she had ever known, never mind the victim of a terrible accident.

Yes, she remembered ennui—the listless, empty feeling òf not knowing or wanting to know what to do about life had swallowed her in the hospital after the accident; before Frannie's Uncle Saul had appeared with a stack of books, a knowing smile, and an invitation to his café on the Pacific Coast Highway.

Café Monstro.

Frannie tried to shake off the feeling as she pulled out of the suburbs and onto the highway. She should be happy. Well, happy enough. The summer after the accident had been transformative—she had found not only herself that summer (and a potential-eating demon that tried to destroy humanity, an ability to channel powerful magic, surfing, and books that could show your future), but a community. Between the surf-crazed Legionnaires and the joyfully eclectic friends she had made at the café, Frannie had discovered a place for herself and powers she was still learning to master and wield.

So, it should be little wonder that after saving the world from a demon aided by the ghosts of Hawaiian royalty and surfing to a hard-won victory with Newpup by her side, returning to Home Economics class in the fall had been a bit of a letdown.

In fact, the whole fall and winter had been disappointing. With her time restricted by class and homework, and with the onset of what the locals called 'cold' weather (the New Yorker in her had laughed at this), surfing had quietly slipped out of her life. As had hot rowdy nights clearing tables at the café. With Newpup off at college and many of the other Legionnaire's returning to school or seasonal jobs, everything had quieted down to a low dull hum. Truly and Betty still came in on the weekends and the odd

Wednesday to practice new songs, Kurt could still be found in the corner with a long cigarette ash dangling as he painted, the bookstore still did some business and there were still sandwiches and coffee to serve—but without Newp to manage the band and direct the surfing, it felt like everything was in a holding pattern until the summer returned.

This was not to say that there had been nothing to do; in fact, after the battle with the Book Man, Saul had doubled down on Frannie's "supernatural studies."

"The Kabbalah is scratching the surface with a pin," he said, as he stacked her arms with books and notes and the occasional dusty looking scroll. "And don't think the goyim don't have their own magics too. They've also got powerful stuff we can use. Fighting evil is everyone's game, no matter what you do for Shabbat. I saw this Imam once—"

And then the story had trailed off in the most irritating manner possible, as Saul's face closed like a window sash, and he stopped mid-sentence. "You saw the Imam what? Turn into a pastrami on rye, what?"

"Never mind," he'd said, brushing the topic off. "Point is, there is more to learn, and not just from our own culture."

"Okay great, so tell me what this Imam did so we can learn from it."

Saul had shaken his bald head "I can't explain it, and it doesn't matter. What matters is protecting the blanks and training you up as a Blankguard."

"What, I'm not one already? Saving the world doesn't get you into the club?"

"I'm not saying that," Saul dodged, looking uneasy. "I'm not saying that at all. I'm just saying there's more, that's all."

And for the rest of the autumn and winter, that's all she could get out of her uncle. Besides more homework.

The memory soured her already unpleasant thoughts. As she turned on Pacific Coast Highway, Frannie clicked on the radio and the slow, thumping guitar sound of Link Wray's Rumble played. Boom, boom, boom. Slowly as the miles slid by and the sun shone down, she relaxed her hands on the wheel. She felt wrapped in love by the little highway, by the sea visible on her right, peeking between the buildings. The sea was always just beyond the shops and hotels and the restaurants, always just there at the edge of her vision. She rolled down the windows and took in the salt air and breathed deeply. It was the very last blooming of the spring, as all turned to white and golden summer.

Summer.

She finally reached the spot that she was looking for and pulled to the right, parking in front of the wonderful, sprawling, five-story Laguna Riviera Hotel. Link Wray went silent, and all was the sound of traffic and waves. As she got out, Frannie stopped for a moment to admire the Riviera's Spanish colonial facade balconies and its enormous, modern swimming structure of glass and chrome in front. Then she looked across the highway, and when she found space enough between the cars, she bounded, the way that she had always bounded towards what had become her home away from home.

Café Monstro.

The café was a small two-story building—really one story with a tiny top apartment that seemed to grow out of the café like an old bowler hat. The building was mostly black, with stained glass windows of ghosts and monsters along the front. The café was guarded by a large statue of the old god Kronos, who held a baby god in his hands the way that most fiberglass statues would hold a muffler. In fact, that was what the baby had originally been, because Kurt had built the Kronos statue out of an old muffler man.

As she opened the dark glass door, she reveled in the fact that there was so much art to see—once your eyes adjusted from the white sunlight into the dark café. When her vision snapped back, the first thing she saw was an enormous plaster-and-papier-mâché Frankenstein monster on a cross against the wall.

This was the relief that she was looking for. The relief of the strange Frankenstein monster statue and the god statue outside, and the many brightly colored paintings of monsters and people carrying torches, the dioramas of creatures and superheroes in wrestling contests and all the zaniness that her uncle and Kurt brought to this place. She hadn't been here in a few weeks—not since it was time to start preparing for final exams. The envelope rustled in her pocket, and with a bit of guilt she admitted to herself that she had also been avoiding the place a teensy bit. Facing down a demon was one thing—delivering news she had for her beloved uncle was another.

"How you doin', kid?" boomed Saul. The man who came toward her with his arms wide was cue-ball bald, with muscles bulging in a bowling shirt and tight blue jeans. He enveloped her in a warm hug. "Look at her, top of her class graduate, beauty and brains, the whole shebang. We weren't expecting you for another hour, maideleh, I thought you'd be celebrating with your folks."

Uncle Saul had been at the graduation but had slipped out as soon as Frannie had walked across the stage, because he had to get back to the café. Just in case somebody came in wanting egg sandwiches or copies of Truman Capote for the beach. Frannie scanned the café. Right now, there were only a couple of people in the place. Even Mutt and Jeff, the undercover police officers who tended to hang out there, wouldn't bother coming in until the sun started to go down.

There was a married couple in their twenties drinking about halfway towards the back wall, on the left, not far from the stage where the band would play in the evenings. There were a couple of teenagers over on the right with milkshakes, and a small family in the center having sandwiches.

Not bad, but quiet. Frannie took a deep breath and just let it out. Just enjoying the environment. It was like she recharged when she was here. "The heat was starting to get to dad, so I took them home a little early. You know how he gets in the sun. So, you got a job for me?"

"Always. Are you planning on working all summer?"

"I'd like to," she said, "if that's alright. I don't have to get up for school or anything."

Saul nodded like that would be perfect with him. "Just you watch. I know it looks quiet, but every year things start to pick back up again around this time, and then you don't believe it."

She believed it. She spent all last summer living it. But it wasn't just the waiting tables in the atmosphere that brought her back.

Frannie looked towards the section in the back, a little door with beads hanging over it and a sign that said BOOKS FOR YR PLEASURE. While she had been working a few hours a week through the school year, the book traffic had been…well, dull. The Blanks, the strange books that drew in the lost, the weary, the people with deep but untapped potential, had sat untouched for months. The patrons that had streamed in over the summer dried up in the fall, as if the spell that brought them in didn't seem to sing when it began to get cooler. She had no explanation for that at all, and it made her worry that maybe it would never come again. Saul seemed to have no such concerns.

The door to the little office off the side of the bar opened. Three people streamed out carrying sheet music, Truly in a hot yellow dress that contrasted beautifully against her ebony skin, and Betty in a deep red flannel nightgown, a red sequined bow setting off her bombshell blonde "do." Both of them had their hair rounded so they looked like the singers they were. Sailing behind them like an All-American dreamboat was bronze, blonde Newp, her… friend? Beau? Boyfriend? It wasn't clear. Her boy Newp. That would have to do.

Newp saw Frannie and waved a clipboard with some paper on it. He said a couple of words to Truly and Betty and they hustled on back to the stage. Then he turned to Saul and Frannie. "How you guys doing?"

Newp had been back in town for about a week and Frannie was still not quite used to how different he looked from when he had left for college the previous fall. She had seen him over the fall and winter of course, his family didn't live far from hers, but their encounters had been strangely formal— holiday parties, an occasional card night among their parents, and a weirdly uncomfortable Seder dinner only a month ago. They had stolen glances at each other, and she had made him laugh when she dropped a matzo ball under the table and made a mess of retrieving it, but the easy friendship of the summer had chilled with the cold months. Now at the beginning of the summer of 1959, Newp had grown some, which she was given to understand was normal for boys going away to college. He had filled out and was more muscular. His face was rounder. He was handsome, but altogether a different-looking person, and somehow, she hadn't yet absorbed that it was still him. But now when he took her in his arms to give her an unexpected and quick kiss, a lot of the old familiarity came back at once with his scent. It shocked her with all its associations, and she wanted to take his hand to run across the highway and out into the surf.

"You're gonna be working?" he asked.

She nodded excitedly, a genuine smile crossing her face for what felt like ages. The voices of Truly and Betty cut through the air as they started working on a song at Frannie guessed they had been arranging in the office. It was a number that Frannie had never heard before she turned around and watched them. For a moment she wished that she could freeze time and listen to Betty and Truly sing forever.

"I'm working tonight." I'd be here all the time if I could, she thought.

She swayed with the music, and the envelope in her pocket rustled again. She felt all the relief flood out of her as she turned to catch both Saul and Newp in her gaze. She pulled the sealed envelope from her back pocket, and sat down on a stool at the bar, gesturing at them to join her.

"So… my parents don't know that I got this."

Saul put a cherry Coke in front of her and looked at the envelope. "Whattaya got there?"

Frannie tilted it towards him. The return address said UNIVERSITY OF GEORGIA NURSING SCHOOL. Newp picked it up and looked at her questioningly.

"You're applying to college?"

"Just nursing colleges right now. Georgia has a really strong program, and they're trying to expand it to make surgical and general practice classes available to women, and—"

"But Georgia is on the other side of the country," said Newp, a little sharply.

"So is New York, and you like me all right," she rebutted, a little hurt at his tone. Saul snagged the envelope and studied it again.

"Nursing," he said. "Where did you get this idea?"

Frannie shrugged, suddenly feeling like she was on the defensive. It wasn't a feeling she enjoyed. "I like helping people. It just seems like the thing to do."

Saul gave her a long look but seemed to stop himself from saying anything. They sat a moment in uncomfortable silence.

Newp rolled his hands in a get on with it gesture. "Okay, so what does it say?"

"I don't know—I waited to share it with you. I'm not sure how my parents are going to react, thought you two might make good guinea pigs…"

Newp and Saul shared a silent look, but Frannie missed it as she cast about for a butter knife to open the envelope. She felt her stomach tighten as she slit the top of the envelope and slid the letter out. Her hands barely shook as she unfolded it. She cleared her throat.

"We regret to inform you—"

Her stomach squeezed and she suddenly became aware of her staring friends. She felt red shame climb up her face. "Well," she managed to squeak out. "I'm glad I didn't show this to my parents."

Newp's face softened, and he gave her a slight side hug. Saul put his hand on her shoulder from across the bar. "Hey, kiddo, it'll be okay. You'll find something that's right for you."

"Yeah… it's just that I need to find a nursing program soon, or else I don't have anywhere to go in the fall. I don't know. I had hoped for some good news today." Frannie crumpled up the letter and thrust it back into her pocket, got off the stool, and walked towards the stage where she could watch Truly and Betty singing. She hoped the beat of the music would loosen the stitch in her chest.

Newp and Saul watched her go, twin expressions of concern on their faces.

"I didn't know she was applying," Newp said.

"Neither did I. I'm not sure we handled that particularly well."

"I just thought that once it was summer and we were all back together, things would be…"

"Settled?"

"Yeah."

Saul shrugged, palms outstretched as though in supplication. "So did I."

From down the bar, the two heard a snort. Kurt put out his cigarette, and lit another through a small, knowing grin. "You do not understand women. That," he said, pointing with the cigarette between his fingers, "is not a woman who will settle. And you two jackasses just gave her the third degree about something she was excited to share with you." he lit the coffin nail, and took a drag, letting out something between an exhale and a chuckle. "Settled." He shook his head and stood up. Saul looked abashed, and a little surprised.

Newp's face was a study in surprise. He stared at Kurt as he walked away, then looked back at Saul. Saul shrugged.

"He's right on all counts. Including us being jackasses."

"Damn."

Newp turned and looked at Frannie from across the room. She stood straight as a post, and, he noticed, a little taller. A little stronger. And, he had to admit, looking a little defeated. With a nod to Saul, he made his way toward the stage, and stood shoulder to shoulder with her in the music. When she didn't turn, he knew Kurt had been right.

"I'm sorry, Frannie. Really, I am."

The set of her shoulders relaxed a little, but she still didn't look at him.

"Want to talk about it?"

She shook her dark curls, and he noticed for the first time the slight depth of red in her hair. Frannie Cohn: there was always something else to learn about her. He reached over and touched her shoulder.

"You wanna go surfing tomorrow?"

She turned, and almost smiled.

"That might be good." She turned to him and closed her fingers over the hand on her shoulder. It's just... I want to do good, you know?"

"Sure."

"I feel like I've been doing good for my uncle, and I feel like I was doing good for the people who came in needing help. But... I'm not sure it's enough. And when the Book Man—when Hooky—"

She saw Newp flinch at the name and stopped herself. Hooky was dead, and the demon who had killed him was locked in a dybbuk box at the bottom of the ocean. Both things were still present and painful between herself and Newp it seemed.

"I just never want that to happen again. To anyone. Not just the stuff with the Book Man, but the stuff before too, the things that happened to him in Korea."

The things the Book Man predicted would happen to Newp. To all my friends, she recalled. The summer was not yet strong enough to warm the chill in her skin at the thought. Newp seemed to feel her discomfort and moved his arm companionably around her shoulder.

"I know. Listen, let's drop it for tonight huh? First real night back at the café and your graduation? We should celebrate! Forget Georgia, tonight you are the First Lady of Laguna, and the first cherry coke is on me."

Her smile came easily now, and she relaxed. Newp was right. The summer was here, and for a little while, everything else could wait. Tonight was for fun. Tomorrow was for surfing. And this moment was for enjoying. She offered Newp her arm with a toss of her head.

"Lead me to the bar, young sir!"

Outside as the sunlight faded below the horizon, the lights of Café

Monstro shone out over Pacific Coast Highway. The old god Kronos stood sentinel over the twilight. The surf followed the ancient pattern, into the land and out to sea, returning and returning endlessly to the shore, as the music and laughter of the young spilled out into the night.

Summer had returned.

CHAPTER 3

FRANNIE LOVED THE EARLY MORNING silence of the café almost as much as she loved the loud and boisterous heart of it in the evening. Despite the late evening she had enjoyed the night before, she felt compelled to rise with the sun and hop on her bike. Yesterday had been a rite of passage, the last official vestige of childhood taken off with the cap and gown. Now was the limbo between schoolgirl and young woman, the time to test the thrilling waters of adulthood. Her time was truly her own, her day to order and organize as she wished. Today she wished to take stock of the café before the sun had warmed the waves enough to grab her board and join the Legionnaires at the beach. It would be good to see them, but not yet. This time was hers.

She reached up to tickle the left foot of baby Zeus dangling from the hand of Kronos, grinning to herself, and unlocked the front door of the café. Kurt had been busy, she noted—the walls were thick with new paintings and sculptures. The enormous papier-mâché Frankenstein on his cross dominated the biggest wall space, balancing visually with the stage space and the bar.

The Secular Trinity of the Café, she thought, music, monsters, and meals. She dropped her keys on the bar next to the cutlery bin and started to cast about for the napkin box. She had just settled onto a stool and started rolling, when a loud curse erupted from the kitchen, along with a clatter and a crackling SPLAT. Saul stepped out of the swinging kitchen doors, muttering under his breath as he marched toward the broom.

"Lign in drerd un bakn beygl!"

"Well, good morning to you too, sunshine," she chirped at him from her perch.

Saul clasped a hand over his heart, and she was stuck between fear and laughter as he jumped at the sound of her voice.

"My God, Frannie if you're trying to give me a heart attack you're succeeding. What are you doing here so early?"

In answer she held up a roll of silverware, grinning as he recovered his composure. "What are you doing, Uncle Saul?"

"If this meshugge hot top decides to cooperate, I'm making breakfast. If it doesn't, I'm making a big mess. Want some?"

"Breakfast or mess?"

He gestured widely, as though to indicate that it was all one, and she laughed out loud at his bemusement.

"I'll have what you're having if what you're having comes with coffee."

Saul raised his hands in the universal sign language of cooks—order received. "Heard, heard, you dig up the mugs and I'll get the pot on. I'm glad you're here, I wanted to talk to you last night, but it didn't seem fair to interrupt your fun. The blue one is mine," he said, as she reached for the mugs on the upper shelf. "The green one with the yellow flower is Kurt's. You can have the brown one with the strawberries, alright?"

Frannie hauled herself up onto the counter to reach the mugs and began setting out a breakfast table for them on the bar. She could hear Saul singing a little congratulatory song to himself as the hot top came to life, and soon they had themselves two tidy plates of eggs over easy, toast, and a slice of cantaloupe each. Frannie doctored her coffee with two cream and two sugar while Saul reached for the salt and pepper.

"Where did you learn to cook, anyway? I know it wasn't the navy, I've heard stories."

"Oh here and there. Mostly here. When Mag—when my ex-wife and I owned the café up the road, you remember the one?"

She did. It had been one of the most terrifying and exhilarating nights of her life.

"We lost a cook early on, got married out in Vegas and left us flat. So, I just had to learn by doing it. That and a couple of cookbooks. Your mom mailed me a postcard with the recipe for her sweet bread on it when you were a little thing. That was a lifesaver, your mom is a good teacher, even on a five-by-seven."

Frannie gently slid an egg onto a slice of lightly buttered toast, careful not to break the yolk. Just as carefully, she glanced at her uncle. "You never say much about your wife. What was she like?"

"Uh. Hmm. Well... she was very... tall."

"Uh-huh. Must've been nice to have a tall person in the family. What was she like as a person? Was she really so bad you're never going to talk about her?"

"Oh! No, no Maggie isn't bad, er, wasn't bad—well—isn't. We just... we were good together, you know, but not good for each other. We went our separate ways, that's all. Anyway, that's the past, and the past is past. What I want to talk to you about is the future."

"Uncle Saul..."

"Eat your breakfast; you chew, I'll talk. Now, ever since we put that demon in the ocean, I've been worried. Not about the demon—that box will hold til the ocean dries up. I've been worried because I should have been expecting something like him. I should have been ready for shedim in general. I've been so focused on the blanks and who they were calling, I wasn't focused enough on what else might be coming. And for that, Frannie,

I'm sorry. I didn't treat it as seriously as I should have, and that was a mistake. One that cost your friend his life."

Hooky. That name had been on her mind for the better part of a year but hadn't crossed her lips again until last night. Now here it was again, and it still hurt to remember that he was gone. The Book Man had eaten Hooky from the inside out, and then had worn his skin like a suit. Hooky, who had taught her the magic of the surf, a power she had used to ultimately defeat the Book Man. Hooky, who was haunted by his own ghosts, had become her own personal specter.

"It wasn't your fault," she said. "I mean, what, you spend a lot of time getting attacked by potential-eating elder shedim? That was one in a million. And we won. Hooky was a hero, and he made sure we won. May his memory be a blessing."

Saul nodded but gestured for her to keep eating her breakfast. He wet his lips with a sip of coffee.

"My point is…there's more to being a Blankguard than I've told or taught you. More than I prepared for. I've always been more of a keeper of the books; I was never a strong practitioner. My gifts lie with leading people to the Blanks, to helping them understand and realize the truth of what they're shown. I've never done more than cast protections or hurl the odd curse. My word to God I was as surprised as you were when we actually brought the Golem to life. And I think a lot of that, Frannie, was you."

She took a sip of her coffee, trying to hide her own surprise. Saul had always seemed so confident, so ready, like he could deal with whatever life dealt him. This confession was uncomfortable, and she wasn't sure what to do about it.

"I think you could be a very powerful rebbe. I also think that you are meant to be a Blankguard—you defended them at the most vulnerable and dangerous hour, and you used their power in ways I would never have thought to or dreamt of. You're young, and clever, and creative, and strong, and I… am occasionally clever, out of that list. Point is," he said, clearing his throat, "I think you need to keep training and studying because the Blanks will eventually be yours. To defend, yes, but also to keep leading the people they call. And because I don't think the troubles are over. If they ever were."

Frannie raised an eyebrow. More trouble? "Something happening that I don't know about?"

"You're seventeen, we could fill a library with all the things you don't know about."

"Ha-ha, I will perish of laughter. For serious, Saul, has something happened you haven't told me about?"

"No. At least, not yet. But Frannie, the reason I tell you this is because it can't just be something you do in the summers"

"Why not?"

"Because being a Blankguard, it's a twenty-four-hour/three-sixty-five commitment. It's a life. A whole life. It's why I run the café and live in it—everything in one place. It's a calling. And I won't be here forever."

"Neither will I. I'm going to college."

Saul was silent for a moment, before waving his hands in the air. "Of course! Of course, you are, bright girl, you'll do whatever you set your mind to, it's my fault for not talking to you before you started applying in places like Georgia."

"I can be a Blankguard in Georgia. You said, the Blanks appear when they find someone. So, if I'm meant to be a Blankguard, they'll appear to me wherever I am, right?"

He blinked, like a cat surprised by a sudden light.

"But you don't need to go, you're here, they're here, there's colleges here, everything is here. That's what I'm saying, you don't have to go anywhere."

Frannie squared her shoulders. "This is exactly why I didn't tell my folks I was applying. I knew you were going to try and talk me out of it. Well, you're not going to—I am going to nursing school, my mind is made up."

"Talk you out, who is talking you out? No one is talking you out, I think it's great, absolutely, you should go. I'm the last person who is going to talk you out of seeking knowledge Frannie. I'm just saying that you can find that knowledge here, what do you need to go all the way to Georgia for? The peaches?"

"That program is the best program. The most modern techniques, the newest technology. It just happens to be in Georgia. I'm not going to settle for just some nursing program, I'm going to apply to the best. And the best is not in Laguna Beach."

Saul was startled at the word 'settle.' Kurt's comment from the night before had certainly come full circle. And, as usual, Kurt's observation had been an absolute bull's eye. He sighed a little bit. Artists. Always seeing the meaning behind everything.

"Okay I hear you but…you're needed here too, you know. There are programs…"

"At the university? Outdated. I already looked. The nearest I would even think of considering is in Los Angeles."

"That's not so far."

"It's a two-hour drive, I'm going to schlep myself four hours a day to school and work nights? Plus, hospital hours?"

Saul felt the argument slipping away from him, and he started to worry. They needed Frannie. And they needed her here. Café Monstro wasn't going to be like…like the others. It was meant to stand. It needed its keepers. It needed young blood. It needed Frannie and Newp.

"Frannie, you're taking this the wrong way, I'm not saying you shouldn't study or be anything you want to be, I'm just saying…what happens if another Book Man does come along? Or something bigger? Or something worse?"

She sat silent, picking at the floppy edge of an egg white, not meeting his eyes. He could see the anger in the lines of her face. She looked so much like his mother, her grandmother, that it hurt just that much more to look at her.

"I need you here. I'm not—"

The bell at the front of the café jingled, and in an aura of bright morning sun stood the dark silhouette, broad shouldered and shaggy haired. Frannie and Saul both jumped in their seats, the intensity of their argument broken by the surprise of the sound. They shielded their eyes as the young man cautiously stepped (slunk, Frannie thought) into the café.

"I'm sorry to bother you," came a mild voice. "Is the café open? I saw the statue and I just…I don't know. Felt like I had to come in."

Frannie and Saul looked at each other. He knew this argument wasn't over, was far from over, but he also watched her face as she let it go and turned toward the young man at the door. With a pang, he realized that indeed, Frannie was on the doorstep of womanhood. His girl was growing, fast. There was so much to tell her, and so little time. And, he thought, an old fool of a man who dithers about how and what to tell her.

It was Frannie who put on a cheerful voice and addressed the young man. "Of course! We were just catching up over breakfast. You're very welcome. Perhaps you'd like to look at a book?"

CHAPTER 4

THE YOUNG MAN TURNED A little bit and Frannie got a better look at him. He was not overly tall, about five-foot-ten, with curly brown hair and large, soft green eyes that she felt she had seen before. He was big, with broad shoulders, but lacked the tapered waist and long lines of body that most of the surf boys had. If the surf boys were saplings, then this was what a tree looked like. She didn't realize she had been staring until she heard Saul behind her clearing his throat.

"Of course, just as she says. Frannie will take good care of you. The hot top is still on if you want some breakfast when you're done. We are a café after all." Saul gave them a smile and started cleaning up the breakfast plates.

Frannie started to lead their guest toward the beaded curtain that separated the café from the bookstore.

"Well, now you've got my name, would you like to trade in yours?" she joked.

He gave a wry half-smile that made him seem older. "My name's Mike. Michael Landry."

"What brings you in, Michael?"

"I…" The smile faded, and he faltered. "I don't know."

For a moment he seemed to struggle with his own memory. Frannie knew exactly what this was, because she had seen it before. As near as Frannie could understand it—and she understood it as well as anybody, she figured—the blank books on the top shelf sent out a silent call to people who needed to hear it. And that call could ring for hundreds of miles. She had known people from the ages of twelve to eighty to wander in, experiencing that strange fugue state, wanting to answer the call. Clearly, Michael was one of those. But she was curious what his problem could be. They swished through the beaded curtain, and as if on some silent cue they both looked up at the shelf above the door that held the blanks. Frannie hopped up on a short ladder (placed there for just this purpose) and selected one with a deep brown leather cover, and a moonstone embedded in the spine. "That's all right, Michael, I can probably help you with that. I was thinking that you might want to look at this one."

She handed it to Michael and waited. She had no idea what the readers experienced, Saul had warned her never to look in a Blank for herself (but not why I shouldn't, she thought with a flicker of irritation). But as the Blankguard, she got to watch the potential life of each person spread out onto the pages, and that experience was nothing short of magic. As he opened the Blank, Frannie saw writing begin to fill in. Suddenly she was flowing in a life not her own, flowing down a river of stars.

This river had small islands, where the great expanse of stars that she was swimming in suddenly congealed. She found herself on one of these islands in a cafeteria in Queens, New York. This wasn't very long ago. Michael was a teenager, and as she hung in space behind him, she could study him and see that he was fifteen or sixteen years old.

He was eating alone because there weren't any other Jews at his school and none of the Christian boys would sit with him. A flood of warmth went through her body, and it reflected in an amber glow in the starry field through which she was flying. There was some sadness here, but this boy at the cafeteria table was serene. She kept moving, because this was not the source of his pain, not the kind of pain that would bring one to a Blank.

The river flowed further back, even though she wanted to just sit down with the boy back at the cafeteria and watch him poke at the eggs on his plate. Maybe engage him in conversation. She felt like she could remain in the cafeteria for a long time with the warm sun coming in through the big glass windows over the cinder blocks. But no, she was being pulled. They were headed back. Back toward...a beach. She could hear the surf. And then—

CHAPTER 5

MICHAEL IS EIGHT YEARS OLD, and Frannie is a ghost hanging over his shoulder as he plays in the sand at the beach. Michael's mother has gotten up from where she has been sitting with him. He is building a castle with a little bucket and looks up to see that she is wandering into the surf in her dress. The dress reaches down to her calves and has white stripes. Michael thinks it is funny and strange that her dress is getting soaked as she steps into the surf.

This is the New Jersey shore, the ghost Frannie realizes. She had been there herself, years ago, on a holiday. The familiarity of it spooks her a little bit.

The water is incredibly cold, but little Michael is not alarmed at all that his mother appears to be going swimming. She keeps moving, stretching out her arms as she wades, and soon the water has reached her chin. But she has still not begun to swim or to turn back. The ghost that is Frannie cannot hear it clearly, but the adults in the party, Michael's father and several others, have now taken notice that his mother has left the beach and for some reason is wandering into the water. They begin to run in after her. Michael is frozen in place, suddenly frightened by the alarm of the adults around him. The only thing Michael can think is that he wants his mother to turn around and look back at him, because he has suddenly decided that if she looks back at him, he will be able to hold her back and keep her safe. But she does not. All he can see of her is her curly hair as she continues moving farther and farther into the sea.

The ghost Frannie begins to feel alarmed, too. There is nothing that she can do because she is not really here, but she can feel the beating of Michael's heart, a heart that is both eight years old and twenty-one years old now—and Frannie has her answer, Michael is twenty-one.

Both of those things are happening, he is twenty-one and standing in the book section of the café and reading a book and he is eight and his mother is growing increasingly numb in the water.

Now several of the men wearing work pants and golf shirts have run into the surf and have grabbed Mrs. Landry to pull her back.

Now there is a skip and a jump. Mrs. Landry is stumbling onto the beach near Michael.

And another skip and jump, and they're still at the beach on the same day, just a little bit later. Michael's mother is distributing sandwiches. He takes his sandwich and mumbles something to her to ask her about going in the water, and she laughs, replying, "What a silly thing to say."

He will remember this moment forever. He will always look at her wondering, is this the day? Is this the day that you do it?

Jump.

Eating eggs alone in yet another cafeteria, because he has moved to California and in the particular neighborhood he is in, there are still not so many Jews. But by this time, he already has the sense that being forced to eat alone is not one of life's great injustices. Now there are so many questions about what he is going to do next.

Because he is a talented young man. He is an athlete who is an expert at the pole vault and javelin and really anything that track and field can throw at him. The ghost floats over him as he runs past in a tank top on the track. His temper and athleticism and drive remind Frannie of the surfers that she has spent so much time with. But the cruel corner of his mouth, the distant look, that reserve, these remind her of somebody else entirely.

The ghost Frannie can tell that Michael's future is not athletics. But what she can see of his future is very strange. She sees him in so many different clothes, she sees his face covered in strange thick hair, and then wearing a cowboy hat, she can see him walking and doing magic and changing people's lives. She sees him as a father, but not really a father. And she could see that he is not going to get very old.

She sees him when his eyes turn... yellow?

The ghost Frannie tumbles down the river of stars and sees all these different versions of Michael. And then—

Michael clapped the book shut and Frannie was sucked back into reality.

"How…" He ran his fingers along the smooth brown cover and then looked at her. "How does it work? Showing all those things like that?"

"It just does," Frannie said.

He flicked his eyes away to look at the shelves, thinking. So far, he had not asked what most people asked: 'so what should I do?' Frannie was relieved because the Blanks didn't give free advice. They weren't a Magic 8 Ball that just answered a question. They gave you a look at your future and your past. And sometimes Frannie suspected that they gave her much more of a look than they did the person who was holding the book.

Finally he said, "I wanted her to look back at me."

"I know. I'm sorry that she didn't."

"What if I had yelled, in the book? In the memory? Or ran into the water? Or…"

Frannie shook her head "It's more like a movie than anything. It just winds back the reel and shows you what already was."

"But then it showed me…stuff that hasn't happened. Is that the future?"

She shrugged, trying to keep it light. "It could be. It's some possibilities for the future."

"Well, what's the point of that?"

Frannie thought for a moment, then looked at Michael. The pain of his mother walking into the ocean was still living in his eyes. That had to be hard.

"I think for people like you, who have seen things that you've seen…I think the point of it is to show you that there is a future. That it's not all darkness and confusion and pain. That there's always the possibility of more. Other people learn that lesson in other ways, but people who are drawn to the Blanks, I think they need to be shown. So it showed you."

He nodded, and started to hold out the book, and then paused.

"Is it mine then? Can I keep it?"

She froze. She didn't know. No one had ever really asked anything like that before, and it had never occurred to her that she might need an answer. So, she told him the truth.

"No one has ever asked before. I don't think so? I mean…they've always been put back?"

He nodded again, and then slipped the book back up on the shelf himself.

"Save you the trouble of getting on that ladder again."

"Thanks."

Michael was still in a daze as they walked towards the front of the café. When they stopped at the bar, he rubbed the back of his head as though he were coming out of a trance. "Boy… I feel like I've been hit."

"I know what you mean. Need a snack, something to drink? I know where Kurt keeps the Oreos if nothing on the menu sounds good."

Michael smiled, a softer smile than she had seen in the Blank, and her heart melted a little. "Tell you what, I'll split something with you if you like, I feel bad for interrupting your breakfast. What sounds good to you?"

Frannie grinned. "Oreos and milk it is. Make yourself comfortable, I'll be right back."

A few minutes later they were settled into a booth, chomping their way through a small plate of cookies. Frannie dipped hers in her milk, then asked casually "So what do you do, Michael? Besides wander into vaguely magical bookshops on Saturday mornings?"

He chuckled. "I'm a senior in college in Orange County. I have a movie audition tomorrow, so I guess that's next."

"Movies? Really?" She clapped her hands. "That's so exciting. I don't really know any actors."

"Oh, well, I don't know how much of an actor I am. But it's a way to pay for tuition, so it's not the end of the world."

She scoffed. "I guess that's one way of looking at a job that everybody on the earth would like to have."

"I guess it is."

Michael popped a cookie in his mouth, looking like he was awake, finally. "So, what do you do, Frannie? Besides show people magic books in weird cafés on Saturday mornings?"

She paused, and wished she had any kind of solid answer. "I work here. And I surf. For now."

"Are you in college or…?"

"Well, nothing now. Nursing school next year if I get in."

"Okay." He thrust his hands in his pockets. Everything about the way he took things in was cool and accepting. The way he said okay, it made it sound like he was trying to figure out where to place her in his world.

"Speaking of surfing…I actually have to get down to the beach. My friends will be waiting for me."

"Oh! Right. Sorry. I didn't realize we'd been talking so long."

She shrugged with a smile "Magic and time are…" she waved her hands around in a circular motion, "kind of vague."

"Yeah, I guess they are."

They sat in an awkward silence, and it seemed neither of them wanted to be the first to move. Frannie felt a strange little flop in her stomach and shook her head as though to clear it. "So, I know you came here because you wanted to look at the books, even if you didn't know that… but this is Café

Monstro. We got good music and decent food, so I hope you come back."

"Yeah, I might do that." He smiled and stuck out his hand. As she shook it, a shock of his brown hair fell over his eye.

"It's nice to meet you, Michael Landry."

"It's good to meet you, Frannie." Then he turned and headed out to the parking lot, where he got into a powder blue Karmann Ghia convertible and slipped out onto Pacific Coast Highway. She watched the car disappear for a moment, and then turned around to head into the café. She was going to need to hurry up and change into her suit if she was going to meet Newp on time.

Michael Landry, her first Blank of the summer. Maybe everything was going to be okay after all.

CHAPTER 6

MICHAEL FELT HIS PULSE RACING as he drove away. He pulled over at the next block as soon as he felt like he was out of sight of the restaurant. He touched his wrist and felt alarm flow through him, which only caused his pulse to quicken more. He breathed, trying to let the cooling air and the sea breeze calm him, and after a moment he pulled the Karmann Ghia back into the street. His palms and the soles of his feet were starting to itch, a bad sign.

Michael drove through the campus of the University of Laguna Beach until he found a parking spot in front of the Department of Anthropology, got up and ran to the third floor. He peeked through a little window in the office door to see Doctor Sutcliffe with a student.

Michael paced in the hall and leaned on the bulletin board. He could feel sweat on his brow and when he checked his pulse again it was still racing. When the student finally left, Sutcliffe came to the door, looking at him. "Michael?"

Michael went inside the office and made an attempt at sitting. He bounced on the edge of the seat.

Sutcliffe sifted papers, barely looking at him. "You seem to be in something of a tizzy."

"I'm worried about what's happening."

"What do you think is happening?" Sutcliffe always had this way of answering questions with questions.

"You know what I mean."

"Why don't you tell me what's going on?"

"I met a girl."

"You're a handsome guy, Michael—I imagine you meet lots of girls. We've got a whole sea of coeds here who I know are booking visits with me because they know you're my assistant."

"I know, but it's... I'm worried that it's going to happen again. I can feel it struggling under my skin, under my teeth, under my fingernails…God…" He wrapped his arms around himself, shuddering. "I'm afraid of what I'm going to do."

"Well, Michael, as long as you're working with me, I can help you make sure that you only do the things that you're supposed to do."

"But I'm afraid that I'll become…"

"Whatever you become when you're working with me is going to be what you're meant to be. You're going to be a better person. I'm going to help you become that, I promise."

Michael's stomach growled painfully, and he doubled over.

"Why don't you start by telling me about this girl."

Michael straightened up a little bit. "She was sweet… at least she seemed sweet. She's a surfer."

"A surfer girl? I didn't know there were surfer girls."

"I didn't either, but she worked at the café, and there was something about her and it made me want to lose control, and then…"

"What?"

"She wasn't scared of me. At all. And that made it worse somehow."

Michael's palms were starting to itch, and he looked at Sutcliffe, a picture of absolute misery. "How long do we have?"

"Two weeks, so long as you don't lose control. My goodness, you are in a bad way, aren't you? I hate to give you one, I know how much it hurts, but do you think you need a treatment?"

Michael closed his eyes. How much it hurt? He doubted Sutcliffe had any idea how much it hurt. The feeling of the blood in your own veins trying to spike its way out of your skin, of being sliced to ribbons from the inside out...Unbidden, an image of Frannie floated into his mind. Frannie, the sweet bookshop girl, sightless and staring, her dark curls soaked with the last of her life blood, escaping in a gurgling gasp from the remains of her strong, slender throat.

"Yes. I need a treatment."

"Go have a lie down on the couch. I'll get it ready."

He did as he was bidden, trying to brace himself for the pain he knew was coming.

Two weeks. They were going to need to hurry, or time was going to run out. For him, for Frannie, for Laguna Beach.

CHAPTER 7

DOWN TO THE BEACH. IT was unbelievable to her that she had not even attempted to go surfing since the beginning of the school year. With every month that had passed, surfing felt more and more like it was a chapter that was closed, and she didn't know how to get back to it. But of course, that was an illusion—it had just been the season of forgetting. But now, in the same way that she constantly felt like she wasn't sure how she was supposed to be around Newp, she felt like she wasn't sure how to feel about the ocean.

First stop was Frannie's car, really her father's big gray station wagon, where her surfboard was sticking out the back window. She grabbed it and hustled across the highway. It was finally time to hit the beach.

The beach had an entrance to it that Frannie thought was just the most. It started out as a winding path defined by gravel and a staircase that twisted its way through grass and sand down a steep cliff to the beach below. The roar of the water grew louder as she left the highway behind.

Once she was down on the beach, the air was so cool that Frannie dropped her board for a second and just stood there with her eyes closed, letting the sound of the ocean and the wind envelop her. When she opened them, she began to walk along the beach, marching to the rhythm of the waves.

It was as though time hadn't moved an inch—everything, and everyone, was right where she had left them in the fall. To the right was a strange little hut that seemed to have been put together entirely from driftwood and old license plates. It had a roof of tin that had been patched occasionally with long grass. Next to that hut were a couple of sawhorses and boards, and even right now there was an expert shaper, a guy who makes and sells boards, bent over a long board that he was slicing with an iron lathe. His name was Go-Go, and he worked in concentrated silence as little chips of board flew away. Go-Go wore a pair of cut-off jeans and no shirt, and his skin was deeply browned.

Go-Go had his back to her, but then as he went around and crouched down so that he could look along the board, he saw her and brightened. Go-Go whooped and threw a fist in the air, shouting, "Hey, Legionnaires! Hey, it's Frannie!"

At once, other surfers started coming in from the waves and running towards them. They were short and tall but all of them seemed pounded out of the same basic mold, wide at the shoulder and narrow at the hip, their bodies so built for surfing that Frannie thought they all looked like human sharks. She laughed with the pleasure of their company and allowed herself to be hugged and lifted and twirled from boy to boy, shouting hello and how-are-you's and where-you-been's at themselves and each other before depositing her gently next to Newp. But as they whooped and hollered on sight, her attention was still back on the little hut, which seemed to throb with emptiness. She was frankly surprised that it was still standing.

The hut had been the headquarters of the surf gang—this surf gang—called the Legionnaires. While the boys and Newp caroused and chatted, Frannie stepped towards the little house. The curtain that hung over the door was pulled slightly aside, and she was able to look in without touching it. She was a little afraid to.

There was still a cot in there, and a framed picture of Gracie Allen, which made her heart melt. Frannie had never met Gracie Allen, but the actress and TV star was a fond love of the leader of the Legionnaires, Hooky, who said he had once given Gracie a surf lesson.

"Everybody thinks she's a dope," Hooky had said, "But she's a fine lady."

For a moment, Frannie just hung there looking into the hut. Then she turned around to Newp and the other surfers. "Nobody's using this?" She gestured with her thumb.

One of the surfers, a boy with coke bottle glasses and a pimple-scarred, muscular chest, said, "No way anybody's using it." This was Brainiac. "That's Hooky's hut."

"Nah." Go-Go wiped some oil off his hands with a rag. "The only person who would use that hut is the leader of the Legionnaires, and right now we ain't got no Hooky."

"Hooky" meant two things. One was a person, and the other was a title.

The title was short for hookeleh, some kind of Hawaiian word meaning big chief. She had no idea if that was actually true.

The person was the only Hooky she had ever known. In the summer before, she had seen him stride across the beach like a suntanned colossus. The surfers made a joke out of worshiping him, but sometimes she felt like maybe it wasn't so much a joke.

For a moment she thought about it all. Hooky, with his straw hat and his haunted Korean War memories. How he'd taught her to surf as much as Newp had, had taken the time to point out the way the waves formed, connected it all with myth and history. And briefly—in a memory that she couldn't completely shut out—how he'd been killed by the creature called The Book Man. But the Book Man didn't get to define Hooky. He was one of a kind, and she ached for him.

Go-Go looked at Newp and said, "Hey, so you're back now — you were Hooky's right hand. Are you the new Hooky?"

One of the other boys said, "Yeah, Newp, are you back with the good news? Are you gonna hold the hut and be the Hooky?"

Newp seemed surprised by this question. Frannie had no idea what he would say. The boys seem to be functioning pretty well without a big chief, but in the time that they had been standing here, now two different people had asked her boyfriend if he wanted to be their leader.

She caught herself again. Boyfriend? Was that still what they were? Everything still felt very much up in the air.

Newp said something that sounded exactly like what Hooky would have said. "Well, I don't know about all that."

"Well, somebody should be using this hut," Frannie said. "If this is going to be the headquarters of the of the Legionnaires."

Brainiac turned towards Frannie and said, "What about you, Fran? You want to be Hooky?"

That made her smile, that one of them would think of her being the leader of the gang. Of course, they knew that she could be. They had seen her doing some very strange things and fighting some very strange creatures last summer, but it wasn't for her. "I don't think I could stay in that hut, and I don't think I could be the leader."

Newp was still pretty quiet. "What's been happening?"

Go-Go said, "Well, most of the summer people haven't come back yet. So, beach is ours for now."

"When did you guys get here?"

"I never left," Go-Go said. "I got a place a mile from here. Me and some of the guys. But it's tight. Some of us sleep on the beach."

Newp turned around and touched Frannie's shoulder, then walked with her towards the hut. He looked in and Frannie watched his eyes. Newp ran his hand along the top of the door frame and turned back. "Guys, I've been thinking."

"What's that?" Go-Go asked.

"That's where I use my brain," Newp said, and the Legionnaires chuckled. "But we all should be doing it. Look, I know it was important for

Hooky to turn his back on the life up beyond that highway, but we all need to find a way to get by. I mean, you guys do know that Hooky at least had an Army pension, right?"

They stared at him. "Anyway, what I think we should do is find a way to make surfing our life. Right? Isn't that what we want?"

Brainiac asked, "What is it you have in mind, Newp?"

"Well, I tell you what," Newp said. "I think we should start offering lessons."

"Lessons?" Frannie asked.

"Yeah, real surf lessons. See…" Newp started to pace, talking to each of them men as he went. "All around the country there are people writing articles about surfing. Okay? And they're putting them in magazines and newspapers… and so people are going to be coming here. And they're going to be watching us out there on the waves. People with their families. So—picture this: we have signs. We put up signs that let people know that if they come to us—if they come to this hut— we can teach them a little bit of surfing. And we can make some money. Go-Go?"

"Yes sir."

"Do you have an extra board or two that would be good for this kind of thing, that are okay to get banged up?"

Go-Go thought about it. For a moment Frannie remembered the first time she had seen him turn this question over, when the late great Hooky had asked if he had a board that Frannie could use. "Yeah, I think I got a couple."

"All right." Newp seemed to be getting more excited now. "We're going to be teaching sons and daughters. Husbands and wives." He pointed at each of the Legionnaires. "And listen, you animals. I don't want any creeping hands. Because the last thing we want is that we have to give any money back because there's complaints. Or worse, that Frannie has to come get any of you bozos out of the emergency room because some father—who probably has scars from Iwo Jima and wants to relive his wartime glory days, has put you in traction. All right? You men understand me?"

The boys all nodded solemnly, and Frannie felt much relieved that they were so readily agreeing not to sexually assault any females. This represented progress. When she was first learning, there were occasional slips of hands that she had to deal with, and she was pretty sure that Hooky may have beaten some of the surfers to a pulp about it when she wasn't around.

"Okay," Newp said. "The first thing we want to do is get our curriculum together."

One of the surfers asked, "What's a curriculum?"

"That's what we're gonna be teaching. So, I'll tell you what." Newp clapped his hands. "Today that's the goal. Let's figure out what it is that you would want to teach somebody who is brand new. Brand new! And then if you think it's easy…"

Brainiac said, "You taught Frannie in like fifteen minutes."

Newp laughed and rubbed Frannie's head. "Frannie's special, she's a freak of nature. Anyway, even if we could do it in fifteen minutes, we get we need to stretch it out to a morning, because remember we're going to have to be charging for it. Brainiac? I want you to go up and get in the car—does anybody have a car to loan Brainiac?"

One of the boys offered up a car and Newp continued. "Brainiac, you go up to Malibu and find out what people are there are charging for lessons, can you do that?"

"Sure, I can do that."

"The other thing we need to do is advertise. And I want to make it big. I saved up over the school year, and I have enough to get us two hogs this time. We need to have a blast off luau to make it official."

The uproar of cheers and hand clapping and back slapping made of all of them grin. Summer was back, and it was good.

"Catscratch, Tombo, I want a flyer done up by the end of tomorrow. Can we get the luau set up for next Friday night men?"

The uproar doubled this time, as Legionnaires left and right shouted offers of help and called out jobs they would do.

"I've got two coolers, I can get the ice, who is buying beer?"

"I can get at least a cooler full."

"I've got fruit from my pop's store, no problem, he throws stuff out at the end of the week anyway."

"Well don't bring any rotten crap, Shekkie."

"Don't bring your rotten face, Chiller, unless you're going to bring your sister too, she's cute."

Over the laughter and the shouting, Newp clapped his hands together. "All right, you men. Let's get to it! Luau Friday!"

The boys began to disperse, chatting in groups of two or three about how they would get ready for the party. Newp grinned and took a deep breath of the ocean air. Frannie turned and asked, "Don't you wanna get some surfing done?"

"Absolutely," Newp said. "Only way to get inspired."

They hit the water and Frannie found herself paddling out to the breakers for the first time in many months. At first her movements were sluggish, and then it was as if her arms remembered how they were supposed to move. She paddled as her body lifted and dropped in the waves.

With every wave she caught, she felt better and better. It was as though her body had been an empty house all winter, and now she was opening up and clearing up, knocking out the dust and throwing open the windows. The sunshine poured into her, and she felt fresh air blowing through her soul. Her spirit was back home, and all her worries about nursing, the future, Newp, the blanks, everything flowed out of her into the waves. This was the magic of surfing, and it was hers.

She sat on the shore a few hours later and grinned at Newp as he handed her a cold Coke and half a pastrami on rye.

"Has there ever been a more perfect day?"

"I can't think of a one. You look great out there, Frannie. I'm glad you're feeling better."

She nodded her thanks around a mouthful of sandwich, and it was

Newp's turn to grin.

"So, what do you think of the surf school idea?"

She swallowed and reached for the Coke. "I think it's a great plan. And a good solution for some of the boys. Oh, I know most of them have families and lives outside of this, but the ones who don't…as long as they don't blow the money, it'll be a big help. And fun, I think."

Newp nodded, wrapping his arms around his knees. "Hooky and I had talked about it before... everything happened. In fact, you were a kind of guinea pig for the idea. You just happened to be—"

"A freak of nature?" Frannie winked to let him know she was in on the joke, and Newp laughed.

"I was going to say a natural, you call it how you see it."

"I think Go-Go is right, Newp. You should be the new leader. Though maybe we should come up with a new name for the position."

They were silent for a moment, watching the waves.

"I want you to do it with me. Share it."

Frannie looked at him sharply, then softened. There was something painful in his face too. Were they all so damaged from last summer? "You don't need me, I—"

"I really do though, Frannie. You're a natural leader. You surf better than most, and they've been surfing for years. You'd be a dab hand at teaching kids and girls that aren't comfortable with the bigger boys, and…." Newp took a breath, and the next part spilled out too fast to be quite awkward. "And I want you by my side. This could be the start of something real, and I don't want it just for myself, I want it for us. To make a life out of surfing."

For a moment, it was a golden and shining idea, and Frannie felt its draw. It would be truly something, she thought. A whole life made of the café and the beach, the magic of the Blanks and the magic of the Surf, two halves making a beautiful, perfect whole. She reached for the idea with her mind, and then stopped cold. The dream was tarnishing before her eyes because she had seen too far into the future. The war the demon had shown her was still waiting, five, ten, fifteen years down the road, who knew? The broken and twisted bodies of boys lay on gurneys instead of surfboards, floating in an ocean of blood. She couldn't stop the inevitable war. But she needed to know how to fix what would remain.

"I love the idea Newp, I really do. It's a dream. But—" she twisted the coke bottle in her hands "I can't do it forever. There are things coming that I'm going to have to be ready for. I have to go to nursing school in the fall. I have to be ready."

Newp's face had gone from sunshine to storm. "Ready for what?"

She shook her head. "I don't know. I just know it's coming, and it's bad. I know that I'm going to have to save lives in ways I can't right now. Surfing can be my heart, but it can't be my whole life. There are bigger things."

She looked at him and mourned the death of the beautiful dream. His face was still closed when she reached out and took his hand. "But it's not here yet. And I can't start school til fall anyway. For the summer, I'm here, and I'll help with whatever you need. We're going to build the premier surfing school of Laguna Beach, okay?"

After a moment he nodded, but something about it made her uneasy. This didn't feel settled, and she felt guilty for bringing him down. Newp seemed to shake it off, however, and squeezed her hand.

"Yes, we are. Come on, the waves are picking up."

The afternoon light was still that of late spring and didn't hold on as long as the summer sun. As the surfer crowd waned, and Newp schemed with the Legionnaires on plans for the surfing school, Frannie found that she was completely alone with the surf. After paddling out, she sat on the board watching the waves, feeling that beautiful sensation of the salt air on her skin. Inevitably she thought about Hooky, and then tried to let the thought ride away on the waves. She spotted a wave and climbed it, knowing exactly when it would break. Just as the wave started to crest, she got up on her feet. Frannie stepped forward, hanging her toes over the end, hanging ten, and spread out her arms. She felt like she could fly, and the sound of the waves ratcheting underneath the fiberglass was a choir.

When the wave began to slow and she dropped down to the sand, Frannie noticed Carol Dolenz walking along the beach with a little dog. She had gone to high school with Carol. The girl waved widely, a 'come in' gesture, the dog yapping and jumping around her feet. Frannie smiled and jammed her board in the sand as she went to talk to her. "Hey Carol! Happy liberation summer, how is post-school life?"

Carol grinned "The first twenty-four hours, not bad! You've certainly taken advantage."

The little dog yipped louder, trying to jump up to Frannie. She bent down to pet the strange dog. "It looks like a sheltie, is it yours?"

"Not mine," Carol shook her head. "Actually, the reason I waved, I was wondering if this was your dog. She was running all around here."

Frannie shrugged. "Not mine. Where did you find her?"

Carol pointed south where the beach narrowed to a stony expanse between the cliffs and the water, disappearing from view. Frannie bent down and rubbed the dog's head again. "She doesn't have a tag."

Carol nodded. "I was dropping off some supplies for the Daughters of the American Revolution." Frannie laughed inwardly at the reference to this old organization. What did they even do? Charity? Dances? She had no idea. "Near the old governor's house at Victoria Beach."

Frannie had some vague understanding that there were mansions up there above the cliffs over by that old turret that everybody called the Pirate's Tower, but she'd never been over there. "Well, what are you gonna do with her?" Then she addressed the dog. "Huh? What are we going to do with you?"

"I don't know… I guess I thought it would take it to the pound." Carol said this as though it was the first time she had actually said the word pound aloud. Carol picked the dog up in the crook of her arm and scratched its head. "But I don't want to turn it over to a place like that. You know what they do in the end right? If nobody comes for them. They put them to sleep," she said solemnly.

Frannie nodded. Frannie had no experience with dog pounds, either, but didn't every town have one? Carol always was a soft-hearted one. In fact, it had been because of Carol that Frannie had wound up coming out to the beach for the first time. Carol had pressured Frannie over and over again to get out of the house after Frannie had healed from a terrible bicycle accident. And finally, Carol had prevailed. Fanny had come out to the beach, although in the end nothing had gone the way that Carol had predicted. Instead of spending the summer sunning and trying to get the attention of boys, Frannie had wound up working at her uncle's café across the highway and learning to surf. So, Carol's good-natured harassment of Frannie in her healing days had changed the direction of Frannie's life.

Suddenly the dog leapt out of Carol's arms and began running. Carol and Frannie ran after the dog as it made a beeline south to where the beach narrowed at the stones. They followed along the rocky shore. Periodically the dog would stop on the wet rocks and bark at the water and then look back at them. But there was nothing in the water at all for the dog to bark at. Soon the Pirate Tower loomed before them, and the dog scampered back and forth around its rusty metal entrance. Finally at the tower, Carol picked up the dog once more, and it shivered in her arms. Frannie petted the dog in Carol's arms and said, "What is it that you're seeing, little girl?"

Just then something caught Frannie's eye. A little bit of wood, about three inches wide and long, painted white, or at least painted white long ago. It floated among the wet stones at her feet. She reached down and shrunk back for a moment, because as she picked it up, the wood appeared to be a carved representation of fingers, like a wooden hand. Like someone had thrown a cigar store chief off the cliff and shattered it.

But that wasn't what made her shiver. Caught in a crack in the wood were what appeared to be several strands of human hair, still attached to a triangular bone shard of skull and skin.

Someone was dead.

CHAPTER 8

IT WAS NEARLY SUNSET BY the time Carol and Frannie finished up with the police. Frannie wondered a little sickly if every summer on Laguna was going to start with a dead body. She made the sign of the evil eye when she thought no one was looking, just in case. The police officer on duty was polite but cursory and took the piece of hair and skull away in a tiny bag.

He did not, however, take the wooden hand. It struck Frannie as odd, until she realized that ultimately it was just a piece of driftwood, albeit a disturbing one. She didn't want to touch it any longer than she had to, so she picked it up between pointer and thumb and placed it carefully in the rocks above the tideline. Something told her that Saul needed to see it. Last summer she would have brushed the thought off as crazy. This summer, she wondered if a new evil had set its sights on Laguna Beach.

Huh-uh, she thought. Not on my turf. Not this summer.

The wind started to pick up, and Carol shivered, holding the little dog tighter. Frannie turned her attention back to them.

"Come on," she said briskly. "You look like you could use a cup of coffee and a slice of pie. My treat. Besides, bands playing tonight, you and

Sandy there could hang out for a while and get warm."

"Sandy?"

Frannie shrugged "I don't know, the pup looks like a Sandy to me."

Carol nodded. "I dig it. Let's go."

Even though it was relatively early, the café was already hopping. They had used the phone to call the police, so it was no surprise to Saul that Frannie was late for her shift. She sat Carol at (in Frannie's opinion) the best booth and had a hot cup of coffee and a slice of strawberry cream pie. She even snuck a good chunk off of the bologna ring for Sandy, and the little dog wagged her tail in appreciation.

As she got settled into her shift, she hummed along with Betty and Truly. Sloop John B always did them in. That was the song that everyone loved to hear, a Kingston Trio number about someone serving on a boat with his grandfather and getting into adventures. It was a song that Betty and Truly loved to sing, even though neither of them had ever served on a boat, and in fact the adventures described in the song were not all that adventurous. The lyrics basically told the story of somebody serving very briefly on a boat and getting sick. Betty had to admit that if she were to join the navy, she didn't imagine that she would last much longer.

Carol and Sandy said good night and promised to visit the café more often as summer ramped up. Frannie bid them farewell and hustled back to clearing plates and glasses, wiping down tables, and soaking in the atmosphere. She had missed this so much. How could she imagine doing anything else?

At midnight, the set was done and Betty and Truly set about gathering up their gear, winding up the cords to the microphones, setting everything aside and in its proper place.

Newp came up to Betty as she was stowing the mics. Her brother seemed to have something on his mind. "What would you gals think about bringing more surf music into the act?" He turned off the amplifiers and helped her move them to one side of the stage.

"What's surf music?" Truly called from the piano as she wiped it down.

"It's kind of like jazz, except it's got a lot of guitar."

Truly tinkled a few bars on the piano. "So… you're talking about instrumentals?"

"I guess so," Newp said.

"We're a folk band," Betty said. "Nobody does instrumentals except maybe Turkey in the Straw."

"Yeah, okay." Newp ran his fingers through his hair. "But it's doing really well in Malibu. When Brainiac drove down there to check on the price of surf lessons, he said he saw posters all over for these live shows. I don't know—if we figured it out, we could split up the set. You could do a couple of numbers and then I could play one of these guitar tunes. You know like… Torquay?" He picked up a guitar and started plunking out a walking baseline. The Fireballs' instrumental song Torquay had come out earlier that year and was hovering around the Top 40, so there were definitely people getting into the groove of guitar-driven songs.

"That's a surf song?"

"It's the kind of thing they're doing at these surf shows, anyway," Newp said. He repeated the baseline and as he came around again, Betty laughed and began to work the piano, playing around the guitar. Finally, she said, "Hey, whatever keeps em putting money in the jar. We can try one tomorrow night."

As they talked, a burst of laughter came from one of the tables. The table had been boisterous all night and Truly raised an eyebrow.

The crowd at the table was a bunch of young folks dressed all in black. Their leader was a beefy teen with a black motorcycle cap and a leather jacket who snapped his fingers at Frannie until she broke free from the bar to take their order. Betty saw Frannie do a little dance because one of other guys at this table reached for Frannie's behind, and Frannie had to jog out of the way.

"Oh God," Newp said. "I need to go take care of these guys."

"I'm pretty sure that Frannie can take care of herself," Truly laughed. That was undoubtedly true, since Truly, Newp and Saul had accompanied Frannie all the way to Hawaii to kick serious demon tail last summer. They never talked about all that, and sometimes each of them seemed to wonder if the others had forgotten that it had happened. But one thing was clear, when everything went down, Frannie was the one in charge.

"Those guys have been giving us a hard time all night," Truly said to Newp. "And every time they get loud, they look around like they're expecting somebody to give them trouble."

Newp wandered off towards the table.

Truly turned to Betty. "Want to get out of here and grab a milkshake?"

"If we can take your car," Betty said.

As they walked across the café, the leader of the gang was holding up his hands dramatically as he talked to Newp, as if to say hey, we don't mean any trouble. Betty waved at her brother as they headed out the door to the parking lot.

The moment they left the front of the café, all sound shifted. The hollow noise of plates and laughter and amplified music was replaced with wind, traffic, and waves.

As they reached the car, Truly asked, "Is that a new nightgown?"

"Yeah." Betty looked down. The nightgown was checkered green and red. "I know it's a little Christmassy, but I like it."

"Works for me if it works for you. I think it's pretty chrome."

Betty smiled shyly at the compliment, and Truly grinned back, opening the car door for her. They got into Truly's car and sat for a moment, enjoying the quiet. In the parking lot pointed out towards Pacific Coast Highway, which rippled with reflected starlight, they could see clear to the ocean. Truly turned on the radio and Tommy Edwards warbled out:

Many a tear have to fall

But it's all in the game

All in the wonderful game

That we know as love

The beams of the headlights ate up the darkness in wide mouthed circles as they drove, and Betty relaxed into the car seat. She loved Truly's company. No one else was quite as comfortable a companion. One thing that Betty liked was that Truly never asked her anything obvious like, have you ever thought about not wearing nightgowns all the time? Truly wanted to know what she felt and thought about things—new songs, new books, new movies. They had gone to the drive-in last week to see South Pacific and decided to stay for the second screen feature of Attack of the 50 Foot Woman. It had been so fun, so normal to sit and talk to Truly about the movies, what she liked, what she didn't. The nightgowns didn't matter to Truly.

But they did, in a way, matter to Betty. Because of course she thought about it. She wondered what it would be like not to get looks everywhere she went. She couldn't put a finger on why, but anytime she put on a dress or a pair of jeans or even a cotton shirt, it was like her skin wanted to get up and run away from her. Only when she was in her flannel did she feel like everything was okay. And in fact, at that point, everything was.

Truly pulled onto the highway, joining a still brisk line of giant chrome vehicles moving up and down. They passed the stairs down to the beach and then a bunch of restaurants and boutiques, and then after a couple of miles, they found a place called Shakey's.

The restaurant was a shining miracle of stone siding and glass, with a neon sign of a heavyset man twirling a pizza in one hand and holding aloft a tray of burgers in the other. The parking lot was full, so they parked on the street next to the entrance of a brightly lit car dealership on the next block. As the two girls got out of Truly's car, Betty rubbed her hands together. "It feels strange going to a different restaurant."

Truly laughed. "We can't spend every waking hour in Café Monstro. I mean, it's like our home, and sometimes you gotta leave home."

The inside of Shakey's was a way different scene than Saul's. Betty knew for a fact that the Café Monstro had only been around for a year or so, but it felt like something ancient and timeless that had been hammered into being with the shields of Hephaestus. Shakey's was now. The lights blazed and the menus were thick and slick.

Betty and Truly took a booth next to the window looking out on the parking lot. The waitress that came to them after a while took their order and didn't seem to know where to look. She didn't want to address Truly, which wasn't new, and she seemed put out by Betty's flannel. They ordered milkshakes, one strawberry, one vanilla.

Betty had the vanilla. She poked at it with her straw and looked at Truly. "What are you gonna do at the end of the summer?"

"Summer hasn't even started, and you want to know what's happening at the end?" chuckled Truly. She sat back and looked around. Betty became aware that a couple of boys several tables down were staring at them. She glanced at them, then shifted uncomfortably in the booth. Truly bristled. "You don't have to look at them, Betts."

"Doesn't it bother you?"

"I'd be lying if I said it didn't…" Truly leaned back in the seat. "But what am I gonna do, not go out? I choose to hang out with a bunch of surfers in Laguna Beach, I know what I'm getting myself into."

"I'm no surfer."

"True enough. Well, then, end of the summer?" Truly twirled the empty straw wrapper around her fingers. "I suppose I'll have to make some decisions about what I want to do and where I want to be. Do I settle down, get a job and a place, or do we—do I, pack up and try my luck back east? There's good music out there, and things…maybe matter less, out there."

Betty was clearly distressed "Oh, no, Truly you don't mean you would break up the act?"

"I mean, I don't want to, Betty, you know I love playing with you. But moms and pops aren't going to let me stay much longer, eventually I'm going to have to fly the coop and find my own. We don't make enough playing for me to afford my own place alone, so I've got to decide if I stay and find a job or go."

Betty reached out and took her friend's hand. Truly looked at her in surprise, and in truth Betty surprised herself with her own fierceness. "Then we will find you a job, and we will figure it out. I don't want you to go. You're the only one who doesn't look at me like they do. You can live with me if it comes down to it, my family won't mind, I know it."

A couple of police officers came in and hovered nearby. It was nothing new, but tonight, Betty noticed, Truly had less tolerance for it than usual.

"We'll see, Betty. There's time. We have the whole summer to work it out, okay?"

When the cops walked by a third time Betty cleared her throat. "Is something wrong?"

The officer looked at Betty, then at Truly, and said, "I don't know, is something wrong?"

Truly shook her head dully. "No, we're just about finished."

They slurped the last of their milkshakes and got up to go pay at the counter. Truly handed her the money, and Betty paid, both knowing that any other arrangement would result in a scene with the cashier. Betty sighed. The nightgowns were one thing—those she could choose to ditch, if she had to, though she never would. Truly had no such options about her color.

They got up and walked out, tired, but at least together. Truly had parked her car on the curb next to the entrance to a car lot that gleamed with steel in the night. As they reached the wide entrance to the lot, stepping around the cars and making their way toward the curb, there was a roar of sound that made Betty jump.

The two girls pulled closer together because all of the sudden four or five motorcycles came in from the highway and into the entrance to the car lot. One of the motorcycles stopped really close to the couple, while more went around behind them. Three motorcycles, each one with a boy at the handlebars. Two of them had girls seated behind the rider. The girls wore long black leggings and leather jackets, and their hair was teased up high.

"These are those guys from the café," Truly said.

One of the three, the same skinny guy who had been making a lot of noise around Frannie, raised up a hand. The other two killed the engines on their bikes. The leader kept his own bike running. He pushed back his cap. He didn't seem very old by his face, but he was pasty and sweaty, with his black hair curling over his eyebrows.

"We're just getting to our car," Betty said nervously, as if she needed to explain herself.

The guy on the running bike answered, "Whose car?"

"My car," Truly snapped. She took Betty's hand and started walking. "Now, if you'll excuse us."

"You?" The guy laughed and clapped his hands. He was wearing black gloves. To the sound was a dull clop clop clop. "What they don't get up to these days. Mm-hm." He looked them up and down, lingering on Betty. "You chicks are the ones who sang at the café."

Betty was looking down and now stuck up her chin. "That's right, we're the Fencers."

"Okay," the guy said. "I like you." He turned to the girl behind him. "Donna, didn't I say that? Didn't I say I like them?"

"You sure did, Eric."

Betty felt herself shivering in her nightgown. Already she was envisioning all kinds of things that she had seen in movies. Without thinking she said, "Is that your name? Eric?" Because she had this idea that maybe if she were friendly, this would go okay.

"Yes, it is." He smiled and swept his arms. "My name is Eric—and these are my Phantoms."

Betty looked at him blankly.

"See…" he pointed at her, then looked at his friends. "See, she doesn't get it. Nobody gets it. You see, pretty girl, the Phantom of the Opera had a name. It was Eric. So, I'm Eric, and these are my Phantoms."

He stepped out from behind his bike, circling them slowly. The other bikers chuckled and watched the show with undisguised relish.

The two girls clung to one another instinctively. Eric stared at them for a moment, no apparent motive at all behind his eyes. "Why don't you take a ride with us." It wasn't a question.

"Ooh, I don't think so," Betty said. She started to step forward, and then one of the other guys was suddenly off his bike and in front of her with his hands raised up, as though to catch her in a hug. "Just… just let us go by." She was scared, now. This was getting bad.

"Why are you wearing a nightgown?" Eric asked. "What's that about?"

Truly spoke up. "She wears it because she likes it. Why do you wear those stupid jackets?"

Betty cringed.

"You got a mouth on you." Eric looked at Truly and the threat was clear.

"Anyway," Betty said. "There aren't a lot of losers around here, either. But I guess there's more every day."

"Oh ho," chuckled Eric. "I like you, blondie. And when Eric and the Phantoms like somebody, they stay liked." He looked at Truly. "You, not so much."

Betty said again, "We just want to get to our car." She didn't know what was going to happen next, but she could feel the sweat on her arms and chest dampening her flannel nightgown. There was a sea of cars between them and Shakey's restaurant, and there was no way that anybody over there could see what was going on.

To get to the highway and the car—even to just keep running—they would have to run through the gang. Which was impossible. Any minute now they were going to reach the moment in a movie when camera always cuts away. Because that's how movies are, they cut away. But real life doesn't cut away.

Then a shadow crossed her eye. There was somebody walking across the highway. Betty couldn't see very clearly who it was, just a figure crossing during a long space between cars. But she was wondering if they could see these guys on their bikes, these guys with their quiet girlfriends, corralling her and Truly backward in the parking lot.

Eric said, "Maybe we're just going to hang around together a little bit. Maybe you can teach us some of that music. What kind of music is it that you sing?"

Truly said, "Folk music."

"Folk music." Eric nodded. "All right, I feel smarter already."

There was a click of heels and then a woman's voice. "What's going on over here?"

By this time, Eric had reached out, and his fingers were brushing Betty's nightgown. He stopped and tilted his head to look back.

The woman who had suddenly appeared was wearing a long gray pencil skirt, a white blouse, and a gray jacket that matched the skirt and heels. She had short blonde hair and a pair of glasses. She could be anywhere from thirty to fifty years old, Betty thought. She was a little taller than Betty.

The woman had her feet planted firmly and her hands on her hip. She had great sharp nails, a carmine red. "I asked you: what's going on?"

"We're having a little get-together," Eric said. "What's it to you, lady?"

"I don't know," the woman said, idly flicking an invisible piece of lint from her sleeve. "It looks to me a lot like the puberty rites of Borneo."

Eric wiggled his head as though somebody had just clapped a book closed in front of his nose. He scowled and turned around all the way. "What the fuck did you just say to me?"

The woman smirked. "In Borneo, when the young men go through puberty, they must participate in a ritual where they act out the stealing of young maidens from other tribes. This is all pretend of course, because these young men have never actually been to war and never actually forced anyone to do anything. I think what I'm looking at here is the puberty rites of Borneo."

Eric nodded his head at the lieutenant next to him. This biker pulled out a knife with a flick, and the blade gleamed in the dark.

"You talk really funny," Eric said. "But maybe my friend Jackie here can fix that."

"Okay," the woman said, walking slowly and calmly toward Eric, cutting off his path around the girls. "Let's talk about that. Let's say you do fix that. Let's say you come after me with that knife. And further, let's say you cut me. Or maybe you don't because maybe I know some ways of dealing with people like you and knives like that." Like lightning, Toni's hand struck out and grabbed Eric by the wrist. She must have touched some secret pressure point because he howled and dropped the knife to the pavement. Toni stepped on it with her stiletto and held it there. "Yes, I know some ways of dealing with that. But you... you're still trying to sweet talk this girl. So, what are you going to do? Maybe you try to cut that flannel nightgown off of her. I don't know why she's in a nightgown, but it should be pretty easy to cut through. And then what are you gonna do? You three guys, and you two women on the bikes, and I just can't tell you how proud I am of you young ladies—you're the only ones who look like you on this entire highway. And somebody will see, and they'll remember you. And I know that you want to commit to bigger and better things than just assaulting these two ladies. And you won't be able to do that anymore. You'll have to find a different turf. If this is even your turf at all."

Everyone had stopped to stare at the blond woman. "Let me break it down for you," she continued. "This is not going to go well for you. So why don't you kids run along."

Eric the Phantom seemed to think about this for a moment, holding his aching wrist. Toni stepped off the knife, and he scooped it up. "Okay, sister. Or maybe I should call you professor. Professor Borneo. How do you like that? School's out for now, Professor. But I'll be doing my homework on you, don't you fret."

He got back onto his motorcycle and kicked several times until the engine ignited. Once more he pointed at Betty and said, "You I like. And when a Phantom likes somebody, they stay liked." He pointed at Truly. "You

I don't like. But it's nothing personal." And then he looked at "Professor Borneo" and said "Oh, but you. You I don't like, and it is personal. We'll see you real soon."

And just like that, the three motorcycles peeled out of the car lot and into the distance

Betty was still shaking. Truly doubled over. "Holy Jesus, that was amazing." She turned to the serene woman with the blonde hair. "I cannot believe that." Truly stepped past the woman and to the curb to watch the red lights of the motorcycles disappearing into the distance.

Then she turned again to the woman that Eric the Phantom had called Professor Borneo. "I don't know how to thank you."

The woman fished a cigarette out of her little purse and put it in her mouth. She reminded Betty of Grace Kelly. "You don't have to. You girls okay?"

"We're... okay," Truly said. "I've never seen anyone handle creeps like that."

"Oh... when I was in the Pacific," the woman said, "the creeps weren't any different. The only thing that's changed is the uniforms."

Betty wasn't sure that they were okay, because she had no idea what they would have done if the strange woman hadn't shown up. She had to do something to stop shaking. She tried friendliness. "I'm Betty." She reached out her hand and the woman took it. "And this is Truly. We sing at the Café Monstro."

The woman said, "That's a bit of a drive isn't it? Up the highway?"

"Yeah," Truly said. "We finished our set and came to get milkshakes over here at Shakey's. Who are you? I haven't seen you around."

"My name is Toni Sutcliffe. I teach at the University of Laguna Beach."

Betty laughed. "Oh my gosh, so you really are a professor! We have a friend whose dad teaches there. Professor Cohn."

Toni nodded. "I think I know him. He teaches comparative literature, correct?"

"I think that's right," Truly said.

"Well, you girls be careful out here at night. That little pissant was mostly hot air and trying to scare you...but that's the first step on a dangerous ladder."

Truly nodded. Betty folded her arms and asked, "So all that stuff that you said. The puberty rites of Borneo. Is that true?"

"Not really," Toni said. "I just latched on to some words that maybe they'd heard of. Honestly that little interaction was just a form of poker if you think about it. I called his bluff, and he couldn't call mine. We win."

The girls laughed. Betty was feeling better already.

"You should come by the café and hear us sing," Truly said.

Betty tried to follow that up with something funny, but she found that she could barely open her mouth and she started shivering. Suddenly she wanted to throw up. She crouched down on her knees and Truly came behind her and put her hand on her neck. "I'm sorry," Betty said. After a moment she groggily got up.

"That's okay," Toni said, "that's normal. It's called shock, and it'll pass in a little while. You should get home and get some rest though." She crushed out her cigarette with her shoe. "And I'd love to hear you girls sing. I'll try to come by tomorrow night, how would that be?"

Truly nodded with her arm around Betty. "That sounds great. Our set starts at seven. We have some people that you would probably love to meet."

Toni smiled widely and shook the girl's hands. "It's a date."

She watched the two girls go. Out of the dark sea of cars, the lone and lank figure of Michael Landry slunk. She held out her hand to him.

"Can you get the scent?

He leaned in, sniffed, and nodded.

"Remember it. I have a feeling we'll be seeing them again."

"You worried?"

"A little. I don't like bullies, and I don't like gangs. I hate them both together. Are you all right?"

Michael shrugged inside his red letterman's jacket. "Just feeling itchy."

"Keep it together. As it happens, we're going to that café you were telling me about tomorrow night."

He froze for a moment, then worked on appearing relaxed. "Oh?"

"Indeed. Print up ten extra flyers about the lecture, I want to bring them."

She turned and smiled in the light of Shakey's sign. "Don't look so worried. Come on, let's get burgers. My treat."

CHAPTER 9

FRANNIE WIPED DOWN THE LAST of the tables while Kurt rolled silverware and Saul counted out the till for the night. It had been a good night, the kind she liked best—mixed crowds, families with kids, and plenty of familiar hellos from the regulars. The biker gang had been a pain in the ass, but they left shortly after Truly and Betty's set, and the rest of the night had been a gentle slope to closing. Mutt and Jeff—the two off-duty undercovers who liked their coffee hot and their pie cold—had congratulated her about school and asked politely about her calling in the drowning that morning.

"Some people just have all the luck, I guess," said Frannie, trying to play it cool.

"Mutt's had that kind of luck his whole life—look at the face he was born with," joked Jeff.

"At least I never had to put a paper bag over it," Mutt shot back, without any heat. He leveled a glance at Frannie. "It's never comfortable, though, calling in a drowning, and this is your second one in a year, isn't it?"

Frannie nodded, picking up the empty coffee mugs. "At least there wasn't a real body this time, you know? It's okay. I'm okay. I mean, if I'm going to surf, these things are going to happen, aren't they?"

Mutt and Jeff shared a glance, and then as if on a silent signal, Jeff reached into his coat pocket and pulled out a card. He handed it to Frannie as though passing a secret note.

"They are. But there are some biker gangs moving in from up the coast, and we're worried that those things might start happening more frequently. We want to be on top of it. So, if you see anything weirdsville, you call this number."

Anything weird. Shit. She had forgotten to tell Saul about the wooden hand. It would have to wait now until after closing.

"Gangs like that group in black leather earlier?" They nodded. "You think they're really dangerous?"

Mutt shrugged "I think they're worth watching. And I think anything worth watching has the potential to go south. So, you just keep a cool eye on things, Frannie."

She had nodded, and the gumshoes had taken their leave. The card sat in her shirt pocket, and she found herself touching it from time to time, like a charm. She tried to shake the feeling of trepidation after they left, but only succeeded in losing herself in the simple work.

In the kitchen, behind the swinging saloon doors, Newp was up to his elbows in dishes and soap suds. He felt Saul rather than heard him, and the older man slipped a fold of bills into Newp's front apron pocket from behind. "Good night's work makes for a good night's pay, boychik. Have plans to spend it unwisely? If not, you should make some."

Newp chuckled. "Ah, but my boss is a slave driver, when will I have time to do anything unwisely?"

Saul joined him at the sink and plunged his hands into the dishes, shaking his head in mock despair. "How painfully true, alas. And I have evil designs to eat up even more of your waking hours. I wanted to..."

Frannie came in just at that moment to drop off a bus tub, and Newp noticed Saul's quick change to address her. "O glorious goddess of dish tubs, bring us no more crockery we pray!"

She shook her head laughing. "Sorry fellas, two more tubs, get scrubbing!"

With a flick of her hair, she was back out the door and into the café. Saul dropped his voice and resumed the conversation.

"Listen, I'm not one for dancing when there's no music. I think you and Frannie should take over the café next year. You make a great team, I trust you, you can run things however you like, everybody's happy."

Newp paused and set down the pan he had been scrubbing. "Not everybody. I love the idea, Saul but you know Frannie isn't going to go for it. She has her heart set on nursing school."

Saul waved his bubble clad hands about as though getting rid of an annoying gnat. "She does, she does, I know. But I'm thinking maybe this is a thing that might pass."

"Or that you think I can talk her out of."

"Doesn't hurt to try."

"I've still got another year of college to go myself before I have my degree, Saul."

"Oh of course, I forgot. But even so…maybe this summer, we try it out a little, huh? I've been thinking about taking Kurt away for a vacation. We haven't had one in…" He scrunched his bald pate in thought. "Ever."

"Sounds nice. Still, Saul, I don't think—"

"You just talk to her. She says no, she says no, but…I think perhaps she'll listen a bit more to her handsome boyfriend than her bald and vaguely ridiculous uncle."

"Vaguely?"

Saul snapped a towel at Newp playfully before leaving to pick up the last two dish tubs. Which ran him smack into his niece.

"Oy! You're in some hurry."

"I remembered something I forgot to tell you earlier, about the drowning. Do you have a minute?"

"I have ten for you. What was it?"

Frannie frowned. "There was something weird about the hair and the scalp. It was wrapped around a piece of driftwood, but I don't think it was just driftwood. It was like a sculpture? Like a mannequin hand. I didn't want to touch it, something about it felt wrong. I wanted you to take a look at it, and then I just got caught up in the shift and forgot."

Saul nodded, pursing his lips. "You think this is some kind of curse, or magic to this thing?"

"I don't know. Or I don't know enough to tell. It just felt bad to me. I put it in the rocks above the tideline, near the Pirate Tower."

"Okay. You want to go look tonight?"

"Maybe? It's a nice enough night, and I'm not tired yet, if you're not."

It was true, she wasn't tired. By rights she should be exhausted by a day spent surfing and a night spent serving, but the truth was after the doldrums of spring semester, the action of the beach and the café had lit her up like the 4th of July. She expected she would pay for the energy expenditure with a long sleep in tomorrow, but for the moment she was ready for anything.

"Okay, all right, let me tell Kurt and Newp. Go dig up a couple flashlights."

In the space of a few minutes, they were headed off down the beach.

Kurt, not one for overt displays of anything except his art, couldn't believe his luck. He handed Frannie two flashlights he had scrounged out of the back office and waved her off. The front door had barely clicked shut behind them when he made his way to the kitchen and started to put away dishes as Newp dried them.

"Hey, Newp."

"Hey, Kurt."

"Do you know anyone that has a truck with a trailer hitch?"

Newp blinked. As was often (always) the case with Kurt, the question had appeared out of nowhere and apropos of nothing.

"Uh, my pop does, why?"

Kurt grunted and stacked plastic fry baskets. "Need to rent or borrow one. I have something important to pick up. A surprise. For Saul."

At that moment, the surprised one was Newp. He had never known exactly what to make of Kurt and Saul's…partnership? Relationship? Friendship. He settled on the word. But he knew the two men meant a great deal to each other. And it was a brave new world. At college, people had all sorts of new ideas about pairing off, and what love might be, and… Newp shook the thoughts off, and turned to answer Kurt.

"Well, I mean, anything for Saul of course. I'll ask him."

"I can rent it for the day, money's not an issue."

"Oh, no, it's all square, Kurt, I'll ask my pop tomorrow. He might ask that I be the one to drive it though."

Kurt appeared to think about this, and then nodded. "Long as I can trust you to keep the secret, you got it?"

"My lips are sealed."

Kurt smiled, an event and countenance so rare that Newp marveled at it for a moment. It was as open and friendly a smile as he had ever seen. Then, like a cloud passing over a dazzling sun, Kurt's face returned to its generally passive and distracted demeanor.

"You let me know, then."

"No problem. Where are Frannie and Saul?"

Kurt shrugged. "Went down to the beach. Said not to wait for them."

"Tsh. Guess it's you and me and the grunt work while the cats are away."

Kurt said nothing more but lifted another stack of baskets in companionable silence.

The cold sand snaked between Frannie's toes, and she shivered. Their flashlights did little to cut the darkness much farther than a board length ahead of them, but the moonlight limned the rocks and surf with its quicksilver gleam. They were silent as they walked, each lost in their own thoughts of what the summer would bring.

"It's just up here, in that pile of—what the hell—"

At first Saul thought that they had come upon a racoon or some other nocturnal creature, but what glared back into the flashlight beams was nothing short of a monster. It hulked over, humanoid but horrifically wrong. The joints bent in unnatural angles, as though bones had broken and set and rebroken into a grotesquery of human anatomy. The head spun all the way around to regard them with eyes that sparked an emerald rage into the lights. He couldn't make out the face in the fierce blaze of the eyes, but what he could make out was a pale, flat countenance with dark...hair? It was all too flat, too smooth, too rounded, like a face painted onto something. Painted on...

Wooden hand. Painted face.

"It's a mannequin!"

"WHAT?!"

With a repulsive twist of its joints, the mannequin straightened and began to run mechanically up the beach. As it did, it reached to re-attach what had been its missing hand to the appropriate limb. On little more than instinct, Saul and Frannie ran after it.

"HEY!" Frannie yelled at it, hurrying to the wet firm sand and sprinting after it. It dodged around a log and Frannie vaulted over it, hoping to close the distance. She expected it to weave, but the mannequin bore a straight line along the sand. She pressed herself forward, hoping for enough speed to snatch at an arm, without any plan for what she would do if she caught it. Like some lithe robot, the mannequin leapt up and over a small rock outcropping, and Frannie was forced to lose precious time going around. Only the up/down motion of her flashlight beam saved her, lighting up the basketball sized rock sailing toward her in the darkness. She dodged to the side but lost her flashlight to the waves. It flickered and died under the water, and Frannie rolled after it, hoping another missile wasn't coming her way. When she raised her head from the water, she knew she was spent, and the mannequin was too far away to catch.

After a few moments Saul reached down to lift her up, and they watched its moon-silvered silhouette disappear around a bend in the beach. They stooped, hands on their knees, panting.

"What…was…that…?" Frannie gasped.

"A mannequin. An….an auto… automaton." Saul heaved. "Did it… throw that…at you?"

Frannie nodded wordlessly, and they stared at the rock. They started to catch their respective breaths and straighten.

"I got lucky."

"Better an ounce of luck than a pound of gold."

"Better my head on my shoulders than smashed to a pulp."

Saul shook his head and whistled. "That was—"

"A golem? Like Emmett?"

He shook his head again "No, Emmett was his own…person, I guess. That thing—"

"You said automaton."

"Right. I've never seen one before. You think Emmett was some big magic, an automaton is something else. Golems you create and then invite the universe into them. That's why I was so shocked it worked, it has to want to come, want to help and obey you. These things, that's binding magic, you have to tie a spirit or a ghost or a soul into it and force it to obey you. That's dark stuff."

They stood on the black and silver beach, gazing in the direction the mannequin had disappeared. Frannie stomped in anger.

"I wish I had a…" she made a vague throwing gesture, and then pulled her arm back as though shooting a bow. "You know? Something."

"Something," Saul agreed.

The waves crashed. The moon shone. Frannie's shoulders sagged.

"This is bad."

Saul nodded.

"This is bad."

CHAPTER 10

IF THERE WAS ONE THING Saul held tightly to that Frannie couldn't disagree with, it was the necessity of sleep. Saul called Frannie's parents to let them know that she would be staying the night in the spare room above the café, as she was too tired to drive home. She had kept a small toiletry kit there and a change of clothes in case she needed to freshen up (or, on one memorable occasion, accidentally tipped an entire chocolate milk down the front of herself). Frannie washed the salty water and sand off herself in the tiny stand-up shower, tied her hair up in a night kerchief, and turned back the covers of the Army cot. She crawled in, mind ablaze, but body struggling to keep the last embers of energy going.

It had been in this room that they had made Emmett, the golem, who had guided them in their defeat of the Book Man last summer. "All is vanity," he had told her once, and the memory echoed painfully in her heart. So, someone was making automatons. Why? For what purpose? Did the mannequin kill whoever the hair belonged to? Was it evil? Who knew that kind of magic? Why—

Her body did what her mind could not, and she fell deeply into sleep. But there were no answers to be found in her dreams, or if there were, they were gone upon waking.

"Frannie!" she heard from down the hall and tried to muffle the reality of the sounds with her pillow.

Nope, she mumbled in her mind. No Frannie here. Please try your call again later.

"Frannie! Wake up! Newp called, something happened to Betty and Truly last night, he wants us all to meet. Chop chop, lambchop, Kurt is making the coffee."

This news perked her up a bit. Saul could do anything, but when Kurt made coffee, angels guided his long artists hands. It was almost enough to coax her out of the warm, comfy cot.

A few minutes later she heard a mug set gently on her nightstand.

"Mfkay. M'up."

"Okay. Newp and the girls will be here in about ten minutes."

At that, Frannie scrambled to her feet, and began to get about dressing.

Seven minutes later, she descended the stairs with her hands wrapped around the mug as though it were a precious jewel. Newp had pulled together two of the smaller tables in the café together, and she could see Betty and Truly nursing their own mugs. Kurt was in his usual spot at the bar, applying papier-mâché to an unrecognizable shape, and Saul was laying out plates of toast, eggs, and fresh fruit. Frannie took a seat, not noticing (though this did not escape Saul's keen eye) that she had taken the place at the head of the table, opposite Newp.

Saul sat, and everyone tucked into breakfast, quiet as Newp relayed the night's events as calmly as possible. Frannie could tell that despite his best efforts, Newp was angry and a little shaken. By the end of the story, so was she.

"They pulled a knife on you?" Saul asked Betty, a deep note of dismay in his voice. Betty nodded, her eyes dropping to her half-eaten toast. Truly took her hand under the table and held it firmly.

"And then Professor Sutcliffe, she had it out of that punk's hand faster than you could think. She just put her hand on his wrist and did some kind of claw move thing, like those Chinese guys in the movies, and bam, he dropped it like the handle was on fire," said Truly, squeezing Betty's hand.

Newp, Frannie and Saul all looked at each other in silent agreement.

"They don't come back here," said Newp firmly. "Ever. We won't ever let them in here again."

Kurt made a sound of agreement from his corner, and Saul and Frannie nodded.

"We'll even tell Go-Go and Brainiac and the rest of the Legionnaires to keep an eye out," said Newp. "I don't generally hold to this kind of stuff, but this is Legionnaires turf. They won't bother you again."

The girls nodded, but it was clear that Betty was still nervous. Newp laid a hand on his sister's flannel-clad shoulder, as Saul spoke up.

"That's not the only bad news, I'm afraid," he said. He nodded at Frannie, and she recounted for everyone the adventure with the mannequin on the beach. As she described it, Kurt stood up decisively and strode toward the bookshop, returning with a small and possibly antique catalogue.

"Like this?" he asked, flipping the book open and pointing to a slightly blurry picture.

"Exactly like that!" Frannie exclaimed, looking closer. From the photo, the build and the unnaturally stiff pose were a dead ringer for the automaton. Saul passed the catalogue around, nodding himself at the painted face and painted on gloved hands.

"How did you know Kurt?" asked Betty, peering at the picture. The taciturn man shrugged.

"Used them in art school when we didn't have live models. They were creepy at the best of times."

"Is this the same bad guy as last time?" asked Truly. "Or something new?"

Frannie started to answer, and then stopped. Was it? The dybbuk box that held the Book Man in his endless prison was only about a mile offshore. Was it holding? Had she and Saul laid strong enough charms? Was there any such thing against an enemy that powerful?

Saul shook his head. "New, I'm pretty sure. The Book Man was a taker—this is different. It's dark magic all right, but the Book Man had to take over human bodies to do his work. This is a spirit or a ghost or a soul that's been bound to the mannequin which means there has to be a binder."

Betty looked up then, frowning "But it didn't hurt anyone, right?"

Frannie glanced uneasily at Saul. "Well…it almost killed me with a rock. I got lucky and dodged. And the reason we found it was because of that hand with the hair and piece of skull. Someone is dead. But it's not clear who, or why, or how involved the automaton is."

They were all silent for a moment. The sun started pouring through the windows, creating a blaze of reflection off of the huge, crucified Frankenstein monster. The strange events of the night before didn't burn away with the morning light, as bad dreams often do, but lingered like the smell of smoke.

Saul slapped his palms on the table, and they all jumped a bit. He grinned a sheepish apology. "All right, enough long sour faces. Time to focus on what we can do and control. Truly and Betty, from now on those creeps are persona non grata at Café Monstro. If we see them, we—"

"Call Mutt and Jeff," interrupted Frannie. "They were worried something like this might happen and gave me their card. In fact, I'll call them and let them know this morning. You'll have the Legionnaires AND the real cops watching out for you."

"Right," said Newp. "You'll be watched. We're on it."

"As for the mannequin, Frannie and I will start hitting the books and see what there is to find out. Meanwhile Newp, you tell the boys and any other surfers out there to stay off the beach at night or stay close to the beach fires. No one wants a repeat of last summer."

"What can we do?" asked Truly.

"Learn those surf tunes and get the crowds in here," grinned Newp. "As your manager, that's a direct order. And I want at least three surf tunes ready for the Luau on Friday."

Betty lifted her head sharply and looked at her friends. "We need to do something for Professor Sutcliffe. She saved us. We need to show her our gratitude. She's new here, and she's coming to the café tonight."

"Then whatever she wants is on the house. Our treat," said Saul.

"I'll invite mom and dad out tonight," said Frannie. "They're colleagues at the University, it might make her feel more comfortable."

"I don't think uncomfortable is a way that she ever feels," said Truly, an admiring note in her voice. "She was the coolest last night."

"Perfect," said Saul, with finality. "Let's get to work."

The morning passed in close quarters and distracted activity. Betty and Truly took the opportunity of the relatively quiet hours to play around with the new song styles. Newp was busy putting the finishing touches on the luau posters and complaining about the price of printing them up. Saul dug through piles of books and papers, pulling out bits and bobs and scraps about binding magic for Frannie to pour over. Kurt manned the café, plying all of them with his heavenly coffee and the occasional plate of store-bought cookies.

Newp came up behind Frannie, who was buried in a tome. "I'm going to head down to the beach, the Legionnaires should be down there for a luau meeting. You coming?"

Frannie looked up and rubbed one eye "In a bit. I think I'm starting to understand some of this stuff."

"That's one up on me, I don't understand how you do any of it."

How did she do it? That thought hadn't ever occurred to her either. From the minute she had nearly died and seen the symbol of Emet floating in the white nothingness, she hadn't questioned any of it—the Blanks, the demons, nothing. Nor had the not knowing bothered her. Now it did, and she frowned.

"Listen, just give yourself a break at some point, okay? Come catch a wave before the shift. I'll be down on the beach if you need me."

She nodded distractedly, then tried to get back into the book. No good.

She turned to a leaf of parchment, then another smaller book, but nothing she picked up caught her and pulled her back in. Saul plunked half a sandwich down in front of her, eating the other half himself.

"You look frustrated."

She picked up the sandwich, then put it back down.

"How does it work? How do we do this? Why can we do this? Why us, why me?"

"I dunno," he mumbled around a mouth full of sandwich. "Does it matter?

Frannie scowled. "Yeah, it matters. I don't know how this works, how we can do this, so how can I change it or make it better or make it work for me?"

At that last bit, a cloud passed over Saul's face. "It doesn't work for you. That's dangerous thinking. It's a tool we use to do a job we can't do any other way."

"Okay great, so why do we have the tool? How does it work? Do you know?"

"No, I don't really know."

"Is there someone who does?!"

Now it was Saul's turn to scowl. "Yes. And they're not the nicest people. Or the most trustworthy. And they're absolutely not anyone that you are ready to start playing ball with yet, do you get me? There are very good reasons I keep the Blanks a secret and you don't see me attending the annual Blankguard Ball and Buffet. So, for now, I think it's best that we keep studying on our own, and if we come across something really bad or dangerous that is directly threatening us, then we can reach out, okay?"

"Is that a thing?"

"Is what a thing?"

"The Blankguard Ball."

"Shut your face and eat your sandwich."

She picked up the sandwich and stood. "I'm going surfing. I need a break. And before you start in again about studying and learning and being ready, rabbi, you better start thinking about spilling all the beans. Because if you don't start telling me, I'm going to start finding out on my own."

She turned on her heel and stormed out, as Kurt joined Saul at the table.

"She looks just like my mother," murmured Saul.

"Acts like her too, from what you tell me."

"Yeah. Just like."

Kurt put a gentle arm across Saul's shoulders, and in an unusual display, kissed the top of his head. "You can't protect her forever. And more importantly, you shouldn't."

Saul sighed, and patted Kurt's hand. "I know. How is the staff coming along?"

"Slower than I like. Of course, first thing in the morning meetings do put a damper on my productivity."

"Point taken. Let me know as soon as it's done though, huh?"

"Beat feet to the kitchen. You have prepping to do. It'll be done when it's done."

"I hate it when you say that."

Frannie couldn't focus. Even the steady beat of the waves couldn't soothe her ruffled mind. She missed wave after wave, her timing completely off. Her thoughts careened from the threats to Truly and Betty to binding spells to Blankguards and back again. A particularly bad mistiming resulted in a nasty tumble, and Frannie hauled her board out of the water in poor temper. She stuck it in the sand next to Hooky's hut, and sat down in a huff, wrapping her arms around her knees. The sun shone but didn't beat the heat down like it would later in the summer, and she found herself getting a bit chilly.

This was all so stupid. She had more important things to worry about. There was some kind of war coming. She remembered the vision of herself elbow deep in the blood and viscera of a young man (boy) who had eerily resembled Newp, and she kicked the sand in frustration. The rejection letter from Georgia had stung, but she was hardly one to give up after just one no.

She would apply again and find other programs to apply to. She would see about volunteering at the local hospital. Maybe if she did well enough with volunteering they would teach her something useful. It was a start.

She dug her bare feet into the warm sand when something touched her toe. She jumped, a little startled, then knelt closer to see what it was.

It was a set of dog tags.

She already knew the name she would find on them.

She turned them over and over in her hands, the motion oddly calming, the slide and slink of the chain echoing the retreat and return of the waves. Frannie wondered briefly if finding them was some kind of message or sign, then shook the thought away. If she went looking for that kind of thing on purpose, she would find it everywhere, and get mixed up. She glanced at the hut, wondering if she should hang them up, or hang on to them.

In the end, she split the pair, keeping one and hanging up the other. She borrowed a leather thong from Go-Go and fashioned herself a bracelet out of the second one. She knew exactly what to do with it—it would become a focus, a touchstone reminder of her purpose. There were greater monsters than the Book Man to defeat.

Soon the sun was sinking, painting the sky of Laguna Beach in rich hues of purple, creamy pink, and gold. The surfers abandoned the waves for the warmth of the beach fires, and Frannie and Newp climbed the stairs toward Café Monstro. The crowds were already starting to trickle in like small flights of moths, looking for the warmth and light of the café.

One such moth was the tall, hunching form of Michael Landry.

Frannie smiled widely and headed over to say hello. If she saw the look of jealous mistrust on Newp's face, she chose to ignore it.

"You came back! I'm glad. How is Hollywood?"

Michael shrugged coolly but seemed to smile back. "Not as happening as this place. What's the big kick about this joint at night?"

At that moment, Betty and Truly started tuning up on the stage, and Frannie's smile widened into a grin. "The hot music act, that's what. Go on and find a booth, I'll bring you a cherry coke in a minute. I'm working tonight."

"Who is that," Newp hissed in her ear as she mixed the drink.

"His name is Michael. A Blank called him in. He seemed lonely so I invited him to come back sometime—maybe he'll make a few friends."

Newp nodded, and Frannie wondered at the expression on his face, then shrugged it off. This was a busy night, and she didn't have time for moods. She grabbed a tray and bustled off. She wasn't going to make tips if she didn't get a wiggle on. School cost money.

Truly and Betty were about to take their first break, when Toni Sutcliffe entered the Café Monstro. She was as polished and professional looking as she had been the night before, short coiffed hair sharply in place and her sensible but stylish heels beating a neat tattoo across the floor. The girls signaled to the others that this was the woman they had been looking for, and Saul intercepted her.

Frannie couldn't catch their conversation from the bar, but she saw both figures relax slightly, and Saul took Toni's elbow in that gentlemanly way he had from his time in the Catskills. Shockingly, he led her to Michael Landry's table, and proceeded to take her order. From the stage, Truly cleared her throat. "This one is for Professor Sutcliffe. Welcome to the café, professor!"

Truly and Betty launched into Unforgettable with twin grins on their faces, while Saul hustled back the order.

"Two cheeseburgers with fries, and a root beer for the lady," called Saul, pushing his way through the saloon doors. Frannie poured the root beer and nimbly threaded her way through the tables, eager to get her own glance at Sutcliffe.

"You're the Cohn girl, aren't you?" said the cool blonde, taking the root beer. Frannie looked up, shocked, and Michael laughed.

"She does that to everyone, don't take it personal," he chuckled.

"You have your mother's lovely eyes, and your father's, do excuse me, rather stubborn chin," Sutcliffe said, grinning. "It wasn't a large leap of logic to make. I met them at the semester faculty dinner."

"Oh! Of course," said Frannie, trying not to feel the butt of the joke. "They've mentioned you, too. I'll be your server tonight; we'll get those burgers out to you right away. And thank you again for everything you did, Truly and Betty are more than just the music act, they're—" she was about to say family, when the gravity of the word struck her. She was saved from an embarrassing pause by Toni.

"I completely understand, and it was my pleasure. There's very little I enjoy more than putting down a creep like that. We ladies have to stick together, don't we?" Toni caught Frannie's eye on the question, and Frannie felt as though she was part of a powerful secret.

"Absolutely we do. Enjoy the music, I'll be back as soon as your order is up."

The order came up at the set break, and soon Toni's table was full to bursting with people—though Kurt hovered at a discreet distance near the bar, filling drink orders as everyone wanted to refill their cup when the music stopped. Truly and Betty were telling the story of their rescue to anyone who would listen, and a number of the Legionnaires were wide eyed with admiration (and masculine appreciation) of the professor. Only Newp seemed immune—his focus seemed to be entirely on Michael Landry.

Frannie dropped off the burgers and made to sneak away, but Truly's voice caught her out. "Frannie is our own resident tough girl. She doesn't take any lip off of anyone either. She's a real surfer girl."

"Surfer girl? I didn't think there were any girls who surfed. What a fascinating subculture this surf-world is, I would love to study it. Perhaps I could pick your brain sometime Frannie?"

Frannie felt herself flushing under the unexpected attention and nodded.

"But," said Toni, slapping a palm on the table. "That's not the only reason I'm here. I'm giving a lecture series at the University while I'm here as a visiting professor—of course I don't really know a lot of people in the area and was hoping you might all come. I promise it won't be boring—it's about tiki culture. I expect it will be the next big trend out here in California. Or at least," she said with a smile, "if you aren't interested in coming, you might all tell your parents. It's tomorrow afternoon at the University lecture hall, east campus. I'm told there will be lemonade. Ah, yes, thank you Michael—I brought flyers."

Toni passed out the flyers and Frannie felt a little thrill of intrigue at the fascinating patterns on the poster—a rough drawing of an ancient wooden god stared off the page at her, surrounded by bougainvillea blossoms. Tomorrow happened to be her day off, and the prospect of learning more about Tiki culture, whatever that was, paled a little in comparison to learning more about Toni.

"I'll be there," said Frannie. "Newp, want to go?"

Newp turned, about to say yes, but a shadow crossed his face. "I can't, I promised Kurt I'd help him with something. You should go, though, it'll be great. And professor, I will trade flyers with you—we're having a luau this Friday night to celebrate our new surfing school. You should come."

"That's the most charming offer I've had in ages. Thank you, Newp."

Betty took Frannie's arm. "Truly and I will be your date to the lecture, if you don't mind the company."

"Okay, great. I'll try to drag Saul along too. He doesn't get enough sun."

As though on cue, Saul called up an order, and the group gathered around the table scattered back to their accustomed positions. Betty and Truly swung into one of the new surfer tunes, and Frannie ran back to catch up on tables. Though Newp kept a weather eye on the door, the bikers didn't return, and the evening passed as pleasantly as it had begun.

Frannie didn't notice when Toni left, but Michael's shadowed form in the booth as the café began to empty was difficult to miss. She waved at him as she wiped down a table nearby. "Told you that you'd have a good time here. Like the music?"

"The music, the food...the view." Michael grinned, and there was something a little startling about his straight white teeth. Frannie felt the blush creeping up the back of her neck and refocused herself on wiping the salt and pepper shakers.

"It's a good place here. The people are good."

"Your boyfriend has me on the cold side of his shoulder."

She hadn't been expecting that and wasn't sure what to say. She looked around for something to clean and came up short, so she started on the next table with a shrug. Michael seemed to take the hint and unfolded himself from his seat.

"He is your boyfriend, isn't he?"

She did not like the tone of the question. Or the question. Or that she didn't have a good answer.

"That's...complicated."

"I don't see why. Pretty simple to me, he is, or he isn't."

She swiped furiously at the table again and didn't answer.

"See you at the lecture?" he asked.

"I suppose so. What's your connection to the professor, anyway?"

"I'm her assistant," said Michael. "You know, carry the heavy stuff, pick up the mail. Hold open doors. It pays the bills when I can't get on sets."

"Do you like it?"

He shrugged. "Suits me well enough. And it looks like it's going to put me in your path a little longer." He smiled again, though it struck Frannie a little off, as though he were not so much smiling as showing his teeth.

"So it does. Goodnight, Michael."

"Goodnight, Frannie."

She watched him go, and the bad feeling that had been dogging her since she found the wooden hand seemed to double down. Something was rotten in the state of Laguna Beach. Hopefully, the lecture would be the cheerful distraction she needed.

Because Michael Landry wasn't.

CHAPTER 11

EVEN A FEW MILES INLAND, at the University of Laguna Beach, the closeness of the sea made the afternoon cool. Frannie walked with her parents towards the lecture hall. Her parents seemed to be in a good mood that echoed her own. "Who are we listening to, again?" called her father, who was walking just ahead of her mother.

"The new anthropology professor," she said. "She's amazing. She said she remembered you and mom. She thinks you're gorgeous mom, by the way." Her father chuckled, and her mother blushed a little, looking pleased.

"I may recall her when I see her," said her father. "But her opinion on your mother is one that agrees with mine own."

They joined a crowd that was making its way through the steel and glass front of the modern lecture hall building and finally found some seats about halfway up from the dais.

A man in a blue suit came down the aisle and stopped for a moment to say a few words to Frannie's parents. "Frances, meet the dean of students, Dr. Herbert," Mom said.

Frannie smiled as she was introduced, then Pop and Mom started talking about plans for the semester and she faded into the background, observing them. She loved watching her parents in their element, because it suddenly made her aware that they had a world that did not involve her at all. It was a thought that only occasionally intruded upon her mind, but it gave her hope, because it meant that there was always another world just around the corner from the one that you think you're living in.

The dean squeezed her pop's shoulder and made his way to the lectern. He adjusted the microphone towards himself and finally said, "It's my honor to introduce this afternoon's fascinating Summer Series talk from an anthropology professor who's only been with us for a short time. A short time, but an extraordinary career! Her articles on puberty rites around the world have contributed to our understanding of what makes man, well, man."

As he was speaking, Toni came out and stood at the edge of the stage, waiting politely. She wore a soft green suit that put Frannie in mind of an Army service uniform. She stopped listening to the Dean because she was now paying attention to how intently Toni was looking out at all of them. The professor was studying them with an intensity that Frannie thought she probably took to indigenous cultures around the world. And she was thinking of how strange it would be to have somebody in bizarre, otherworldly clothing appear in your life and follow you around and start asking you questions. Like: why do you wear your hair the way you wear it? Why do you wear the clothes that you wear, why do you choose the mate that you choose? If this professor had done exactly that and written those kinds of articles, then there were people around the world who viewed her as a frightening and intrusive stranger—a stranger with a magnetism that was hard to deny.

Frannie tuned back into the introduction in time to hear the dean refer to Toni as "former nurse Lieutenant with the United States Army, Pacific Theater." Her heart skipped one, then two beats. Here was a woman who had been, and done, and seen the things Frannie only knew from her nightmares and visions. Here was a woman who had lived the future that Frannie feared was coming for herself. Was it too much to hope, given the themes of the lecture, that this was a woman who also had an understanding of magics?

After a healthy applause, Professor Sutcliffe stepped up to the lectern. The house lights were lowered, and a familiar, bright white beam that indicated that slides were about to begin cast a great rectangle on the screen behind her.

The first slide that the professor showed was a bright pineapple-colored drink.

"This is a Mai Tai," she said.

Click. "This is a palm tree"

Click and click. "And this is a drum, and this is a native god. All of these things are recognizable, but our ideas about them are not based in any reality connected to the item. Our understanding of these things is, in a word, fake. Our concepts are based—more or less—on what people outside the items' original culture observed when they were serving in the Pacific—people like a lot of you and, I have to add, like myself."

The professor smiled and stood straighter. "I served for two years in the United States Army as a nurse, and sometimes I find it difficult to recall that my time in the Pacific was barely over fifteen years ago. For those of us who have seen war, time and place are much more fluid and more difficult to define, I think. But I digress."

When Frannie thought about it, it seemed everyone was touched by war. Hooky, the mentor whom she had adored, had been haunted by his time in Korea before coming to the California beaches. It was strange to walk around and realize that about every man that she ran into who was an adult fifteen years ago had probably spent time overseas. That would be true unless they had some really good excuse, either a responsibility, like being the sole caregiver of a family, or an illness that would exempt them from service, or some special job that they had to do at home. Her own parents were immigrants from Germany and had found their way here during the war. But her uncle, who had emigrated decades earlier, had wound up in the Pacific just like Professor Sutcliffe.

"Those of us who served in the Pacific theater know that our existence there was always one of two things. Sometimes it was ugly and terrifying. Most of the time it was boredom in paradise. As is only natural, we wanted to bring home only those memories which brought us joy or pleasure. So, when we returned, we started to recreate what we remembered—but centered in our own culture. We took those things which were beautiful, or comfortable, or novel, and refashioned them in a framework that functioned under the mores of our Western sensibilities."

Click. A surfboard.

Click. Small clay statues of exotic gods being used as begonia planters.

Click. Flowered skirts, Hawaiian shirts, Bermuda shorts.

"We call this exoticism. And there is no greater practice of it than in the exoticism of the South Pacific. After my time serving in the war, I have been shocked at how all of these things we observed have become a part of our culture here. We set up backyard barbecues to make our lawns look like jungles—jungles not as they are, but as we imagine they must be, or remember vaguely. We make masks to indicate gods we simply invent, or we mix aspects of different gods together because we like how it looks on our living room wall. I don't say this to insult American culture, but to point out that whether we find it comforting or troubling, most of our 'tiki culture' is fake."

The professor expertly paused for silence.

"But this is all very harmless, isn't it?" she asked, waving an arm at a new slide depicting a backyard luau barbeque, complete with torches and faux grass skirts. "This is just fun and charming. We're not hurting anything, we're just playing dress up, like children putting on a play in the barn for their parents." Click. The image shifted now to a wooden tiki statue, roughly three feet high, holding a drinks tray on its flat head at some garden party. "No one really believes that this little statue has any power, that it's connected to any sort of actual god. We infantilize cultures outside of our own. We chuckle and shake our heads, because of course we know that these images are just representations of things that aren't real."

Toni paused again, and Frannie felt a strange tension in the room amongst the older adults. She felt like a storm was here, like lightning was gathering in the lecture hall.

"Things like this—"

Click. A washtub Mary appeared. Frannie recognized the Catholic Yard shrine from her friend Carol's house. She had thought it delightfully quaint at the time. Frannie started to realize where Professor Sutcliffe was going with the lecture, and her mouth went dry.

"Or this—"

Click. What Frannie had to assume from context was some kind of prayer rug appeared to be acting as a hallway runner in the home of a short and smiling blonde woman.

"Or this—"

Click. Frannie didn't recognize what the small altar covered in marigolds was, but she recognized the dress of the woman sitting at it as Spanish in origin.

"Or even these—"

Click. There was a gasp, and she felt the outrage in the room roll like thunder. Her own heart gave a leap, and then dropped to her feet. This was a split slide—on one side, a plain Christian cross hanging on a wall above a vase of fresh flowers. On the other side, a gently shining brass mezuzah, almost identical to the one that guarded her own front door, that her father lovingly ran his fingers over every time he left or entered the house. She felt her own gorge begin to rise. How dare—

"How dare I compare your personal beliefs to those of the Pacific Islanders, the Tonkans, the native Hawaiian peoples? How dare I suggest that your religious iconography is comparable to this?" She clicked again, and the slide reverted to a wooden mask adorned with floral leis. "How dare I show you images of your own personal totems and tokens, in relation to silly tiki items?"

Toni Sutcliffe stood in a circle of light in a dark room, growing the storm around her, almost seeming to revel in it.

"Friends…can you imagine how it would feel if you found yourself in a foreign land, and discovered your own sacred things to be hung up for display, as an aesthetic, as a curiosity? To see them distorted and disfigured to fit the pleasures of a people to whom they do not belong? For some of us, this has already happened. For others, they cannot imagine such a thing. For all of us," she said, pausing meaningfully, "I must beg you to understand—people do indeed believe in these things. And belief, that is a very powerful force in humanity. It is not my aim to insult you, but to bring understanding to the items that belong to other cultures than our own."

Frannie felt her chest let go, and her legs seemed suddenly very far away from her body. In the darkness, in the eye of the storm, Toni's eyes had found her own. The world narrowed, and all that Frannie could see were those blazing green eyes.

"Not only this—but that in the act of creation, a kind of belief may also arise. It's easy to say to ourselves that the statues and masks and the trappings of tiki culture are all fake, completely removed from any belief structure. That can be true of this generation. But what of your children? And theirs? Let me tell you a story from my own childhood. My brother believed, when we were children, believed with all of his heart, that the tulip tree in our front yard was the luck of our family. He had heard an old native story about trees protecting the land, and those who lived under them. He…worshiped is not the right word, but his belief in this tree was deep, and binding. He insisted on being wed beneath it. The year he and his wife welcomed their first child, it bloomed the day of the birth. The day his second child was stillborn, the tree was hit with a lightning bolt and lost a large limb. He had arborists specially hired to save the life of the tree. Nothing could dissuade him from his belief."

"One day, his third child, a son, who was more than a bit of a daredevil, climbed the tree. We don't know how it happened, or when, but when we found him at the foot of the tree, he was already gone. My brother was enraged, broken, betrayed. He went and got an axe. While his wife wept over the body of their son, his daughter tried to stand between him in the tree. You see, she also believed in the tree. My brother's broken belief caused him to get the axe. His daughter's faith in the tree put her in the path of the first swing."

Toni stopped, and the whole room was breathless. Toni's green eyes never wavered from Frannie's brown ones.

"When everything was over, the tree had been chopped down. With the bodies of my brother, my niece, my nephew, and my sister-in-law beneath it. It seemed impossible that this could be the case. The police said it was impossible, for the tree to fall just like that, for everything to... impossible was the word everyone used. But friends, what is belief? It is just that—to have faith in the regular occurrence of the impossible. It is belief that often saved the lives of soldiers I tended on the front lines. Soldiers who should have succumbed to their injuries, but believed in a God, or a power, or even just in the words of the nurse holding their hands. Belief in the ability of doctors, of science, to save lives, this belief was just as powerful as the chaplain at prayer. It is not the type of belief, or in what, that holds the power—but the act of believing in and of itself. For glory, for tragedy, for power, or simply because it is what we have been raised to believe. Tiki culture is fascinating, and yes, it is fun, and yes it has evolved past the original and true objects of worship in their cultures of origin. But—"

Toni's eyes swept the audience, and Frannie felt herself fall out of the spell, shaken.

"What new things might we soon believe in? What new power might we give to these new idols? To what new ideologies do you give the power of your belief?"

That was it. The lightning strike. And when it came, the room was divided into thunderous applause, and looks of unsettled disgust. Toni Sutcliffe was a polarizing force.

Frannie needed to learn more.

The hall cleared out in a wave of chatter, angry arm waving, and some beatific grins. It was easy to see who had been impressed by the lecture, and who had been affronted. Frannie and her friends made their way slowly to the stage, waiting for those who wanted a moment with Professor Sutcliffe to clear away. Frannie pulled Truly and Betty aside.

"I looked for you earlier but couldn't find you—"

"They made us sit at the back," said Betty, flushing a little. Truly looked off into the distance, but Frannie could feel the shame and anger rolling off her in waves. "It was all right though because that gave us the best view. She was a real hot dog of a speaker, wasn't she? I'm not sure I understood all of it, but it still gave me the shakes just to hear her. Wow."

Truly nodded silently, relaxing a bit into admiration, and relaxing further when Betty took her hand to pull her into a smaller circle with Frannie. "Do you think she's like you, Frannie?" Betty asked with shocking insight.

"I don't know," said Frannie, surprised. "But I want to find out."

"I bet she is," said Truly. "She knows things. Like you know things. I believe it," she added, a bit cheekily.

Saul joined them with Frannie's parents. Frannie tried to catch his eye, to see what his thoughts might be, but Saul was unusually cagey. She thought he seemed unsettled. Perhaps the lecture had reminded him too much of his time in the Pacific.

The crowd had disappeared, and now it was just their little group. Toni turned a beaming smile on them and held her palms out wide.

"Well, friends. I did promise you lemonade. Shall we take it in my office?"

CHAPTER 12

NEWP COULD BE WRONG—KURT was almost impossible to read in even his most obvious moods—but the older man seemed nervous and unsettled as they climbed into the cab of the truck. It wasn't until they had made it a solid ten minutes down the Pacific Coast Highway that either of them said anything.

"Radio?" asked Newp, hoping some music might ease Kurt's nerves.

"Nah," said Kurt. "Can't get into this new stuff."

Newp nodded, and they drove on in silence for another half hour. Which was about as long as his curiosity could take.

"So, what's the big surprise we're picking up?"

"It's at the marina."

"Mmm," said Newp, nodding.

"Take the next exit."

Terse, taciturn Kurt could barely seem to keep still. A man's business was his own, Newp firmly believed, but the uncharacteristic nervousness in Kurt was starting to spill over and spook him.

"Everything okay, Kurt?"

Kurt grimaced, and placing his hands on his legs, firmly rubbed his hands down them, as though to try and warm himself. "Just nerves. Turn right at the next cross-street."

Toni's office was as neat and tidy as she was herself. The only untidy thing in it was Michael, who it seemed had been tasked with making and serving the lemonade. It was clear that domestic tasks were not his general purview, and Frannie tried hard not to chuckle as he spilled and dripped his way through pouring tall cool glasses of the stuff. Frannie's parents had politely declined, not wanting to "crash into your party, as you cool cats say," her father had quipped charmingly.

The room was small and packed with books, artefacts, strange masks and beautiful carvings. Saul found himself a place against a bookshelf, smiling but reserved. Frannie was happy to let Truly and Betty take the two chairs and leaned a hip on a small typing desk while she sipped her (slightly too sweet) lemonade. Toni sighed and relaxed into a small stuffed velvet chair behind her desk, and Michael mirrored Frannie's position on the big desk.

"Well, that was exhausting. What did you think of the lecture?"

"I think you made a lot of people pretty angry," said Betty, taking a sip of her lemonade as though to hide behind the glass. Toni laughed delightedly.

"That may have been the idea, a little bit. Not to make them angry, necessarily, but people who have an emotional reaction to what you say are unlikely to forget what you said."

Truly tilted her head. "Was that true? About your brother?"

The professor nodded, and Betty looked heartbroken. "I'm so sorry. Your whole family."

"Thank you. As I said, belief is powerful, and dangerous. But not always a bad thing. We just have to know how to channel it, how to use it properly, how to believe in the right things."

"And what would those be?" asked Saul from the corner. Everyone looked at him with some surprise. His tone had been sharper than Frannie would have expected in mixed company. Toni, however, nodded graciously.

"The kind of intelligent question I would expect from a man of your experience. Personally, belief in justice. Belief in love. Belief that all things serve the Greater Purpose. And of course," she said, gesturing at her office "belief in oneself and one's goals. There is so much we can do if we just believe we can do it."

Saul didn't necessarily smile, but he did nod respectfully.

"Unfortunately, that system doesn't always work out for the professor. She believed in my ability to make lemonade, and you're all paying the price for that belief," joked Michael. They chuckled collectively.

"But, belief did bring me here, Michael," said Toni. "In fact, that's the reason I'm here. The university has a very ancient and rare artefact in its collection, a piece of a larger relic called the Delta of Enoch. When the Temple of Serapis was endangered during the burning of Alexandria, the Delta was divided into three pieces, and carried in three directions away from the sea by the monks of the Temple, for fear the relic would fall into the hands of Caesar. I've been able to track two of the pieces—one that eventually ended up here at the University. The other I genuinely think is somewhere here in Southern California, carried here by the Mormons and sub-factions of their groups as they moved westward. The third..." she sighed and shook her head.

"Dead end," said Michael. "Somewhere in Liberia."

"Right now, the grant money will only cover Southern California. Maybe someday I'll chase the third piece down."

"What's so important about it?" asked Frannie, setting her glass down.

"It's one of the few things we know survived the burning of the Great Library," Toni replied. "If we could put the whole thing back together, who knows what we could learn? It could be the next Rosetta Stone of ancient history." She suddenly emptied her own glass and smiled brightly at them all. "Would you like to see it?"

"It's even better on the inside," said Kurt, beaming at a speechless Newp. "Would you like to see it?"

Newp, who knew nothing about boats at all, could still recognize how beautiful the little yacht was. The bright white of the boat contrasted with the gleaming red and gold honey of the wood deck, the brass fittings seemed to glow gently, every pane of glass sparkled. Ropes coiled neatly on the deck, and the small set of stairs leading down to the galley and living quarters was spotless. Kurt reached out a hand and pulled Newp aboard, to give him a short tour. Very short, given that there was just enough room for the two of them to move around the boat.

"This is the surprise for Saul?"

Kurt nodded, running a loving hand along a deck rail. "We're not getting any younger. And Saul…" he looked away, far away, before shaking his head and looking back at Newp. "Tomorrow doesn't come with any guarantees. Though you'll find that out for yourself one of these years. Anyway…this is part of why I want you and Frannie to take over the café this summer. I want to take Saul away."

"It's beautiful," said Newp, and he meant it.

"It's beautiful!" exclaimed Betty. The Delta of Enoch was a wedge-shaped, intricate weave of delicate rose gold wire and semi-precious stones, which had been inscribed on their faces with arcane runes. It stood in a glass case on a small glass pedestal, about the size of a dessert plate, gleaming in the natural light that poured in from the white translucent skylights in the main hall of the University museum. Frannie could identify neither the stones nor the runes, but something that hummed within her like a tuning fork picked up resonance in the presence of the item. She shared a look with Saul, silently in agreement—this was big magic, whatever it was.

Truly knelt in front of the case to study it a little closer. "Moonstone, rose quartz, beryl, topaz, and blue tourmaline."

"How do you know those are the stones?" Betty asked,

sounding surprised.

"I got an A in Geology my last year of high school, didn't you know that?"

Betty looked surprised and a little ashamed, and Truly laughed. "I'm just foolin', Bets. It's on the description card."

Truly paid for her teasing with a lighthearted smack on the shoulder, as Saul stepped forward to take a closer look. Frannie wasn't sure she wanted to—the power radiating from the Delta made her wary.

"It was believed," read Saul, "that the complete Delta was capable of returning the dead to life, and of locking away unwanted spirits and ghosts. The origins of the Delta are unknown, and it has no mention in history until 337 B.C.E when it is listed as one of the treasures of Alexander the Great. The Delta was split to protect it from looting and destruction during the burning of the Great Library of Alexandria. The locations of the other two pieces are unknown, and they may have been lost to history or destroyed. This piece of the Delta is on loan from the Vatican Archives as we celebrate the Summer of Mysteries series."

"It is a beautiful thing," said Toni, standing next to Frannie. "Imagine what it might be like when joined with its sister pieces again."

"It's a beautiful thing," said Kurt, and clapped a hand on Newp's shoulder. It took the better part of an hour to get the boat up on the trailer and hitched to the truck, but the hard work in the warm sun made both men feel happy and relaxed. The drive back was uneventful, though slower than the drive out, as the added weight and length of the boat behind them made Newp nervous on the highway. In another hour they had put the boat in at the Laguna marina, and it bobbed gently in the waves. They stood shoulder to shoulder, admiring their handiwork.

"Saul's going to love it," said Newp.

"I think so too."

"Is um… I mean with Saul…is something wrong?"

Kurt seemed about to reply, when he stiffened and turned away from the boat toward the shore. He spun back to Newp, and his face frightened.

"Get in the truck, something's wrong."

Truly was the first to notice that something was wrong. While the others admired the Delta, she made her way quickly and quietly to Frannie and Toni.

"Those men, in the corner, you see 'em?"

Both women straightened, but neither was so naive as to turn unnaturally to look. Frannie pretended to swing her gaze over a painting, but instead was clocking a group of three average sized people, heavily dressed in long khaki pants, long sleeved shirts, trench coats and fedoras. Twenty years ago, they would not have looked out of place, and indeed even now Frannie may have missed them if she wasn't looking too closely.

"That's a lot of heavy clothing for a hot day like today," Truly muttered.

"Good eye Truly," said Toni. "I think we'd better alert security, they may be—"

She didn't get a chance to finish her thought. As though on some silent command, the three figures turned simultaneously and began to walk in lockstep toward the Delta. Frannie barely had time to register what she was seeing before she made the connection—the heavy sunglasses the figures wore were not enough to disguise the strange green blaze in their eyes.

"Mannequins!" she shouted, and ran to join Saul beside the Delta, Toni and Truly at her heels. They were too late to get between the mannequins and Betty, who turned at the sound of Frannie's shout. Betty's shock registered on her face for a brief moment before the lead mannequin swept its arms through the air, hitting Betty and sending her skidding across the marble floor into a bookshelf. Truly screamed, and Saul clapped a hand against the glass of the display case, muttering furiously. There was no time to hesitate—the mannequins were headed straight for Saul.

Frannie took a running leap at the first mannequin, hoping to knock them all to the ground like bowling pins. She wrapped an arm around its hard, slippery frame, shouting the first thing she could think of. "Shteyner af zayne beyner!" she cried, the stones-on-bones curse, and the mannequin dropped to the ground beneath her, landing on her arm. She almost screamed with the pain, before yanking her arm free. The second mannequin was grappling with Toni, though it was clear the professor was no match for the inhuman thing. It smacked her upside the head with its wooden hand, and the heavy thunk of the blow made Saul wince and falter. Toni went down in an arc of bright red, and Frannie hoped to God that the blow hadn't killed her. Frannie struggled upright, trying to shoulder into the third mannequin as it ran past her, only to watch it change direction with a horrible twist of its knees. From the corner of her eye, she saw a dark brown blur flying through the air, only to watch Michael Landry fling himself into the third mannequin.

Or rather, what had been Michael. What was there now was a mass of rippling muscle, fur, and sharp white teeth. Teeth that buried themselves in the neck of the mannequin, as the sudden full weight of the creature bore the automaton to the floor. There was no time to wonder at the transformation however, as the second mannequin was getting too close to Saul.

She didn't think, there was no time. She shoved thoughts of an injured Saul out of her head, and felt the rage and power growing, burning to get out. She cried her fury, throwing her uninjured hand out toward the mannequin, as though throwing a heavy stone at her enemy. "Zol es im onkumn vos ikh vintsh im, let him splinter and crack, let him rot asunder!"

There was a cracking sound, and Frannie felt the power leave her as swiftly as it had come. The mannequin slowly dropped to the ground, a pile of trench coat, hat, and wig. She turned to look for the other two. In the far distance, she could hear Truly's voice shouting to hurry. Toni was getting to her feet, but the first mannequin was already standing, moving toward her. Michael rolled and snarled and snapped across the floor and into the bookshelves, disappearing from view with the third mannequin. Frannie rushed toward Toni, but the woman held up a hand, palm flat in the air as though pressing against a wall, and her voice seemed to come from somewhere deeper than the floor.

"You will stop," she said, in the deep voice, and the mannequin slowed to a halt. Frannie felt a frisson of power from the other woman, and almost stopped moving herself. All she wanted to do was obey that voice.

"You will leave," said Toni, rising shakily to her feet. The mannequin turned and began its quick unnerving walk toward the main exit. Just then, Truly and two security guards rounded the corner. The mannequin plowed through the guards, scattering them like bowling pins, and continued out the door.

Truly bolted for Betty's side, and Frannie whirled to Saul.

"Quick!" she hissed, "Gather it up!" She and Saul bundled the mannequin into its coat. Saul stuffed it into a broom closet with shaking hands, looking at the trail of wood splinters it left in its wake. "Mein gott Frannie, what did you do to it?"

"I cursed it. I think. I just…" she made the throwing motion again, then shrugged. When she did, her left arm lit up with fiery pain from her wrist to her elbow, and she clutched it to her side with a groan. Truly lead Betty over to the group, and Toni looked worriedly around her.

"Michael, where is Michael? He might—"

"Forget where," snapped Frannie. "What is Michael?"

"Bleeding. A little," came a voice from the bookshelves that could have belonged to Michael had he smoked for fifty years.

Toni sighed with relief, but the relief was short-lived. Newp, Kurt and the two security guards bounded up the steps. Newp ran to Frannie, wrapping a gentle arm around her shoulders, while Kurt grabbed Saul's shoulder. "The kids all right?"

Saul nodded wordlessly.

"You all right?"

"Will be."

"What in the blue hell happened?" said a security guard, a stocky older gentleman whose name tag revealed him as MURRAY.

"Those thieves attacked us!" said Toni, straightening her blazer solemnly.

"My word, Professor, you're bleeding!" cried the other security guard, a slightly younger version of Murray. His name tag announced him as M. JUNIOR.

"We came down with the professor to see this artefact," said Saul grimly. "When some men tried to get through us and take it. They struck the professor, and the rest of us came to help her."

Toni raised a slow eyebrow at Saul but remained silent.

"How many were there, sir?" asked Junior.

"Th—" started Truly.

"Two, sir," Frannie chimed in quickly. "We saw the one run out, the other disappeared into the stacks, is there a back way he could have gone out?"

Junior nodded, "I'll go check."

"I'll come with you," said Newp, and the two younger men ran off to check the doors.

Murray frowned at the small group. There were more than a few cuts, bruises, bumps and injuries among them. "Everyone's banged up. are you all okay, do I need to call the medical office?"

"No, that won't be necessary," said Toni, looking to the others. Frannie thought she could hear Michael step further backward into the book stacks but couldn't be sure. "I'm fine. These wonderful people saved my life. And saved the Delta! I'll be commending them to the university for special honors, I hope you will sign on them with me, Mr. Murray?"

"Of course, of course. But professor, you're still injured, shouldn't we get you to—"

"We're headed right off to the hospital now, just to be safe," said Kurt, stepping in. "We'll just get everyone out to the truck. Those thieves may come back, you may want to file a report with the police."

"Absolutely, of course," said Murray "Professor, we can call you for your statement at your office, can't we?"

"Yes, certainly. I'll have my assistant notify you when I return."

"We can worry about that later, Professor," said Saul. "Let's get you to the hospital."

The small crowd moved toward the exit, Frannie hanging back until the guard was out of sight. She walked quickly to the bookshelves and stepped into their shadows.

"Michael?"

A rustling.

"I'm here," replied a husky voice. "I'm all right."

"I took down one of the mannequins, we put it in the closet. Can you get it back to the café? Or are you too hurt?"

"I'm fine. I can handle it. I'll meet you there. It may take me a little while. Your friend and the other guard are coming back. Get going."

She thought she saw a glimpse of a shaggy head in the shadows and turned away quickly. Whatever was going on with Michael, it was beyond her at this moment. They needed to get back to the café, and quickly.

"Where is everyone else?" asked Newp on his return.

"They went to get the vehicles, I stayed back to wait for you. Come on, we need to catch up."

Without a backward glance, they followed the rest to the doors. Behind them, a clawed and furred hand opened the closet door, and disappeared inside.

CHAPTER 13

LESS THAN TWENTY MINUTES LATER, they were recovering in the closed café. Kurt's miracle coffee was passed out to everyone in short order, along with aspirins and bandages as needed. Truly sat in an empty round booth with Betty's head in her lap, stroking her hair and whispering soft and comforting things. Toni Sutcliffe needed no such ministrations.

"Where is Michael?" she barked, almost running toward Frannie as she and Newp entered behind the others.

"On his way. He said he was all right; he's grabbing the mannequin I broke."

"Frannie's fine, though, thanks for asking," snapped Newp sourly, locking the door behind him. "I'll be right back; I'm getting you ice for that arm."

Toni rubbed her face with her hands exhaustedly. "My god, I'm so sorry, you're hurt. She needs witch hazel for that bruise, if you have any, and you'll need to elevate it for a little while, rest it. I'm sorry, I'm just worried about Michael—"

"I would be worried, too, if my assistant was a werewolf," Frannie shot back. Her arm pulsed with dull pain and the skin was hot and tender to the touch. She doubted if anything was broken, but it felt like she had dropped a brick on it. Toni's face snapped up, panic stricken.

Saul put a cup of coffee in Toni's hand, then wrapped an arm around his niece's shoulder. "Smart girl, I knew something was off about him."

"You think?" said Newp, wrapping Frannie's arm tenderly in a towel filled with ice. She winced and tried not to make a sound.

Kurt came out with cups of coffee for Newp and Frannie. "No one's perfect," he remarked, settling himself into a booth of his own and sipping from his personal mug.

Toni stared around at them. "You're all taking this really well."

Truly snorted. "Professor, after last summer, there's not a thing you could say that would shock us."

"I dunno," said Betty, sitting up slowly. "I think the mannequins are weirder than the guy who wanted to eat the books."

Toni's head whipped toward Betty, and Saul muttered a quiet oy vey to himself.

"Books? A book eater?" She turned to Saul and Frannie and gave them a genuine smile. "You're Blankguards. I thought you had all died out long ago. Real, live Blankguards!"

"And who are you?" said Saul, in a voice of quiet steel. Everyone in the room looked to him—they had never heard such a tone out of the gentle older man. "Polidorium? Hexen? Black Towers? New Templars? And do not," he said in a low growl, "even think of lying to me, or I will curse you six ways from Shabbat."

Frannie was dumbfounded. Who was this, and what had he done with her beloved Uncle Saul? Who were all these... groups, she guessed... that he was naming? What did she mean, she thought the Blankguards were all gone? It was like some dark whirlwind of information whipping around her—she felt like she had learned more about the strange new world she was inhabiting in the last exchange than she had in a whole year with Saul. What else was he hiding from her?

Toni held up her hands. "I'm a free agent. You can ask anyone you like. Ask the Vatican if you want. I think I made them a little angry when I refused to work for them. Though talking to them may be a bit more challenging for you, as one of the Chosen People."

Saul snorted. "I have a direct line to Monsignor Matthias if I want to use it, so don't mistake me for some idle threat."

Something passed between the two adults that Frannie couldn't quite translate, but it seemed to her that Saul had won the exchange. Toni put her hands down with a slow nod.

"That's good news. Maybe they'll be some help in protecting the Delta, should it come to that."

Newp slid up beside Frannie, putting a protective arm around her waist, and for once she leaned into his shoulder, soaking in his strength. His arm tightened in a hug, and she allowed herself to acknowledge how good it felt to be held, protected. She was tired and cranky, and she hurt, and she had a long evening of yelling at Saul ahead of her.

"What's a Delta?" whispered Newp.

"Piece of magic we were looking at. But it's not a bad question. Hey—" she said, breaking into the conversation. "So why don't you tell us what you really want with the Delta? It's clear you know it's magic. What do you want it for, and what can you even do with it?"

"Cure Michael, for starters," she replied. "Save lives if I can. I was a nurse before I was ever anything else. But to help Michael, I need the second piece of the Delta. One piece is powerful, but not powerful enough to take the wolf out of him. And if we don't find it quickly—"

"Then things are about to get very, very bad," said Truly. They looked at her, and she shrugged. "I like scary movies at the drive-in. I've seen The Wolf Man; I know what's happening."

"Was that the sad one where I cried at the end?" asked Betty.

"Yes, honey."

"Oh, no, I don't want that to happen to Michael. How can we help?"

"We figure out who else it is that wants this piece. Maybe they already have the other piece, or know something about it," said Frannie, straightening. "Exactly how fast do we need to find this other piece?"

"It's twelve days until the full moon," said Kurt quietly from the corner.

Frannie crossed her arms, chewing on her bottom lip. Suddenly, seamlessly, she was in charge again. She wasn't even aware when the shift happened, only that the decisions came quickly and easily, as did commands and requests. Only the older adults seemed to acknowledge the power shift between themselves.

"Professor, we're going to need everything you know about the second piece. We're pretty solid researchers. Newp, until we figure out what the hell is going on with these meshuga mannequins, we need Legionnaires keeping an eye on the café. I don't like that we found that wooden hand on the beach, I feel pretty sure someone is dead at their hands on our turf. Michael is going to bring back the one I tore down, hopefully we can learn something from what's left."

"How can we help?" asked Truly, with a quick second from Betty.

"I'll need help getting my research down here from the University," said Toni. "And we'll need to make copies of it as quickly as possible."

"I can type eighty-two words per minute," said Truly. Newp was astonished.

"You never told me that!" he exclaimed. She shrugged.

"A keyboard is a keyboard; you just play the words instead of the notes."

"That's excellent. I'll need a new assistant, anyway. We can't risk Michael around campus this late in the game. Are you up for the job?" cut in Toni.

"Are you going to pay her the same as Michael?" asked Betty. It was Toni's turn to be surprised.

"Of course? Why shouldn't I?"

Betty nodded. "That's all right, then. You should do it, Tru, you'd be the cat's pajamas. You're so organized and smart, you always keep me and the band on track. You've been looking for a job. This would be so perfect!"

Truly was unconvinced. "They almost didn't even let us into the lecture today, Bets, how do you think I'm going to get away with working there?"

"The sad and unjust truth is," said Saul, "that a lot of people don't look too closely at anyone wearing a tag that says 'staff' on it. Especially people from the fringes, like us."

It was true, and Frannie hated that it was. She thought back to last summer, how devastated the girls had been when the Ed Sullivan show had canceled on them for being a mixed band. It was hard enough being Jewish sometimes—she had been called the names and felt the stares. She couldn't imagine how hard it was for Truly.

Toni nodded encouragingly, and Truly reluctantly agreed. At that moment, there was a loud thump sound at the front door. Kurt got up to check and returned with his arms full of busted-up mannequin. He shook his head at the unasked question—there was no sign of Michael. Frannie sighed.

"Let's get to work."

CHAPTER 14

"IT LOOKS LIKE TERMITES AND wood ants fought a war inside it with wood rot bombs," said Saul, once they had laid the mannequin out on the floor of the upper room. Though it was still mostly recognizable as a mannequin, it was only just holding together at the joints. The green eyes blazed, and the arms and legs occasionally twitched, but it seemed Frannie had done enough damage that it could no longer command it's rotting body.

"What did you do to it Frannie?"

"Cursed it, zol es im onkumn vos ikh vintsh im, then I just yelled all the worst things I could think of happening to a man made of wood. I guess it worked," she answered with a shrug.

Saul whistled low. "I guess it did. And you didn't have to touch it at all?"

Frannie shook her head and repeated her throwing motion. "I just threw it. Like…you know how when you're in a big room full of people, but you can make your voice heard to a specific person? Like that. Just focused my voice."

The green glowing automaton twitched and writhed a bit, making them both jump. Saul clutched his chest.

"Gott in himmel... Well, anyway, now at least we can test your theory about binding magic, eh? Where do you want to start?"

Frannie pursed her lips and frowned. "I'm not sure. I wish we still had Emmett. What I think is happening is that a soul has been bound to the mannequin, because that would give it life, or at least allow it to move, right? Like how all the things floated around in House on Haunted Hill."

"You mean it's haunted. Yeah, that could work. But I'm also not sure... let's be honest, Frannie, if that's not black magic, then paint me purple and call me colorblind."

"Okay. So, if we unbind the spirit from the mannequin..."

"Then you have an angry spirit floating around and a stack of bad firewood."

"No good."

"No good."

They paced, occasionally stopping to look at the mannequin. Saul searched it for symbols or sigils, to no avail. He sighed and sat down on the cot.

"Let's think backward from the problem. If we were going to do this—" He gestured at the man shaped mess on the floor. "—how would we do it?"

Frannie ran a hand through her hair, blowing out a breath through puffed cheeks. "Well...you wouldn't want to just bind a soul to something as strong as those things wound up being. You'd want to be able to command it first. Bind the mannequin to you, then bind the soul to the mannequin, so you can command it?"

Saul shrugged "Makes sense to me. Okay, so first thing is release the mannequin from the schmuck who did it, then release the soul?"

"You got any kind of incantations for this uncle?"

"Not a one. But we could try inverting the language of a binding spell. Think of it like unlocking a dybbuk box instead of locking one, you just turn the key the other way, right?"

"I guess so. What's the worst that could happen?"

It didn't take them long to find out.

After rearranging the wording to unlock the spell, they stood apart, one at the head and the other at the foot of the mannequin. Together they chanted slowly, feeling out the shape of the spell. It hurt, and Frannie dug her nails into her palms—it was the psychic equivalent of pulling off a deep hangnail, and she hoped they hadn't used up all the aspirin.

"Mi'avdut le'cherut, mitzrayim le'chofesh. Amen!"

Saul and Frannie both winced as the spell unraveled, a mix of fresh pain and relief. The relief was short lived as the mannequin began to scream.

"DEAD, I'M DEAD, OH GOD IT'S KILLING ME! CHARLOTTE, RUN, RUN, OH GOD NO NOT THE WATER, PLEASE!"

The voice was loud and male, but had a deep and unsettling sound, like someone calling words down a hollow trunk. The painted-on mouth didn't move, but the individual limbs danced and twitched with furious, desperate energy, throwing off splinters and chunks of rotting wood as though the very floor were shaking.

"Hey!" shouted Saul, "Hey listen, you're okay, calm down, you're all right!"

But whoever was trapped in the mannequin was beyond hearing. The soul rattled and screamed and sobbed, babbling about the waves and the sand and the darkness, reliving the cold wet death over and over again.

"He can't hear us," yelled Frannie over the din. "We need to let him go—do it again!"

They took up their places once more, repeating the unbinding. If the last unbinding had been like a hangnail, this was being tortured by having nails ripped off with pliers. Tears ran down Frannie's face, and she and Saul were both panting out the words.

"Mi'avdut le'cherut, mitzrayim le'chofesh."

The mannequin rattled and bounced and screamed, the sounds tearing into Frannie's mind and heart. The sound was suffering and fear and every bad dream that she had ever suffered. She wept, and screamed back, unleashing a deep power of desperation and terror.

"Chofesh, chofesh, CHOFESH, SHALOM!"

With a clatter, everything ceased. The silence of the room was as terrifying as the noise had been. In the center of the room, the mannequin was still, the green glow extinguished from its painted eyes.

Frannie had been to exactly one funeral, that of her friend last summer. She stared at the mannequin the way she had stared at the body, waiting for it to move, to twitch, to breathe. She sobbed, both for air and from pain and exhaustion, and sank to her knees. As bad as she was, Saul was in worse shape. He was positively gray, one hand held tight to his chest as he walked backward to the cot to sit. They didn't know and couldn't guess how much time had passed before Truly and Newp were pounding on the door.

"We're all right, we're all right, I'm coming," she said, standing on unsteady legs to open the door. She let them in and was too tired to resist their fussing as they walked her to the cot to sit next to Saul.

"What the hell was that?" Newp demanded fiercely.

"She was right," panted Saul. "Someone bound a soul to that mannequin to animate it."

"And it sounds like they murdered someone to get that soul," Frannie said quietly. "And maybe someone else. Someone named Charlotte."

"Jesus," said Truly, staring at the remains of the dummy. "What do we do with it?"

"Burn it with salt," said Saul.

"I'll get Brainiac up here with some of the boys, they can use it for the bonfire tonight." said Newp.

"The kosher salt, from the green jar in the kitchen, not the other stuff."

"Right." With a kiss to Frannie's forehead, Newp headed out with a purpose.

Truly rubbed Frannie's shoulders and narrowed her eyes at Saul. "You need to sleep, old man," she said, trying to make her tone playful instead of scolding, and failing miserably.

"These women," complained Saul. "Always right. I need to go lie down."

Frannie held out a hand to stop him. "We can't do that every time they turn up. It's impossible."

"I know," he said solemnly. "We'll think of something. Rest for now."

He walked slowly and carefully out of the room, as Truly took over and bundled her into the cot.

"That goes for you too, young lady. Take a nap. Everyone is safe, Betty is napping too, and Toni cleaned up everyone's cuts and bruises. Get some rest."

Get some rest, thought Frannie darkly. What other impossible things do they want me to do today?

She was asleep within moments.

She didn't know and couldn't guess how much time had passed between Truly tucking her in and Betty shaking her awake. Her usually sunny friend's face was frowning and clouded. She tugged gently at Frannie's shoulder.

"Frannie? Honey you need to wake up. We found out who Charlotte is. And who that poor person in the dummy was. We called Mutt and Jeff— Charlotte Nagle and Tom Chambers never came back from their date three days ago."

Frannie opened her eyes and stared at the wall. After a moment she said, "Charlotte Nagle is blond, and the dog that was with them didn't come back either, am I right?"

Betty's eyes widened in surprise, but she nodded.

Frannie sighed and closed her eyes tight against the throbbing pain in her head. "Then we better tell Mutt and Jeff that we can be pretty sure they're dead. And that we can at least return the dog to the family. Is there any aspirin left? Or maybe a hacksaw you can cut my head off with? Everything hurts."

"You know, that's almost exactly what Saul said. You look a lot better than he does, though. Kurt doesn't say much, but I think he's really worried."

"Where's Newp?"

"Down at the beach with the bonfire. They're burning the dummy just like Saul said."

"Good. Everyone else okay?"

"The professor and Truly went up to the University to start copying the notes about the Delta. They might not be done until tomorrow night though, there are a lot of notes. Saul told everyone to go home and get some rest, he doesn't think we're in any big danger—those things were after the Delta, not us. Oh, and Toni is going to have Michael watch the Delta for now, since I guess he…well…what she said is that 'he can't be seen in polite company right now' because it'll scare the pants off everyone. And if he's away from people it's more…safe. Also, Saul says he put a ward on the Delta, whatever that means."

"It means he put a protection spell on it that will zap any goons with bad intentions. What about you, you okay?"

"Just some bumps and scrapes. I'll be fine. I'm going to go pick Truly up and drop her home. Can I give you a lift too?"

It wasn't a bad idea. She could do with a hot bath and a night in her own bed. Saul had taught her a simple ward she could put on her door and window too. It seemed the more questions they were able to answer, the more questions appeared, like heads on a hydra. Why Tom and Charlotte? What happened to them? Why was the Delta so important? Who was controlling the mannequins? What were they going to do about Michael?

"Werewolves, murderous mannequins, a magic hunk of metal, bad bikers, a surfing school… It's like we're in a comic book," Frannie said.

Betty smiled and chucked Frannie under the chin. "Good thing we have our very own super heroine. Come on, let's get you home. I think your cape needs washing."

A hot shower, a cool breakfast (fresh fruit and strudel, her favorite) and a good nights' sleep took most of the edge off her headache, and she was almost cheerful the next morning. She had nearly forgotten the worries of the night before, until her mother ran an affectionate hand through Frannie's dark curls at the breakfast table.

"Liebling," said her mother gently. "I have a worry."

"What's wrong, mom?"

"A young lady and her beau went missing a few days ago…they think at Laguna Beach. It's all over the news this morning. Poof, vanished." Her mother waved her hands like a magician for emphasis, then leveled a serious look at her daughter. "I just want you to promise that you are never alone down there, all right? Stay close to Newp, or your friends, and if there is no one at the beach, you go back to the café. Hurst du mich?"

Frannie struggled through a sip of coffee. It was no secret in her family that she and Saul had abilities beyond the norm. Her parents had even witnessed part of the battle with the Book Man. Why was this warning coming now?

"I hear you mom, I do, and I don't want you and pop to worry…" *but I already know what happened to Tom and Charlotte, and I'm not keen on it happening to me.*

"We're your parents, that is our job. And we are very good at it. I know you are a very strong and powerful girl—but we took you out of Germany, out of New York, to bring you away from danger and pain, not to its doorstep."

For a moment, her mother looked tired and a little sad, and Frannie felt her throat tighten. She had never wished until that very moment that she was a normal teenager, with normal troubles and nothing more dangerous in her life than a handsy date at the drive-in movie. She stood and wrapped an arm around her mother's shoulders.

"I'm sorry, mom. I promise, I'm being as safe as I can be."

Her mother took hold of Frannie's injured arm gently and held it out between them. The arm was ablaze with purple and green mottled bruises all down its length.

"How safe is that, liebchen?"

"Um…"

Her mother stood, wrapping Frannie in her arms. Mother and daughter stood in the early summer sunlight, holding each other tightly. Her parents were affectionate, but not usually overly emotional. Frannie rested her head on her mother's shoulder and soaked in her scent.

"Maybe this is something you think about while you are running about, eh? Just stay safe. For me."

"Mom, stop it, you've got me all verklempt."

"Well, have another piece of strudel and some more coffee. It will settle you down. Remember we are having dinner party tomorrow night for the English department. Should we invite your friend the anthropologist also?"

Frannie hesitated. After all that had happened in the last 48 hours, a dinner party was unsettlingly normal. Would it be irresponsible of her to stop working on the Delta mystery for a social gathering?

"I'll ask her what she thinks, I'm seeing her today. I think. But I have to head down to the beach first and see how the surf school is coming along."

"You working tonight?"

"Yeah but not late, it's Tuesday, we close early."

"Okay. Be careful?"

"I promise mom. I love you."

"I love you too."

She followed her mother's advice about the strudel and coffee, then headed out the door. Her mood was more melancholy now, and the sunshine did little to warm her spirits. She hopped on her bike, hoping the ride would work the mood off. Her board was safely ensconced in Hooky's Hut, where it would stay for the remainder of the summer, so she had little she needed to carry beyond the rucksack with clothes, sandals and beach towel that lived in her bike basket.

How much danger were they in? What if they just walked away from Toni and the Delta and let it be? But then what about the innocent lives of Tom and Charlotte? How many more 'souls' would this…necromancer? Maybe that was the word. How many more souls would they need?

How many more mannequins did they have out there?

And then there was the problem of Michael the Werewolf. The last thing

Laguna Beach needed was a werewolf on the loose.

Are you listening to yourself? Do you hear how coo-coo bananas you are?

But the thoughts followed her like a cloud, and nothing cleared them up. She needed some space.

She needed to surf.

CHAPTER 15

HE NEEDED TO EAT.

No, that wasn't the right word. He wasn't hungry—he was ravenous. There was nothing in him but empty wanting—want for flesh, want for blood, want for the soft crack between his teeth as vertebrae shattered and hot life flowed out and into his mouth. The wanting raced through his body, down his spine, ached between his legs—want for release, for death, for life, for the sweet joy of the hunt and the wretchedness of its' ending, which was always victorious exhaustion.

Beneath this, beneath the pure vital energy of the wolf, lay Michael. At the film studios when he had work as an extra, he had seen the special effects people at work. He had watched actors and actresses pulling on the tight suits, the heavy, unbreathable masks, the thick glass goggles or helmets or monstrous gloves and boots that gave the appearance of claws. He had seen people he knew disappear under the monster, only to pop back up at lunch time asking for pastrami on rye and laughing through the sweat and stink of the costume.

This dual life of his was the opposite. When things were good, when they were under control, he could put on the Michael mask and walk around, acting like a man. He could be close to others, enjoy the sun. He could admire the beautiful curve of Frannie Cohn's neck without wondering what it would be like to sink his teeth into it, to sink himself into her death. He wanted this life, this gentleness, he wanted to live as though he didn't have to fear himself.

But the wolf always came back out, no matter what he did. It was always hungry, no matter how much it ate, no matter what it took from the world.

He hadn't fully transformed, he knew—he was in the middle place, the limbo between full moons, and the strange hoary existence between man and beast. He was enough Michael to hide, to know that he had to resist the urge that screamed at him from every nerve ending, but he was wolf enough to sometimes slip those bonds of reason and drop to all fours, stalking, waiting, anticipating the bite. If he was fully transformed, Michael and any ability for memory would be gone. It had often been a blessing that he had no memories of what he did as the wolf.

It was why he never read the newspaper.

He let the wolf roam through the sparse forests near the shore. It was safe enough for now, still early in the week so the beach would be mostly free of small children and families. Maybe he would get lucky, and he could sate himself on a deer, or a dog, or some other inhuman sacrifice. It was easier to take control after he had killed, to put the Michael mask back on. But the closer the full moon drew, the less effective killing was. It was a thin tightrope to walk.

He kept to the tree and rock shadows, letting the wolf think they were stalking, hunting. How long could he keep it distracted? Could he make it to Sutcliffe for a dose of nitrate? He had managed to drop the mannequin off last night because the pain of his injuries had kept the wolf at bay, but the smell of Frannie hung around the café like a perfume, and he knew he had to leave immediately. It had been a long, tortured night in the woods after that.

A long night. He was tired, and tiring. Could he sleep? The sun was beginning to warm the rocky outcrops and the clear air of the forest. He had kept the mannequin's trench coat, and now he made himself a small den, jamming the trench coat between rocks and the branches of a tree to create a little lean-to. He crawled in, curled up, and tried not to dream about the death of Frannie Cohn.

She parked her bike at the top of the stairs leading down to the beach and chained it to a fencepost. She had learned the hard way last summer that riding the bike down the sandy path was not worth the agony of walking it back up. She made her way to the hut, waving idly at Legionnaires who appeared to be applying paint to a wooden sign. Board under her uninjured arm, she turned toward the ocean—only to be faced with Toni Sutcliffe in faded green tropic fatigues.

"Professor!"

"Good morning Frannie. I'm sorry to disturb you, but your young man up at the café said I might find you here—you like to surf when you're upset." Toni turned and took in the ocean view. "I can see why. It must be very peaceful and cathartic."

"He's not my young man."

"He's not?" Toni looked surprised and tilted her head. "How odd. That was the impression he gave me. In any case, I was hoping you might show me where you found the mannequin hand."

Frannie's mood was souring by the second. "How do you know about that?"

"Truly told me all about it. It's an exciting few days you've had, it seems. Is this normal for a Laguna Beach summer?"

The younger woman laughed bitterly. "It's a thrill a minute down here at Laguna. Why, if we don't find at least three dead bodies a summer, it hasn't been a proper season."

Toni caught the tone and softened her stance. "I'm sorry Frannie," she said. "I didn't mean to be flip. I've seen a lot of death and destruction; I forget what it's like to encounter those things as a young person. I guess that means I'm a bit jaded to it all. If you want to just point me in the right direction, I'll have a look around and leave you be."

Frannie let out a pent-up breath. She was acting a fool. It was hardly the professor's fault that the last three days had been a roller coaster. She certainly wasn't at fault for Frannie's bad mood. Frannie stuck her board in the sand and sighed.

"Sorry, Professor…"

"Please, call me Toni."

Frannie nodded. "I'm sorry, you're right, it has been a wild few days. I'm maybe not handling it the best. I'd be happy to show you the spot. But why don't you come out and get a wave or two with me first? Consider it an olive branch."

"I'd love to, but I'm afraid I don't know how."

"That's all right, we're starting a surfing school down here on the beach. You can be my first student. And you're a teacher, so maybe you can teach me about teaching. Saul likes to say, 'all knowledge is a blessing, when it's not a curse.'"

They laughed together at Frannie's impression of Saul. Toni looked out at the surf, gleaming in the sunshine. "You know…it wouldn't be a bad place to chat, after all. Very private."

"Some of the most important talking I've ever done, I've done waiting for a wave. Come on, let's get you a board."

Go-Go had clearly been hard at work—he had a small pile of boards already shaved and waxed, waiting for new students. They picked one out at a good height for Toni, and she stripped out of her fatigues to reveal a white bikini. Frannie shot a warning glance at the Legionnaires as they whistled and clapped, and they soon settled down with only slightly apologetic grins on their faces. Frannie really couldn't blame them—Toni Sutcliffe was one stunner of a woman.

They paddled out slowly, Frannie explaining the basics as they went.

Toni was a quick learner, and it was barely half an hour before she was up on her board, riding down a small wave near the shore. As Toni's confidence grew, so did Frannie's and soon she paddled them out a little further toward the larger, steadier waves.

"You're a natural, Toni," said Frannie admiringly.

"I spent a lot of time in the water in the South Pacific. There wasn't much else to do between shift duties and wounded calls but enjoy the island and what it had to offer. In a way, this feels very familiar to me. And exhilarating! I think I'm in love."

"Surfing was sacred to the Native Hawaiians. Sometimes I think it's like a cross between prayer and worship and play, like all those things can just live at the same time in your mind."

They sat on their boards, soaking in the warm sun, waiting for the tide to begin pulling the next good waves. Frannie crossed her arms in front of her and lay on her board, looking at Toni.

"Can I ask you a question?"

"Of course."

"Do you… I mean… was it worth it? Being a nurse? Do you regret it? Only—" she said quickly "Lots of people who come back from war seem to regret the experience, even the ones who didn't fight."

Toni nodded thoughtfully. "Are you asking because you've also started down that path?"

A nod.

"Is there anything I can do to talk you out of it?" Toni said jokingly, but the smile died as she saw the clouds cross Frannie's face.

"No. I don't regret it. But then, I also don't really believe in regret," said Toni solemnly. "Your choices are what make you, and you make your choices based on what you believe to be the most important thing in the moment. To regret your choices implies that you didn't really make a choice you truly believed in. And if that's the case, then are you really in control of your own destiny?"

Frannie was silent, trying to decide if she agreed, when Toni continued.

"When my brother and his family died, I needed to escape. I was young and didn't know what to do with pain—I thought it was something to run away from. The army was a way to get out, see the world, a way to reinvent myself and to forget my past. There are no tulip trees in the tropics," she said, with a sad smile.

"But you can't outrun pain. And you can't outlive death. So, I learned to deal with both, on their own terms. So many young men, and women, died. But so many more lived because I was there with my skills. You had to let the deaths go. You learned to use the pain of that loss to fuel you, to keep working to save the next one, and the next one, and the next. No, I don't regret it, and I don't think you will either. But you will have to learn to make a friend of pain, and to make your peace with death. Otherwise," she added, and for the first time Frannie noticed a smudge of weariness under Toni's eyes, "you can go absolutely mad."

Frannie felt the waves before she saw them and broke the spell of Toni's reverie. "Come on," she said. "We'll ride these waves over as far as we can. It'll make our walk to the Pirate's Tower a bit shorter, and I can show you where I found the hand."

They paddled out, Frannie shouting out tips just like Hooky had done for her. By the time they came back into shore they had tried for three waves, caught and ridden two, and Toni had only tumbled once. They made their way to the shore, grinning and exhilarated.

"How long until I learn how to hang ten like you?"

Frannie laughed "How many times are you willing to wipe out?"

Frannie showed Toni how to stick her board in the sand, and they began walking toward the curve in the bay, toward the trees and rocks that shadowed the path to the Pirate Tower.

Michael woke with a scent in his mind. The wind kicked up from the ocean, crossed the beach, and wound its way gently through the trees. She was here.

With a growl that shook his whole frame, he tore out from under the trench coat and raced to the edge of the cliffside. His ears pricked up through his matted fur, and he could hear her voice just under the sound of the ocean waves.

When he saw her round the bend to the tower, all control was gone. The wolf had won. He streaked down the side of the cliff, and there was no turning back.

"It was about here," Frannie said, pointing to the heavy driftwood log and a pile of stones. "We didn't find any—"

"FRANNIE, RUN!" screamed Toni, who grabbed the girl's arm and began to race along the beach. Frannie searched for the source of Toni's fear, stumbling in the loose sand. She caught a dark shape racing down the cliffside from the corner of her eye, and her blood ran cold.

Something was coming for them—fast. Something like a wolf.

"The tower!" cried Frannie, "Get to the tower, it has a gate!"

She pulled Toni toward the wet sand at the surf—it would give them more traction and an edge to their speed. The blurry shape was moving closer, but slower through the dry sand past the tideline. She could see the tower ahead, it's bottom gate held open with a heavy rock, about fifty yards away. Her legs pumped, and her chest burned. Surfing was a completely different set of muscles, and she had stopped running on the track team her junior year. Beside her, Toni ran with the grim determination of a trained warrior. They just might make it.

She could feel rather than see the shape pulling up parallel and slightly behind her, knew that its hot wet breath was almost close enough to raise the hairs on her neck. It was getting too close; it was closing the distance. Frannie pushed her body harder, breath ragged and thick in the humid air. She heard Toni yell, and barely registered the word before obeying—she ducked as a handful of wet sand flew through the air, over her head, and into the creature's face. It tumbled, making a sound like a cross between a growl and a pained whimper. Frannie struggled to regain her feet, and Toni yanked her back up.

Only ten yards now. Ten yards to the gate.

The howl tore out of the creature's throat, and Frannie knew the sound would live in her nightmares for the rest of her life. The women held each other up as they cleared the last few feet, Frannie and then Toni diving through the gate. Together they yanked it shut as it screeched on its rusty hinges. It wouldn't be much protection for long. Frannie cast around for something, anything to hold the door shut.

"Here!" said Toni. She had found an iron staple still driven into the wall near the door. Frannie spotted a length of chain half buried in the sand. As one, the women looped the chain through the bars, and started to run it through the staple.

"Hurry," Frannie sobbed, her hands trembling. She could see it clearly now, running for them, jaws awash in white foaming spittle and yellow eyes ablaze. You would never know that it was Michael Landry under that fur, those teeth. All she could see was teeth and bloodlust.

Toni yanked the chain tight, and together they tied it into as tight a knot as they could through sweaty and shaking hands. Not a moment too soon, as the werewolf hit the gate and it rattled like bones in a jar. The women clung together at the base of the stairs, gasping for breath.

For the moment, they were safe.

And completely trapped.

CHAPTER 16

"DON'T MOVE," SAID TONI, BACKING away from the gate. "And stay where he can see you. I'm going to climb the stairs and see if there's a way out. Don't let him bite or scratch you, I don't have any wolfsbane in this bikini."

Frannie was shocked into a brief, barking laugh as Toni disappeared around the curve of the tower. She stared out through the bars at the beast.

"Knock it off Michael," she said, voice shaking. "Or I'll throw a curse at you, don't think I won't. I bet I could make you allergic to your own fur if I tried hard enough."

The werewolf snarled and leapt at the door, tearing at it with his fangs. She could see one of his bright shining teeth rip away out of his mouth and clatter to the stone floor of the tower, red and bloody. She choked back a scream. The werewolf barely seemed to notice the missing tooth. The foam at its mouth was turning pink with blood.

She heard Toni swear from above them, and then her footsteps beating a tattoo down the stairs.

"Any luck?"

"I have an idea…but you're not going to like it."

"I'm usually the one that says that. Try me."

"There's a door at the top, like this one, but it's latched from the outside. There's a window slightly below where the door landing is. If you boost me out the window, I think I can get to the roof of the tower and drop down on the outside of the door."

"What's the part I'm not going to like?"

"The second part, where we use you as bait to trap him in here."

"You're wrong. I don't dislike it, I hate it. How do we do that?"

"I'm going to open the door at the top. You're going to loosen the chain down here, then run. He'll try to break in and chase you. While you run to the top, I run to the bottom and lock the bottom door. You get up here before he does and lock the top door."

"What's to stop him getting out the window?"

"It's too high without a boost, he can't do it on his own. Especially not as a werewolf. They're not the brightest but they've very…"

He snarled, and bit the bars again, spattering them with bloody, ropey slobber.

"Focused."

They both jumped as the wolf bashed against the bars again.

"How come I'm the bait and you're the escape artist?"

"You going to climb with your arm like that?"

"Scheisse. All right, come on, professor."

It took less effort than she had expected to get Toni up and out through the ancient window. The woman moved like a jungle cat. She crept to the top of the tower and watched while Toni unlatched the door as silently as she could.

"Okay," she whispered. "Are you ready?"

Frannie struggled to steady herself. Her legs felt like jelly after their sprint across the beach. Could she do it? She heard the snarling from below, and felt her belly drop to her feet. Yes, with that thing behind her, she could do it.

She nodded. "I'll yell when I do it, so you know to start running down the cliff to the bottom, okay?"

"Okay. You can do it Frannie. I believe in you."

Frannie took a deep breath and started back down to the bottom. Outside, the werewolf was pacing back and forth in the sand, and it made her shiver how unnaturally it moved on all fours. It wasn't quite a wolf, and it certainly wasn't a man, and whatever it was in between was a nightmare.

Slowly, carefully, she started to untangle the chain. The werewolf froze, watching her. She kept eye contact with it as she pulled it halfway out of the staple, leaving the door free but the chain ready for Toni.

"Okay boy," she said, taking a deep breath. "TAG, YOU'RE IT!."

As though it understood the signal, the werewolf leapt at the door, bashing it inward. Frannie scrambled up the stairs, flying around the curves and past the window. She could hear it, feel it behind her, catching up, gaining. I can make it, I can make it, she chanted manically in her head. She grabbed the door frame and used it to turn her momentum around, whirling to close the door shut. The monster's head slammed into the door, and the weight of it almost pushed Frannie off balance. She shoved her shoulder against the door and slid the latch home, falling away from the door as the werewolf went crazy, bashing itself into the door like a wild, trapped thing. Everything had happened so quickly, did Toni have enough time to shut the bottom door?

"Michael," shouted Frannie. "I know you're in there. I know you are! Remember? We ate Oreos, we talked about the day your mother walked into the ocean, we read your book together. Michael, you pay attention to me now!"

She could see the ears twitch toward the staircase. How good was his hearing? She had to drown out the sound of Toni moving the door and the chain.

"You want to eat me, don't you?" she called, picking up a stone from the ground. "Eat me all up like the big bad wolf. Well guess what? You're not a big bad wolf. You're a scared little boy alone on a beach, you're Michael Landry, you're the assistant to Professor Toni Sutcliffe, you're…" she was rapidly running out of things she knew about him. "You're my friend, you're Michael, and so I name you to your true nature and self! Return to your proper form, shedim!"

She hadn't expected it to work, necessarily. It was, like everything else today, a long shot. But the werewolf slowly straightened upright, and she could see that the eyes were fading from yellow to a golden brown. The snout and fangs and ungodly fur were still there, but something had tipped the scales back to a more human affect.

Until the sound of the chain rattling against the lower door sounded.

With a cry, Frannie hurried to pick her way down the cliff as the werewolf turned to race down the stairs. The going would have been easier, if she were not in a panicked hurry to get down. She could see Toni tying furiously with the chain, as the werewolf harried the bars. Frannie jumped the last few feet, rolling in the sand, before getting up and helping Toni tighten the last metal knot. They stepped back, breathing heavily, as the werewolf paced inside his makeshift cage.

"Well," said Toni, puffing a bit. "That was exciting. I should holiday in Laguna Beach more often."

CHAPTER 17

LOOK DOWN ON LAGUNA BEACH, down from the top of the Riviera hotel. It's a beautiful day in late May. For the natives, the weather still holds a touch of chill, but for visitors the balmy 75* weather is perfection. There is a slight but warm breeze holding steady on the shore, fluttering sundresses and pennants and the tall grasses that bend. Far off around the curve of the bay stands a stone tower, its age and purpose lost to all but the most avid of local historians. Just below and to the right of the Riviera is the Café Monstro, just a hop across the highway from the steps that lead down to Laguna Beach, where surfer boys gather around a pair of makeshift huts in ever shifting groups as some take their boards out to the water, and others come back in for a rest and a soda, and to watch the girls who have gathered on their beach blankets to watch them in mutual appreciation. Beyond all of this, the endless and timeless sea, answering the ancient call of the moon with its tides.

On the beach, the boys plant their hand painted sign: "Surf Lessons, $5, Two Hours. Friendly and professional! Hooky's Legionnaires."

In the café, Saul sits heavily down, and rubs at his left shoulder. It's been bothering him all week.

In the penthouse suite of the Riviera, a table is cluttered with maps, notes, old books, and arcane symbols. Housekeeping is not permitted in this suite.

In the tower is trapped a werewolf.

In two hours, everything will fade into twilight.

Hurrying along the shore, the small figures of two women make it to the main beach.

Toni threw on her fatigues with the speed of long familiarity. "I'm going to run up to my office and grab the silver nitrate. It'll bring him back down faster. Otherwise, all we can do is wait for morning. How are we going to keep people away from the tower?"

"I'll handle it," said Frannie, "No problem. Probably. We'll figure it out. How long will you be?"

Toni glanced up at the highway, then back at the tower. "At least an hour. Possibly more if traffic is bad."

"We'll handle it, go. I'll meet you at the café."

Frannie picked up Toni's board and returned it to Go-Go. "Go-Go, we surfed over to the tower, and some of the stones on the tower started collapsing, it looked really dangerous. Can you just keep an eye and make sure no one goes over there? I'll tell the other Legionnaires. Just for an hour, that lady is headed to tell the beach patrol about the tower so they can rope it off or whatever."

"No problem, Fran. How did the lesson go? She looked really good for a first timer."

"She's a natural. I don't think we'll always get that lucky. She's going to come back for another lesson later, I let her have the first one free. I'm not sure I'm the best teacher, but we did okay."

"Sounds good. We're doing pretty well. As long as he keeps his hands off the ladies, Brainiac is making a killing. He's actually really good with kids, you know?"

"He is?"

"Yeah, they love him. He had a little girl, maybe ten, up on a board in the shallows. She rode one all the way in. They had a ball."

"That's fantastic! Brainiac, who would have thought. Okay, great. Newp at the café?"

"Yeah he is."

"Thanks, Go-Go. Need anything?"

"Pastrami on rye wouldn't be the worst."

"You got it."

She tried to make her walk to the steps look casual instead of exhausted. She pulled aside a few of the older boys, Tombo and Catscratch, and told them to keep an eye on the tower. The stairs were a real struggle, and she pretended to stop halfway up to take in the view. Really, she needed to catch her breath.

Kurt leaned back in his chair, shrugging and stretching the kinks out of his neck and shoulders. Clay had always been his medium, clay and paint and sometimes decoupage for the bigger stuff. Carving wood had never been his strong suit, but he thought he'd done all right. For a goyim hack artist, anyway.

Saul, with the preternatural instinct he had always possessed, picked that moment to peek around the corner. He grinned impishly, and the years fell away from his face. For a moment, Kurt was reminded of how they met. Saul was on a trip with a bunch of Florodora girls from the Catskills, because he had gotten them a contract for a show in Cuba, and they were on a steamer. It was one of countless jobs that Saul had done.

Kurt had noticed Saul right away—it was hard not to recognize the showman in him. Kurt was younger than himself, a skinny thirty-something with black hair cut short and a thousand cowlicks. He didn't know who had spoken first, himself or Saul, but as always it was Saul's words he remembered instead of his own. He wasn't sure what Saul had asked, but in his mind it was something like, "So, what's your story? What are you doing heading to Cuba?"

Kurt told him he had a sister who was doing some missionary work. Saul had asked, "Are you a missionary?"

"Far from it, but I guess I'm a decent brother."

"Are you the kind of brother that likes coffee and Danish at 2:00 AM? I'm friends with the kitchen manager and I'm starved."

They spent long hours of the voyage together after that. Saul had been with a lot of women, and in fact would eventually marry one. But as he later told Kurt, his mind would keep going back to this artist. It was the reappearance of the artist that signaled the end of his marriage. And he still had a fear that crept in every now and then that Kurt would leave, go away, head somewhere and not tell him where it was going. It was the most unmanly feeling, but there it was.

"Is it done?"

"It's done."

"I would ask the angels to bless you, but how can you bless a blessing? You are a blessing, my love."

Kurt rolled his shoulders again, and the clicking and crackling sound of it drew Saul over to him. Saul rubbed his strong hands into Kurt's shoulders, working the tension away.

"Will it work?" asked Kurt, a note of concern in his voice. "I mean, I'm not Jewish, I was just going from the drawings and the letters you gave me."

"I don't think it matters," said Saul. "You made Emmett. It was Frannie who brought him to life. I think it's going to work like gangbusters. You'll see. What's that?" he asked, pointing to a smooth yellow lump on the workbench.

"Surfboard wax."

Saul laughed, the deep hearty laugh that Kurt loved. Saul's laugh was like a cozy fireplace in a blizzard; nothing made Kurt feel quite so safe and warm.

"Of course, it is. Which end is which?"

"Does it matter?"

Saul nodded. "They hold different spells."

"This is the business end, then. I carved a closed book on this end and an open book on this end. It just—"

"Felt right. I know.'

Saul wrapped his arms around Kurt, and they studied the long wooden staff together. He rested his head on what remained of Kurt's soft black hair.

"It's a work of art. Just like you."

Kurt drew him down for a kiss, then gently pushed him back to standing.

"You still look like death warmed over. Go back downstairs and sit. Take two aspirin. I'm going to finish it up."

Saul nodded and made his way toward the stairs. Kurt frowned at his retreating back. Saul didn't necessarily look like an old man, but he was starting to move like one. It worried him.

He turned back to the staff and began rubbing the wax into the carved surface.

The day was beautiful, the lunch crowd dispersed back to the sunshine, and to her relief, the café was empty. Saul was just coming down the stairs as she entered, and Newp was handling the floors.

"Michael is a werewolf and Toni and I have trapped him in the Pirate tower. We need to keep people away from the tower somehow until Toni can dose him with the silver nitrate. Or something."

The men stopped to look at her. Then they looked at each other.

"Do I want to know the story behind this?" asked Saul.

"No, you certainly do not," she replied.

"Leave him there," said Newp.

"What?"

"Kurt said there were what, twelve days til the full moon? And isn't that when they go bonkers? So, he's going to be dangerous soon anyway. Leave him in there, everyone is safer until the full moon is over, or the professor figures her stuff out and cures him."

Frannie stared at Newp. "We can't just leave him in there for two weeks! He needs food, and blankets, and…"

"And we need a safe beach. Don't werewolves eat people? You want to wake up some morning and Brainiac is down there with his throat ripped out?"

Frannie looked desperately to Saul for help, but the older man only looked thoughtful.

"He's not wrong." Saul shrugged. "That's a good place for him, until we're past the worst. We can feed him. We have blankets."

"And how are you going to keep people away, huh? What, are you going to put some kind of invisibility over the whole tower?"

"Wall up the doors," said Newp with a shrug.

"Now, now, we don't need to be so harsh as that. I can go put up… well, kind of the equivalent of a stink bomb. Instead of warding to protect, you can ward to make people avoid an area. Or we could just convince everyone that it's haunted," he said with a chuckle.

Frannie stomped her foot. It was a childish gesture and she regretted it immediately, but she was angry. "Why aren't you taking this seriously, either of you?"

"I'm totally serious," said Newp, arms crossing over his chest. "Also, I don't see why he's our problem. The Professor is the one with the pet werewolf, let her deal with it."

"He's our friend!"

"He's your friend." said Newp. "And I'm not even sure why."

"I…he's… a Blank called him, and…"

"And so what? I don't see you making friends with anyone else who reads a Blank. In fact, this is the first time one has ever stuck around. Don't you wonder why that is?"

Frannie stilled, dangerously. "Do not make this about me. He's a person. He's a werewolf on Laguna Beach, and if we didn't know anything else about the situation, that would still make it our problem. You said so yourself, you want the Legionnaires winding up dead? Or more summer people?" her voice choked as she fought back tears "Or anyone?"

Saul raised his hands between them. "Children, I love you. This does not solve our immediate problem. Frannie, take me to this tower, I will set up the wards. That will keep people away. Newp is not wrong—though he is your friend, he is also a threat, and a danger to himself and others. How would your friend feel if he woke up after the full moon and he had eaten all his new friends? That is not a fate you want for him. I'm sure your professor means well, but this is now a community issue, am I right?"

Her lip trembled, but she nodded. Newp put down the broom, a look of contrition on his face. "Frannie, I'm sorry, I didn't mean to—"

"You absolutely meant to say those things. *What you don't see with your eyes, don't invent with your mouth.*"

Newp's lips tightened, but he said nothing else. Saul raised a reproving eyebrow at Frannie, who turned toward the door.

"Come on then, let's deal with this."

"Wait!" called Kurt from the stairwell. "Take this!"

In his hands was a long red oak staff, covered in carved Hebrew script, arcane runes, glyphs, and tiny carved pictures that she couldn't make out from a distance. He held it for a minute, almost reluctant to let it go, then handed it over to Frannie.

"Kurt, what…"

"I'll explain it on the way. Thank you Kurt."

The artist nodded, with a tiny smile for Frannie, before disappearing back up the stairs.

"After you," said Saul, holding the door open.

Betty grunted and heaved another banker's box of files into Truly's car. "Is there more?" she panted.

"No, this one is the last. You did good Bets, thanks for the help."

"I vote we make Frannie and Newp unload all of this."

"Seconded."

They hopped in the vehicle, and Truly started making her way through the twists and turns of campus streets toward the highway.

"You typed up all this in a day?" asked Betty, looking at the boxes.

"No—the professor does all her stuff in triplicate. I only typed up half of the last box. The rest is her stuff. 'Pertinent to the location of the second piece,' she said."

"Geez. That's a lot of pertinence. Where are we even going to start?"

"Well," said Truly, flipping on her turn signal to join the highway. "The good news is that most of the stuff in the boxes is background stuff—I think the word she used was 'provenance' or something like that. Anyway, the stuff I was typing up yesterday and this morning was all stuff about this area, and a group called The Knights Templar. There's stuff in the research that suggests these Knight fellas hid it nearby."

"Knights like... Errol Flynn and Robin Hood and that stuff? Those knights?"

"Kind of. But like, only a few of them were those kinds of knights. A lot of them were scholars, really smart guys, and they were really good at being bankers. That's mostly what they did during the Crusades, bankrolled and fundraised stuff because they were really trustworthy and good at keeping secrets. But the French king—I don't remember his name—anyway he got really bad into debt with them, so he betrayed them and had a bunch of them killed and had the group disbanded by the Pope, so they had to go into hiding."

"You mean it's like a secret society now?"

"I guess. I mean if they're still around, I wouldn't go poking my head up, if the last bunch got burned alive at the stake."

"And these knights got the Delta all the way to America and hid it?"

"They really got around, says all the stuff I read."

"Wow."

"I mean, not them, not the ones from the Crusades. But their descendants. Anyway, she's narrowed it down to a fifty mile-ish radius of right here, at Laguna."

"This is wild."

They rode in silence for a little while, the warm sun and soft breeze pleasant and sweet.

"Listen, Truly…have you thought more about what we talked about? About…whether or not you're going to stay? I know we can find you a job, and I'll get one too, and—"

"The Professor paid me a month in advance. So, for right now, I'm not going anywhere. And Betty…if I didn't have to, I would never leave you, you know that right?"

Betty nodded. "I know. At least, that's what I believe. And that's the whole point, isn't it—what you believe."

Truly's smile was like a beautiful spill of pearls across her face. "I believe we are owed burgers, fries, and at least one chocolate milkshake for all this hard work in the hot sun."

Betty leaned back into the sunshine with a grin. "I believe you're right."

"Do you know what this is?"

"That's one of those things that Little John uses," Frannie answered, "in the Robin Hood movies."

"Yeah, it's a Bo staff. Take a look." He tossed it and she caught the staff, twirling it once just for fun. When she let it land with a smack against her palm, she studied it up close. It was about four feet tall, and the carvings were inlaid with gold paint. It was slick and smooth to the touch, but held to her hand, almost like…

"Is this board wax?"

Saul grinned "Kurt has a sense of humor, you know."

She spun the staff again and the gold shimmered beautifully in the dimming light of the sun. She whacked it against her palm again, bringing it to a stop. "Looks like you've carved a bunch of curses into the staff. I see some stuff from the Sefer Yetzirah..." she ran her fingers along the golden ruins. "Go to hell, get choked, explode. This is sort of the greatest hits of the curses, isn't it?"

Saul nodded. "With all this going on, I thought you could use some new tools. It has wards too—I know you're not as strong with those, but I thought one or two might be useful. Do you know all the curses still?"

"Why would you think I didn't?"

"I just don't know how much you've been keeping up with it. Have you been practicing?"

She waggled her hand. He knew exactly what she meant by practicing. She remembered the day that Saul had declared that he didn't want her to study, he wanted her to learn, to spend every waking hour reading from every dusty tome there was and learning all of the magic that she was able to bring out. Because it was one thing to man the book section and cater to whoever came in, to see their future. It was another to know that the same magical pull that was bringing lost people there, was also capable of bringing evil.

And no, she had not really been practicing. She had been lucky in the past week.

"Okay," he sighed as they walked. "You and me, we're gonna start doing ninety minutes a day. I want you to relearn everything, as if you've never read the curses before. But!" He gestured a give me that with his fingers, and she tossed the staff. He caught it and whipped it around and held it up. "I want you to start focusing them with this. If you're using the staff, you can defend yourself." He went towards her and whipped the staff over and tapped the back of her shoulder and she felt it push against her back. She kept from moving forward, because she was strong, but she understood what he was indicating. "You can pull people towards you," and now he whipped the staff over and tapped her chest, and then lightly tapped her forehead. "But more than this, you can focus your curses into the staff, and you can wield them when you're facing a foe."

"Ho boy," she said. "I could also just carry a shotgun like Truly did in Hawaii."

"I don't really like either of you carrying guns."

Frannie nodded. "I get it, you don't like guns."

"You want to know the truth? I don't really know anybody who has seen war that does." He shrugged. "Sometimes they are necessary, but for you, you are our warrior of purity. You need a pure weapon, and you need pure focus, so: start learning this, will you?"

She wasn't sure what was bringing all of this on. Really, all things considered, they had handled the mannequins and the Michael problem just fine. And those were recent troubles; she didn't know much about wood carving, but she had to imagine that Kurt had been working on this for weeks and weeks.

"Uncle Saul, this is neato and all, but is this really necessary? You said yourself, the Book Man was a once in a lifetime kind of demon, a huge one. Is this a little…overboard?"

"Just call it a feeling," Saul said.

"I need to be applying to college," Frannie said. "I don't know how much time I have to go around playing warrior."

"Is that what you think this is? You think we're playing a game?" He didn't say it in a cruel way. He said it as though he had been slapped. After a moment, he continued. "I know you got things to do. I know you're a girl who reads, I know you're very smart. And I know that you're very frustrated that you haven't gotten into a college yet. But you have to trust me that you're the kind of special that we need around here. And while you're here I need you to continue developing your abilities. I'm not always going to be around. Somebody's going to have to do this when I'm gone."

"When you're gone? You're not going to be gone anytime soon." She said this in a jovial way, but what she was really thinking was, what if I'm gone? What if I go off to college myself, who's going to watch the place then? "Saul, when I go to college, do you expect me to keep being a Blankguard?"

"We become Blankguards because we're called," he said. "I have a feeling that you will be one, whether you want to be or not. I just want you to be ready."

"Are you ready? Because we're almost there and I have to tell you... its...not good."

They drew closer to the tower, Saul struggling to keep pace in the sand. Frannie gave him the staff to lean on as they rounded the corner—

Straight into a pair of glowing green eyes.

"Vey is mir!" muttered Saul.

Frannie, however, was nothing but enraged. The mannequin stopped moving toward them and appeared to stare for a minute.

"Screw this whole fakakta day!" Frannie growled, and took three quick steps forward, swinging the Bo staff with both hands.

"Shteyner af zayne beyner!"

With a bright glow of golden light, the staff whacked against the side of the mannequin's head with a satisfying thunk. The mannequin collapsed to the ground, and lay there still, seemingly dazed. She tossed the staff to Saul and began to pile rocks on top of the wooden man.

"Watch my back for more!" she said, rolling and piling the heaviest stones she could manage on top of it. After a minute or so it became clear there weren't any others, and she took the staff back, perching herself atop the chest of the automaton.

"Go cast your wards, I've got this one all locked up. Don't I, Pinocchio, you schmuck?"

She tapped on its head with the staff, making little hollow sounds, and grinned.

Saul nodded, looking pleased, and went to take a look at the tower. Frannie stared down at the mannequin, who regarded her blankly. She looked at the staff, a thought taking shape. She stood, staff still pointed squarely at her enemy, and regarded the situation. She decided to wait for Saul.

After about ten minutes, he made his way slowly toward her. "He's asleep," said Saul. "And you were right, whew is he ugly. My mother-in-law would think she was looking in a mirror. We're going to want some silver chains for those doors though. They should hold in the meantime. And no one will want to come around here—anyone that doesn't see truly will think the place looks dangerous and will believe it smells of decaying fish. Think it'll be enough?"

Frannie nodded, and waved Saul over. "So, the staff…does it make my powers bigger? Amplify them, like a speaker?"

Saul shrugged. "I don't know. The only way to find out would be to practice. Why, what were you thinking?"

"I'm thinking about unbinding this soul from its master and seeing if this one is any calmer than the last one. Or at least we can find out who it is."

"I don't know if I'm strong enough to do all that again Frannie."

"That's why I'm going to do it. Besides, I cursed him and covered him in heavy rocks. I don't think it's going anywhere."

Saul shook his head but gestured for her to continue.

She flipped the staff to the unbinding spell. As she read it out, the symbols began to glow softly gold once more. She spoke the words louder, more firmly, and the glow increased. Grinning, she began to chant, growing the light, the power. It was enthralling, and she swung the staff in a slow arc over the mannequin, watching the light trail in the air behind the staff.

"Mi'avdut le'cherut, mitzrayim le'chofesh. Amen!"

There was that ripping feeling inside of her, like tearing off the thick, translucent layer of skin just above the nerve. She bit her lip through the not-quite pain, but it overwhelmed her senses and left her feeling nauseous. She tapped the mannequin with the staff, and then made a swooping motion with it, as though tossing whatever was holding it trapped away off into the surf. The feeling began to pass, and she shook her head to clear it, standing over the mannequin.

The previously blazing green eyes were now a soft, glowing blue. They were still deeply unsettling in the wooden face, and she didn't find the change comforting, but the change was there all the same. The mannequin stared at her, and the discomfort grew. It didn't scream or move or anything like the last one. It just lay there, watching her.

Finally, after a long silent moment, it raised its arms over its head in the universal sign of surrender. Frannie looked at Saul, who was just as surprised as she was.

"What do we do?" Frannie said.

"I'm not sure," said Saul. "I've never been on this side of that gesture before."

They looked at the mannequin, who raised its arms slightly higher, as though to emphasize the point.

"Can you…hear us?" asked Frannie.

Slowly, but very clearly, the mannequin nodded its head.

"Holy shit. Okay. If I take these rocks off you, are you going to freak out or try to kill us or…generally be trouble?"

Faster, this time, the mannequin shook its head. It pointed at Frannie, then at her bruised arm.

"Yeah, that's from last time we met, which is why I'm feeling not so confident about letting you up, Pinocchio. Saul, what do you think?"

Saul rubbed at his arm. "I think we go get Newp, he's going to be more helpful if this goes south than I am."

At the mention of Newp, the mannequin seemed to light up even further, and jabbed a hand in the air. The carved thumb was mostly upward facing.

"Did you just try to give us a thumbs up?" said Saul.

A nod.

"Because you know Newp?" Frannie exclaimed.

A nod.

"Oh god, I hope you're not one of the Legionnaires, crap, okay, it's safe, Saul, help me get these rocks off of him."

Together they cleared the wooden body, and the mannequin stood. It looked around, as though a little confused, then turned to face them.

"Who are you?" asked Frannie, afraid of the answer. She was racing through the names and faces of the Legionnaires, and when she had last seen them.

The mannequin pointed at her arm again, then at itself, then pointed down the beach, and started to walk.

"Whoa, wait, wait, buster," said Saul. "You can't just go wandering down the beach looking like that."

"Do we still have that trench coat from the other one?"

"Up at the café."

"Okay. I'll go get it. You take the staff, and you—" she pointed at the mannequin, "—no funny moves, okay?"

The mannequin nodded and shrugged, and the motion caught her off guard. Something was very wrong here.

She was back within ten minutes, carrying the trench coat, a battered wide brim fedora, an equally questionable looking pair of jeans, and a plain white t-shirt.

"Sorry, buddy, Kurt didn't have any spare shoes or socks kicking around."

She placed the clothes on a large flat rock, and then stepped back to stand next to Saul.

"Everything okay while I was gone?"

"Sure, everything's fine, he's very good at charades."

She shook her head and took the staff back.

Finished, the mannequin turned to them. In the dimming light, it could almost pass for a person. As a finishing touch, Saul unfolded a pair of sunglasses from his back pocket and wedged them between the wooden head and the hat band.

"A very hip cat."

Suddenly, the mannequin grabbed Frannie by the upper arm, and started walking quickly down the beach. Saul yelped in protest, but Frannie turned to reassure him. "It's okay, I think it's taking me somewhere, just follow us."

The mannequin nodded and moved faster down the beach. Frannie struggled to keep up, but there was a sudden desperation in its movements that she couldn't deny. They moved faster, too fast down the beach and Frannie called, absurdly, "Stop!"

Instead of stopping, it simply let go of her arm, and walked with its straight and strange mechanical gait straight into Hooky's hut.

Slowly she approached the hut. The wooden man there had slowed down, moving his knees in the sand. His eyes glowed as he kneeled. Frannie slowly moved to the corner, putting her hands on the license plates hammered into the walls.

The wooden man continued to move a knee at a time, then it rounded the corner of the hut and stopped, pitiful and strange.

What are you?

The wooden man had reached the front corner of the hut next to the little curtain that blew with the wind. It put down its hands and struggled to raise itself up, using the side of the hut to hold itself until finally it was able to balance on its two feet. And then it did the strangest thing that Frannie could imagine a wooden man doing. It rolled its shoulders, first one and then the other. And then hesitantly stepped forward with its left wooden hand reached out towards the curtain of the hut.

Frannie yelped, because this thing was going to destroy one of the last memories of her mentor, and she called out, "No!"

The wooden creature tore the curtain off its pins in the doorway. Frannie felt as though she were being torn, herself, but as it kept moving, bending forward into the hut, she felt an idea that she didn't want to feel. A thought that she couldn't dare think.

Frannie peered into the hut. As usual there was the cot there where she had sat shivah for Hooky, when the surfing chief died, when her uncle Saul had come and talked to her and talked about the ways that would pay homage to those who have passed. The wooden man was standing at the side of the cot and approaching a long shelf that ran along the wall. Frannie knew its contents completely... there were a couple of photographs and the wooden masks that Hooky collected, carvings of strange beings with tongues stuck out, amidst colorful bottles, a whole panorama of glass and ribbons and paint. There were a couple of old wine bottles with candles stuck into them that she knew Hooky had prized. One was supposedly used by Vincent Price in a movie, another he said he had got in Japan.

The mannequin turned its entire upper body and extended its arm and she saw that it was ready to let its arm fly back. She called out, "No!"

But the creature swept all the bottles and trinkets aside. The sound of glass breaking was barely audible in the hut with the oceans roar. Frannie leapt and grabbed the mannequin by the arm. He was not going to destroy everything in the hut, she wouldn't let him. But the mannequin paid no attention to her as she pulled at its powerful arm. She was lifted almost off the ground entirely as its two hands reached out to the shelf again. She watched the fused fingers close on either side of a photograph that was pinned to the wall behind the bottles. The wooden fingertips crimped into the photograph's metal frame, so that the glass cracked as the mannequin pulled the photo away. Frannie let go as the creature stepped backwards, still holding the photograph. The wooden man turned towards her, stiffly staring with its strange glowing eyes, and let the picture drop to the cot. And then it turned its head towards Frannie, stretching out its arm as best it could and pointing at the photograph. Frannie didn't need to look close to know what it said. The photo showed a beautiful, gray-haired woman with an impish smile, and an inscription that read:

TO "HOOKY" WITH LOVE,
GRACIE ALLEN

CHAPTER 18

NO, THAT'S IMPOSSIBLE.

Could it really be him? The wooden man stood there in silence. How? How could this creature be Hooky? The rational part of Frannie's brain said of course not, no, for some reason this animated wooden man was simply a moving creature of magic, and not... But of course, none of that was rational at all. She was already spun well off the edge of normalness.

She found herself hunching a little bit, holding out her hands as if she were talking to a rabbit or something dear that might fly away. "Okay. Okay. I don't know what to do, but can you... Can you come? Can you come with me? Back to the café?" The mannequin stared at her. "We can figure out what to do."

Hooky's body had been destroyed long ago. He was killed by a demon called the Book Man just after Hooky had rescued Newp. And his body had been defiled when the Book Man wore Hooky's skin. Was it possible that Hooky's spirit had lingered, and now found its way back... here?

Then a strange hum came into the air that crackled so much that Frannie could feel it on her skin. The creature's eyes suddenly blazed stronger and it seemed to stand up even straighter, its arms falling back to its sides. Something subtly changed and Frannie had the distinct impression that she was going to lose whatever clues she was looking at. She put up her hands on the wooden chest. The mannequin was even as tall as Hooky had been. But whatever recognition had seemed to be there in the glowing eyes had suddenly gone.

The mannequin bent down to duck under the door and stumbled out into the sand. Then it began to pick up speed, moving like an automaton southward. Marching towards the cliffs.

"Wait!" Frannie called. She had to stop it. She ran around and got several yards in front of it waving her arms. "Wait, if you really are..."

It shoved past her like a freight train. She grabbed its arm, and it dragged her a few yards and she fell into the sand. It was under whatever control had held all of the mannequins together. Well, she needed to capture this one. She felt certain more than ever that even if it might not be... she had to find out.

She was faster than it was, though, so she just needed something to hold it. She scrabbled to her feet and ran back towards the hut, looked around and found the curtain that the mannequin had torn down. She picked it up from the sand and twirled it several times in her hands as she began to run. She was forming it into a rope. By the time she was happy with the twisted curtain, she was close enough to tackle the wooden man. She set her mind to ignore the hammering that her body would take, and she landed on top of it, smacking it into the sand, her knees grinding into the beach. As she sat atop its back, it kicked mechanically, its head moving back and forth and mouth in indignation. She flipped around and used the curtain to tie the creature's feet together and then fell to the side. She grabbed its wooden hands and tied those as well, so that finally what she had was a hogtied mannequin. She grabbed the mass of curtain where it met the feet and hands and began to drag the creature back up the beach.

Saul had caught up by now and was watching her in bemused silence. He gestured with both hands, as if to say, 'what is this?.'

"Saul, it's Hooky."

"What?"

"The mannequin. The soul inside it. It's Hooky. But it's gone weird again, help me out!"

They managed to wrangle the staff through the curtain and carried the struggling mannequin between them like a hog for roast. The ridiculousness of the situation struck Saul, and he started giggling.

"This isn't funny."

"Oh, I don't know, you're not back here."

"What are we going to say if someone sees us?"

"We'll just tell them it's a new art installation by Kurt."

They hauled it up the steps and up to the highway and dragged it across the road, avoiding traffic as they did so. As they hauled it past the plants and the statue of Kronos, who was pretty much a giant mannequin himself, she also felt the hysterical giggles start to bubble up inside herself. She looked back and the creature was holding up its head to keep its chin from dragging on the highway and she could see that its shoulder was getting scraped up. She snorted but adjusted the staff on her shoulder to lift it higher.

They came to the café just as Truly and Betty were moving the last of the banker's boxes out of the car.

"What in…." Truly said.

The café door flew open, and Kurt strode out to throw a tablecloth over the mannequin, then held the door and ushered everyone inside. There were a few patrons reading, sipping coffee, and a couple enjoying a milkshake together in the far corner. Saul, smooth as ever, raised his voice so everyone could hear.

"Where do you want the new art piece, Kurt?"

"Upstairs Saul, to the workshop, it needs some work yet."

"I'll get the doors," said Betty in a voice that matched Saul's. "I can carry the paints on this hip, you go ahead and stay down here, Kurt."

In a strange procession they made it up the stairs and into the suite of rooms at the top. Frannie dropped the mannequin and pulled out the staff, and then stood on its chest as it writhed. It wasn't as strong as it had been, but it was still an effort to keep it from escaping. Frannie yelled, "Truly, I need help." Truly ran up and pressed down. That seemed to be good enough. It moved, but clearly wasn't going to overpower the two women. Betty put down a heavy box, and then joined them holding down the mannequin.

"What is it?" she asked.

Frannie pulled back the tablecloth with one hand to reveal the head of the mannequin, "More important, who is it: it's Hooky, trapped in this wooden body. I unbound him for a little while, but I maybe did it too fast, and it didn't hold. I gotta do it again."

Betty and Truly looked at each other wordlessly. Then Truly spoke for both of them.

"We're going to get Newp and Kurt up here to help you. We can run the café, right Saul?"

"Absolutely, you two powerhouses are the most capable girls I know."

"What about Frannie?" said Betty, not wanting her friend's feelings hurt.

"She's not a girl, she's a force of nature. I'll help her hold him down, go!"

Saul put his hands where Betty and Truly had been holding and looked up at Frannie. "I think I know the problem. You ended with amen, right?"

"Yeah, what's the problem with that? Means 'so be it.'"

Saul shook his head. "It's a call and response. You can't 'amen' yourself. Someone else has to. That might be why it faded off; you didn't cap it right."

"It worked last time!"

"We also released that soul almost immediately last time."

He was right. Frustratingly so.

"Okay, so what we need someone else to say that?"

"A group would be better."

Kurt and Newp thumped up the stairs, then Kurt took up the right arm and Newp the left, moving Saul down to the legs.

"What's going on?" asked Newp.

"The soul in this mannequin is Hooky, we have to get him unbound from the person controlling him."

Newp shook his head. "Frannie, Hooky is dead."

"His body is dead. The spirit in here is Hooky. He showed me the Gracie Allen autograph, who else but Hooky would know about that?"

Newp started to speak again, but Kurt cut him off. "What do you need us to do?"

"I'm going to do the unbinding spell again, and when I stop talking, I need you to say 'amen' and mean it, okay?"

Kurt looked at the others "I'm not Jewish, can I do that?"

Saul nodded "It doesn't matter. All that matters is your belief in what Frannie needs to happen. Ready?"

The men bore down, and Frannie lifted the staff again. God, she was tired. How much more could one day, one week, throw at her?

The staff lit up with the golden glow, and she braced herself for the feeling she knew was coming. She wasn't sure she wouldn't throw up this time. She was too tired. But this was Hooky, and she could free him. She had to.

"Mi'avdut le'cherut, mitzrayim le'chofesh. Meldung, Hooky, chofesh!"

She brought her arms and the staff down as the men chanted Amen. There was a bright flash of the golden light, and she felt herself thrown off her feet, though she never felt herself land. She opened her eyes and stood, to see Newp and Kurt helping Saul off the ground. On the table, the mannequin sat up, shook its head, and turned the blue glowing eyes to Newp. Newp froze, scarcely breathing, when the mannequin wrapped its arms around him. Frannie leapt forward, terrified that she was about to watch it squeeze the life out of Newp, when Kurt put a hand on her shoulder.

"It's a hug, kid," Kurt said. "And I think you could use it, too."

As naturally as rain, the three men, the young woman, and the wooden man gathered together in a group hug. Outside, the sounds of a summer night droned on, unheeded, in a rare and stunning moment of peace.

CHAPTER 19

LATER, WHEN THE STORM OF emotions had passed and they had spent an incredibly frustrating half hour trying to talk to Hooky via mannequin charades, Kurt finally spoke up.

"Okay, this isn't working. Those hands," he pointed to the stiff, carved, posed digits of Hooky's wooden hand "don't work. So, he can't write. And he can't talk."

Saul had excused himself down to the café for some peace and quiet work, so it was up to Frannie to make the sassy remarks.

"Sure, and if he only had a brain, we'd be halfway to Oz by now."

She plopped herself glumly into a folding chair, while Hooky stood against the wall and Kurt paced. Newp, who had been leaning in the door with his arms folded, suddenly looked up.

"The last one talked. Why can't he talk?"

"The last one had one of those hinged-jaw mouths," Frannie snapped bad-temperedly. "This one doesn't."

Kurt shot her a look with a raised eyebrow that suggested she cool it, and she slumped petulantly back.

"Well," said Newp, ignoring Frannie's tone and regarding the mannequin with a considering look, "What if we gave him one?"

Kurt looked from Newp to the mannequin and back again.

"You know," he said, "That might just do it. Hooky, why don't you come with me for a while. I think we can do something about that pretty quick. The hands, though...that's going to take a bit longer."

Hooky shrugged, and tousling Frannie's hair as best his mannequin hand would allow, he followed Kurt to his artist's workshop, leaving Newp and Frannie alone.

Newp resumed his position against the door, looking at anything but Frannie. "You okay?"

"Yeah, great, terrific, I'm the tops."

He turned his glance on her, and she felt a sudden pang of remorse. It wasn't fair to treat Newp like that. It wasn't his fault that there was someone out there ordering crazy wooden men around, or that Michael was a werewolf, or that she didn't—

That she didn't what? Want to be here? She did. She wanted more than anything for this to be all there was to life. But if the last few years had taught her anything, it was that you couldn't always have what you wanted, no matter how much you wanted or worked for it. It just wasn't meant to be.

She loved Newp. He was an undeniable part of her life, a steady rock. He was smart, and capable, and didn't panic. He was a good leader, a kind heart, and a hell of a surfer. He was as close to a best friend as she'd ever had.

She just didn't know what that meant in her life.

"The professor called. She's out of silver nitrate and is driving around trying to find more. I told her you and Saul were handling the problem, and that seemed to make her feel better."

Frannie ran a hand over her face. "I'm sorry Newp. And thank you. I'm just so tired. The last three days have been non-stop, and I just..."

She started to cry, silently. She hated crying. Newp quietly pulled up a chair next to hers and put an arm around her. He didn't say anything, and for whatever reason, that seemed to be exactly what she needed.

"I just don't know what to do," said Frannie, after a while. "What evil schmuck is trapping souls in those mannequins? How do we stop them? What do we do about Michael, what…" she threw up her hands, overwhelmed. Newp took them in his own.

"We start with the things we can control, Fran. It's just like showbiz. You can't control what's going on in the audience. You can only control what you play and how you play. What can you control?"

She sighed. "We can help Toni find the other part of the Delta. That solves the werewolf problem. But it makes the mannequin problem worse if that's what they're after."

"Why do you think Hooky was down there by the tower? Isn't that weird?"

"Maybe they're tracking Toni, that's the last place she was."

"I think we need to ask the professor what she thinks she knows about the dummies. But you're right, finding this Delta thing is something we can absolutely do. Betty and Truly brought all the paperwork here. We can start researching right away."

"I can help."

Hooky stood in the doorway, his blue eyes glowing softly. Below the carved nose, Kurt had painted a gently smirking mouth. Frannie and Newp stood, gaping, as Hooky's voice poured out of the motionless lips.

"Hey, Newpup. Hey, Angel. How are we saving the world tonight?"

CHAPTER 20

THEY COULD HAVE TALKED FOR hours, but Frannie's exhaustion was clearly taking over. Hooky, with his trademark no-nonsense style, informed her that he would answer all of her questions when she had rested, but for now she was limited to one.

Frannie and Newp sat in the folding chairs, heads bowed, thinking.

"Who did this to you?" asked Frannie.

"That's question one," said Hooky's voice. "And I don't know. The last thing I remember is watching you put that demon thing that ate me in a box and dropping it into the ocean. After that everything is kinda… blurry. I think I've mostly been surfing. Time…doesn't really matter, over on this side of things. The dead side. I mean, I am dead, right?"

Frannie and Newp nodded uncomfortably.

"Okay, so. Yeah, the last thing I remember before waking up in this thing, is surfing."

"So, ghosts can surf," Newp observed.

"I guess."

"Well, that's comforting. If we get killed, we'll just hang ten in the afterlife."

"My turn," said Hooky. "What exactly is this body I'm in, and why?"

They did their best to explain what they knew, which was not much.

"So, this Delta thing, we need to find it before the other dummies do?"

"Yeah, the professor needs it to cure this guy who is a werewolf," answered Newp. "Who Frannie and the professor trapped in the pirate tower this afternoon."

Hooky shook his wooden head. "I feel like I should be shocked that you just told me there is a werewolf, but I don't think I'm in a position to call bullshit on anything anymore. So...am I just stuck like this forever?"

Frannie and Newp looked at each other, and then Frannie shook her head. "No—at least, I don't think so. We captured another one, and Saul and I were able to unbind it from its maker, and also unbind the soul from the mannequin, though I don't know what happened to the spirit after that, to be honest. I hope it found some peace."

She didn't know how she could tell, since the painted-on face had no inherent expression, but Hooky looked thoughtful. "Okay. It's good to know I have an exit, if I want it."

"Now," he said. "Newp can fill me in on everything else since I died. You are going to bed. No arguing, Angel, you look like death. No pun intended."

"He's right, Frannie," said Newp. "We've got this, get some rest. The café won't get busy at night until Thursday, so just rest up."

She looked at her two men, and it was as though nothing had changed. Her heart ached for both of them, but her body ached for sleep. She nodded and curled up in the cot with no further urging. Newp assured her he'd call her folks, and kissing her forehead headed downstairs.

"Don't worry, Frannie," said Hooky. "We'll sort all this out. Get some sleep."

She did and slept soundly through a busy evening.

Truly and Betty set up the room as silently as possible with a folding table, chairs, and the boxes of research from Toni's office. Satisfied that

Frannie wasn't going to stir after accidentally dropping one of the boxes with a loud 'THUD' on the floor, they started unpacking and organizing the information.

"Let's put the most recent stuff out on the table, and the stuff about the Knights over here on this chair. The rest can go in the corner. It's mostly lore about the Delta. I'm not sure we're going to need that so much," said Truly quietly.

"Okay," Betty replied, shifting piles of papers around.

They moved like they sang, in a gentle harmony together, unfolding maps, shifting files, taping xeroxed pictures and images to the walls of the room. Betty held up a scrap of paper, tilting her head slightly as she read it.

"What is it, hun?"

"A poem, I think. But it's written in that old-ey English, like Beowulf. Remember when we had to read that for Senior English?" She shivered. "Gave me the creeps, that old Grendel and his mother, living under all that swampy water."

She rubbed at her arms as though she could feel the chill. Betty hated being wet, or cold. Both were intolerable.

"Let me see?"

She handed the paper over, and Truly took a turn studying it, then shook her head. "I don't get it either. That's for bigger brains than mine. Maybe Saul will know what it means."

"I'm worried about him. He still doesn't look good."

"Me too, Bets."

"Maybe we shouldn't play tomorrow night. And cancel the luau."

Truly paused, then shook her head. "It'll be all right. Newp will handle things. And we need the money."

Betty yawned, and stretched like a cat, the thick ruff collar of her flannel nightdress giving the impression of a lion's mane.

"Well, I think Frannie has the right idea, then. Besides, you have to work tomorrow, don't you?"

Truly nodded. "I'm excited. I know it's only temporary, but I'm hoping maybe it'll lead to something else, you know? I've been hoping—" she trailed off and shook her head smiling.

"What?"

"Just an idea I have, I'll tell you about it sometime. For now, we need to get ourselves home."

Betty stooped to kiss Frannie on the forehead, while Truly turned out the light.

In her dreams, Frannie surfed down a river of stars.

Alone.

In Kurt's workshop, Saul and Kurt regarded Hooky solemnly. Kurt scratched at his curls and let out a sigh.

"I think we're going to have to replace those hands with some articulated ones if you're going to stay in this…thing for any great length of time," he said, plucking a cigarette from behind his ear and lighting it.

"I mean, I'm not sure there's a lot of choice at present," said Hooky, from the painted mouth. Saul shivered a bit—the effect was spooky. "Frannie and Newp said there's a werewolf on the loose?"

"Loose isn't exactly correct," said Saul. "We've got him locked up in the Pirate Tower, and I warded it to keep people away. Toni Sutcliffe, the professor they were telling you about, she apparently has some kind of silver nitrate stuff that's supposed to keep him under control, at least until the full moon. But I'm inclined to think that tower is just the right place for him. In fact—" said Saul, looking over to Kurt, "We should probably take some food down there and show Hooky where it is."

"That's another thing," said Kurt. "Are you going to get hungry, or sleep?"

"No idea," said Hooky. "So far so good on either front. I don't feel hungry or tired. To tell you the truth…I genuinely can't feel anything. I know where my feet are because of the sound they make, does that make sense?"

Saul and Kurt both shrugged. What was sense, anymore?

"For now," said Saul, and looked apologetic "And I don't mean to be ordering you around now that you're back on the material plane, but…for now I think that it might be a good idea for you to stay up here in the daytime. And generally, try not to be seen. Not only because it's…well, spooky, but because we also don't know who the strong caster is that bound you this way in the first place. Which as you can imagine, is something of a big problem. It would be bad to accidentally run into them, eh?"

Hooky nodded. "But," he added, "Probably a good idea to put me on werewolf feeding duty. It can't, y'know, eat me. I'm just a walking chew toy."

Plan made, the three walked down the stairs and hung a tight left into the kitchen, where Saul made the biggest sandwich he could, and wrapped it in wax paper. Kurt meanwhile went to work on Hooky with some tools and hardware.

"You sure you can't feel anything?" asked Kurt, picking up a hammer and some short box nails.

"No, but I won't say that the way you're holding that hammer and nails isn't making me nervous, friend."

"You don't have any ears; we need to give you something to hang your hat on. Literally. And probably a fake beard sometime, but sunglasses will do for now. Bend your head sideways and tell me if it hurts."

Ten minutes and a pair of sunglasses later, and the three of them were walking out the door. Newp had assured them that he could handle things himself, given the quiet and small group that was in the café this evening. Saul offered up a grateful prayer for small blessings, then laughed that the café doing slow business should be a blessing. Joke is always on you, sayeth the Lord.

When they arrived at the Pirate Tower, the werewolf was nowhere to be seen. After a quick panic and a check of both doors, Saul caught a glimpse of thrashing tail on the stairway. "Well, that was a bit more of a heart attack than I wanted tonight," joked Saul, but something in Kurt's glance was reproving.

They let Hooky put the sandwich between the wide bars, before gathering a short distance away.

"What will you do now?" asked Saul.

"Keep watch on the beach, I think." said Hooky. "I'm not tired. I'll come back in before it gets light out. Then…I guess I'll help with the research. Though I'm not sure how much good I'll be, I never was much of a brain."

"Well, stay out of trouble, okay? I would never hear the end of it from Frannie."

"That kid is a—"

"Force of nature," they said together, and laughed. Hooky saluted, then wandered off down the beach, a strange dark figure in a long trench coat and fedora.

Saul turned to head back up the stairs, and Kurt stopped him.

"Saul, you don't look good."

"You're no catch yourself. Too skinny."

"Maybe we should call Magda."

Saul bristled. "I'll call Monsignor Matthias before I call Magda. It's a bad idea."

"I'm just saying—"

"And I'm just telling. No. No Magda. Unless something takes me out of the game. Understood?"

Kurt tried not to be hurt, but the tone—and the idea of Saul being incapacitated—stung.

Saul wrapped his arms around the smaller man.

"I'm sorry, Kurt, I'm sorry. I'm just a stupid old faygeleh. If it gets bad enough, we'll call, okay?"

"Okay. Listen, tomorrow morning—can you keep the café closed? Just for an hour? I want to show you something."

"Okay, sure. We can do that."

"Okay."

"Now help me up these meshugge steps."

CHAPTER 21

FRANNIE WOKE EARLY TO THE sound of soft snoring. She was puzzled, until she looked down at the floor. Curled up in some spare blankets with a booth cushion for a pillow was Newp. Frannie had to smile. He was sweet. She leaned down and brushed the beginnings of a curl from his forehead— the usual short back and sides his father insisted on was starting to grow out into its wild summer mane. Her fingers brushed the curl, and suddenly she remembered the dark brown wildness of Michael Landry's hair. She pulled her hand back as though she had burnt her fingers. Michael! The tower! Toni!

Frannie sat bolt upright when a familiar voice cut through her panic.

"What's the rush, Angel?"

She looked around and was surprised to find herself at the center of an investigation. Papers, books, articles, newspaper print, maps and pictures covered nearly every surface that wasn't herself or the floor. There was a table in the middle of the room covered with more of the stuff, and standing at the table, dressed in an old undershirt and paint spattered jeans, stood Hooky the Mannequin.

It was hard not to stare. It was even harder not to give into sorrow, or anger, or just plain grief. Instead, she rose carefully, avoiding the sleeping Newp, and joined Hooky at the table. He had what appeared to be two stacks of papers in front of him and was carefully (clumsily) shifting them from one stack to the other, one at a time.

"I was worried about Michael, he's still down at the tower and—"

"We fed and watered your pet werewolf, don't worry. And I spent most of the night watching the place. Not much else I can do. I can't really go out like this in the daylight."

"Hooky, I—"

"Don't say you're sorry. It is what it is, Frannie. And honestly, it's a lot better than it could have been. Anyway, Saul said the professor called and said to keep Michael in there, she was having trouble finding...whatever it's called, the silver stuff. She said she'd try again this evening when the pharmacy restocks."

"Okay. OKAY," she said, blowing her breath out in a puff of air that made her bangs dance. "Then I guess...what's all this?"

She gestured at the stacks of paper, accidentally knocked over a small coffee mug full of pencils and pens and swore quietly under her breath while Hooky chuckled.

"This is the research Truly and Betty brought down from the university. I had Newp make a stack of all the most recent stuff," he said, pointing to the pile on the right, "and then when I've read it I move it to the left. This Delta thing really probably is somewhere in the area. It's just hard to tell how big 'the area' is."

She scanned the papers, looking up at the wall of pictures. She walked to a picture of the piece owned by the university and tapped it thoughtfully. "What do you know so far?"

"That piece was found in Alexandria in the 1930's at an archeological dig. The only reason we know what it is, is that another piece was cataloged by the Knights Templar as Crusade loot during the second Crusade. They labeled it as a Holy Relic. They said the piece they found let them speak to the dead through objects."

Frannie looked him up and down, startled.

"Yep, that's what I thought too. Whoever is after the piece at the university, I'm willing to bet they already have one. They're going for the trifecta."

"What happened to the piece the Templars had?"

"That's the piece we're looking for around here. Your friend the professor seems to think that it was smuggled over to the U.S. by the Templars at the founding of the Colonies to keep it out of the hands of some other group—I have no idea how to pronounce it."

He pointed as best he could at a word Frannie had only heard once before. "Polidorium. Saul knows who they are."

"I guess they're bad news if you're a Templar. From there it traveled west, I guess based on these articles—about every thirty years or so, someone wound up talking to a dead person through a candlestick or something, and bam, it makes the news, and then all mention of it disappears for another thirty or so. Every time, the newspaper article is further west. The last one—" here he gestured at a stack of yellowed and crumbling newspaper clippings "is from a town called Salton, in 1900."

"Salton? Like, the Salton Sea? Mom and Pop have been invited up there by friends, it's like the dead sea of the Americas or something."

"I guess. I'm not from here myself…it's just where I washed up."

They stood quietly together for a few moments, pretending to look at the research, when the tension finally was too much.

"But Hooky I am sorry, it's my fault you're dead, if I hadn't—"

"Bullshit. It's the Book Man's fault I'm dead, and that's the end of it. Did you eat my guts and bones and all the things I could have been from the inside out? No. He did. You were a seventeen-year-old kid trying to fight monsters and learn to surf and recover from almost dying. Nothing that happened was your fault, you did everything you could do. You built a golem, for Pete's sake."

"It was a busy summer."

They laughed together, and the tension eased a little bit.

"This has been a pretty busy summer too, huh? Newp filled me in last night. Seems like it's been nothing but go since you graduated."

"Yeah," she sighed. "You could say that."

"For him too."

She looked up, startled.

"Starting the surf school, getting the luau ready, half running this place, werewolves trying to make time with his girl, his mentor shows up as a life-size wooden mannequin…"

She stomped her foot, then winced, worried she might wake Newp.

"No one is making time with me. And I don't recall ever agreeing to be 'his' girl. I am my own girl, thank you very much."

Hooky raised his wooden hands in surrender "Easy, Angel, I'm just calling it like I see it. His feelings are pretty clear."

"I have a lot bigger things to worry about than Newp's feelings!"

"I think maybe you better tell him that."

"Yes, thank you, I take all my relationship advice from temporarily possessed dress forms."

They both froze, Frannie in horror and Hooky in surprise. Before she could babble out an apology, Hooky started laughing, deep and hearty, and the sound woke Newp.

"Mmmm? Wuzzit?"

"Nothing," said Frannie quickly. "We were just looking at the research."

"Mmmf…Gotta open the café, Kurt is taking Saul somewhere for an hour."

"I'll do it," said Frannie, practically racing out of the room, her face beet red.

Hooky and Newp looked at each other. Newp wished, not for the last time, that the wooden face had any other expression than a smirk.

"Women," said Hooky with a shrug. Newp looked at the empty doorway, where Frannie had disappeared, and shook his head.

"Women."

CHAPTER 22

"IT'S TOO EARLY FOR THIS," grumbled Saul, holding tightly to his mug of coffee as he clambered into the old Studebaker.

I'm worried it's too late, thought Kurt, as he turned the key in the ignition.

They drove in companionable silence for a while, and eventually Saul relented and took Kurt's right hand as he drove.

"Sorry, I'm just so tired lately," he murmured apologetically. "Where is it you're taking me?"

"It's a surprise," said Kurt.

They pulled up to the marina, and Saul lifted an eyebrow.

"So far, very surprised. The Marina?"

Kurt didn't answer but got out of the car and waited next to it for Saul to get out.

The Marina was empty at this time of the morning. Saul stepped out, waving his arms. "What is this?"

Kurt walked silently ahead of him and stopped in front of the small yacht. He took off his painter's cap and aimed it at the boat. "This," he said, "is a thirty-foot Chris Craft El Capitan Cruiser. It's top of the line. Just two years old."

Saul ran his hand across his bald head. "Where did it come from?"

"Well, it belonged to a friend, but he had to leave the country, so he wanted to get rid of his boat."

"But how did you…"

Kurt said, "I got it for a song. Actually, that's not true, I got it for art."

Saul went over and climbed over the wheel well of the trailer and into the boat. For a moment he stood on the deck, his arms extended rocking slightly. He reminded Newp of Gene Kelly in his sailor outfits. Saul turned around and ran his hand along the sails, which were still bound down. "It's got an outboard motor, oh, fantastic. We're gonna go fishin'. But what's the occasion?"

Kurt said, "It's May 23rd."

"May 23rd?"

Kurt nodded. "May 23rd is when I met this fellow on a steamer headed for Cuba."

Saul smiled wide and jumped down and embraced Kurt. This was a public display of affection that Kurt was not entirely comfortable with, but he did manage to say, "Happy Anniversary."

"You want to take it out? A baby like this." Saul slapped the hull of the boat. "It's gotta be in the water."

In ten minutes, Saul the sailor Kurt the artist were on the water for the first time in years.

Frannie offered up a silent prayer in praise of Kurt and his coffee. Not only had he made coffee, but he had made enough extra that she could safely open the café without scrambling to make her own poor imitation. She was equally grateful that the morning delivery of pastries had already arrived because no one would be getting hot food until Saul came back.

Cooking, she had discovered to her chagrin, was not one of her skills. Cast a curse? No sweat. Scramble eggs? No thank you.

She toasted a bagel and lathered it with cream cheese, inhaling the sweet dark scent of the coffee. As she lifted her breakfast to her lips, as though on a silent cue, the café door swung open in a blaze of light. She decided to take the bite anyway.

"Good morning," she said around a mouthful of bagel. "Welcome to Café Monstro. I'm sorry, we—"

"Good morning, Frannie," said Toni, laying a leather sachet on one of the stools. "Sorry to hit you right in the eyes with the light."

Her eyes adjusted, and she could see the more casually dressed Sutcliffe had opted for khaki and cream today.

"That's all right, professor. Coffee? All I can offer for breakfast is pastries though, Saul is out for a bit."

"I think I could be friends with that cherry Danish and a cup of coffee."

"Coming right up."

Frannie busied herself with the business of mugs and plates, while Toni settled herself at the bar.

"I checked on Michael—from a distance. He's still very…lupine."

Frannie set the plate and mug in front of Toni. "Beg pardon?"

"Wolfy. I'm quite concerned, usually it doesn't last into the sunrise. Then again, I'm working from very sparse experience and research where Michael is concerned."

Frannie cupped her mug with a look of surprise. "How long have you known him?"

"Only two months. I met him when I was interviewing for the summer position at the university."

"And how did you—"

"Find out he was a werewolf? It seems the condition is triggered much the same as an anger or fear response. I was checking out the library, and he had been working in the gardens and lawn department. I startled him one evening while he was trimming the rhododendrons and let's just say, the teeth were concerning, but the fur was an absolute shock."

Frannie snorted a little into her coffee, and Toni winked before taking a dainty bite of Danish. "This is delightful! Where did you get this?"

"Saul is friends with a couple of bakeries in the area."

"Saul is friends with everyone."

"Not everyone," said Frannie, setting down her mug meaningfully. "He's certainly not sure about you. And I have…a lot of questions."

"That's fair," said Toni. "So do I. Shall we trade? You ask one of yours, and I'll ask one of mine."

"Okay. What do you know about the mannequins?"

"I remember that they used to have similar ones at the department stores when I was a very young child. They always spooked me. As for the ones that attacked us…" Toni shrugged. "I'm guessing an automation spell? But that would require someone puppeteering them, which means they would need to be able to see the space, and there could only be one puppeteer for each mannequin, so it would have to be a group of them—"

Frannie shook her head excitedly "It's souls, someone is binding souls to the mannequins to animate them and then binding the mannequin itself to their will."

Toni slapped the table "Damn, that's clever. And evil. It gets around the puppeteering problem, they can just be ordered to do something, and they have a soul to power the movement. Damn. How did you figure that out?"

Frannie couldn't help herself—it was really something to be receiving compliments on her work, especially from someone as worldly and experienced as the professor. She felt her spirits take an immense lift.

"Saul and I just sat down and tried to figure out how we would do it if it were us. Reverse-engineer, you know? Once we figured out how to unbind the spells—"

"Unbind?"

Toni's face was pure astonishment, and Frannie's ego took another pull at the cup of her admiration.

"Yeah, it's a lot of effort and you pay for it with a huge headache after, but it can be done. I didn't know there was another way to do it, you mean there are spells that let you actually move stuff around?"

"I mean, I've never cast them myself, but I've seen it done, usually by witches or shama—"

The door opened with a soft bell chime, and an older woman wandered in with the vaguely lost look that Frannie knew as intimately as she knew the taste of her own tears.

This woman was being called by a Blank.

Toni followed Frannie's gaze. "Is she?"

"Yeah," said Frannie, taking a big bite of her bagel and swig of her coffee. "She is. Do you mind?"

"Not at all, I'll tell anyone who comes in that you stepped away to the ladies room."

"Newp should be down soon anyway. You all right?"

Toni raised her Danish as though in salute and went back to enjoying her breakfast.

Frannie smiled widely at the woman and began what she thought of as the Ritual of the Blanks—the welcome, asking if they were looking for a book, telling them there was something special just for them. She watched, riding gently on the river of stars as the woman's life poured out onto the page, scene after strange and lovely scene of a life well lived. She placed a gentle arm around the woman's shoulders as she shook slightly and smiled at her as the woman told her about her plans to write her own book about her life.

"It will be a good book," she said. "A book for young people like you. A book about the value of peace."

"I can't wait to read it," said Frannie, carefully replacing the Blank on the high shelf above the door. She led the woman out into the café, to find Toni watching them intently. Frannie sold the woman a writing journal and pen set (along with a cookie "for the road") on her way out. After warming her cup of coffee back up, Frannie returned to the counter.

"That must be truly amazing," said Toni. "Magic like that. Maybe I could look at a blank? For my research. They must be—"

"Absolutely not," came Saul's voice from behind them. It sounded stronger than it had in days, and it made Frannie jump a little.

"Blanks are for Blankguards and for those who are Called. Anyone else messing with them is verboten."

Maybe it was the stressful few days they'd had. Maybe it was the note of chastisement in Saul's voice. Maybe it was the strength she got from feeling admired and appreciated by Toni. Whatever it was, Frannie turned sharply on Saul.

"Why? Why can't I show her a Blank?"

Saul's face hardened. "Because it's verboten, that's why."

"That's not a reason. What is it going to hurt, showing Toni a Blank? Is there some great curse that will befall us, or does it mess up the magic, or what?"

Toni reached out a hand "Frannie, it's okay, I don't—"

"No, it's not okay. You want me to be a Blankguard so bad, but you don't want to tell me the rules. You teach me the magicks and you want me to use them, but you don't want me to know about who and what else is out there using them! I am not a child anymore. You want to play by the religious rules, my bat-mitzvah was years ago."

Frannie's eyes blazed as she glared at Saul, then turned back to Toni.

"Who are the Polidorium? The Hexen? What's a Black Tower? Who—"

"Please forgive my niece," said Saul firmly to Toni. "She sometimes forgets that the café is open to the public."

Frannie's voice died out, shamed into silence. She felt the heat rise and prickle all the way up her face, past her cheeks, and sting her eyes. Toni shook her head, though Frannie wasn't sure at whom.

"No, it's my fault, I'm sorry. I just stopped by to check on Michael and get some breakfast before my morning classes."

"Of course. I'm sure we can continue this conversation at a later time and in a more appropriate setting," said Saul, and Frannie felt the sting of humiliation again. She stared down into her coffee mug, feeling control slip away from her.

"Absolutely. Your Danishes are the best I've had. I'm sure I'll be by later to listen to the girls sing."

With that, Toni disappeared out the door.

In a fit of pique, Frannie scooped up the dishes and brushed past Saul. She would not cry, she would not…

He followed her into the kitchen, a tired look on his face. "Frannie, sweetheart, you—"

"I don't have a single thing to say to you. To any of you. Someone was Called this morning and I showed them a Blank. I did my job. I'm going surfing."

She swept past him again, ignoring his pleas that she wait and talk to him. She wasn't going to spend any more time this morning being humiliated. She hit the door like a thunderbolt and was gone into the morning sun.

"I'm not going to say I told you so," said Kurt, handing him a dishcloth. "But I told you so."

Newp was, generally speaking, a man who kept things simple. You looked at the steps of a job, you knew what they were, you did them and you did them well. Manage a café? Simple. Keep lists, keep it stocked, keep the flow going. Manage a band? Easy. Make set lists, keep the songs fresh, don't let go of hits or favorites. Manage the Legionnaires' surf school? No problem. Make a list of tasks. Delegate them to capable men. Use the strengths of each individual to strengthen the group. Above all, in each of these arenas, the most important thing was advertising.

Laguna Beach was liberally papered with flyers. He had sent Truly a stack to put up at the university on her breaks. He sent Betty out in the car to hit all the local burger joints. He sought out families on the beach and handed them flyers himself. Everyone, and he meant everyone, was going to know about the Luau Friday.

Newp liked to keep things simple.

Eric and the Phantoms liked to complicate them.

The bikes idled outside the malt shoppe as Eric and his entourage sauntered out, wiping grease and salt from their hands. A flutter on the cork community board caught his eye, and he reached out a grimy hand to pull it down.

"Who wants to go to a party Friday night, huh?" he said, half laughing, entirely serious. The gang nodded and made the expected sounds of approval, and Eric stuffed the flyer into his leather jacket pocket. That girl he liked, the one in the pretty pajamas…it would be nice to see her again.

The handle of his switchblade pressed into his side through his pocket next to the flyer.

Yeah. It would be really nice to see her again.

In fact, he didn't want to wait.

"I feel like dancing," he said. "Let's go catch the music at Café Monstro tonight."

"Didn't they kick us out?" said a newer, and nominally stupider of the group, named Clarence.

"Sure, they did, sure they did," said Eric, and the more experienced members drew away slightly. In a flash, Eric had pinned Clarence against the concrete wall of the burger joint. "Which is why it'll be a surprise party when we show up. When we show up," he said, speaking to the group, "in our Sunday best instead of our riding gear. Get me?"

A young man nicknamed Meatball nodded. "They wouldn't recognize us from their own mothers, we'll be so squeaky and square."

Eric let go of Clarence, pointing at Meatball. "Ten points for the big brain. Go home and clean up, kiddies. I'll see you at the café tonight, 10 PM sharp. Bring your dancing shoes," he said, winking.

The motorcycles roared away. Eric and the Phantoms disappeared down the highway, leaving exhaust and dread in their wake.

Truly wiped her brow and shook out her aching hands. Even with all the windows open and the wide bladed fan running above her head, the noon heat promised a long hot summer to follow. She stood, wiping her hands on her trim white trousers, and walked to the window, hoping to catch a breeze.

It had been a busy morning transcribing student lists and preparing coursework outlines. While she was glad that she wasn't just retyping research and filling banker's boxes, that had at least been a little more interesting than the general assistant work she had been tasked with today. But with a whole month's pay in advance, beyond the extra she made from the café and other gigs, the work was worth it.

If she was very lucky, she could sign the papers on Monday.

She was doing a little happy jitterbug with herself when the door swung open to admit Toni. Truly stopped, embarrassed, but Toni only laughed and did a little dance herself.

"I know the feeling, no need to feel embarrassed. What made you so happy?"

"Oh," said Truly, trying to be nonchalant. "Just some good news is all. I think I found an apartment."

"How exciting!" said Toni, dropping a pile of books on her desk. "Ready to fly the coop?"

Truly smiled. "It's a pretty full nest. Mom and Pops have a lot on their hands with my sisters and my cousins. One less chick around might not be so bad, you know? Besides, the rule in my family is, 'turn eighteen, find your own scene.'"

The professor stacked and unstacked several files as she spoke. "I'm sure they'll miss you, though?"

"Oh, I won't be far. And you should see us at holidays, we pack a place with family from all over. It's a real party. I'm sure I'll see them plenty."

"Well, you've certainly shown yourself to be more than capable here. I'm glad to have you. Michael can't type to save his life."

Truly returned to the desk, adding a new file to Toni's stack. "How is he?"

Toni shook her head grimly. "Still a wolf, mostly. I've never seen it this bad before. It worries me." She turned and gave Truly a smile "But don't you worry. Saul says they have it well under control, and I believe him. Unless…" this time her gaze was a little more secretive, but Truly felt as though she were in on the secret. "You don't have a bit of a thing for Michael, do you?"

When Truly made a face, Toni laughed. "Oh, he's fine," said Truly. "I'm sorry, I didn't mean to be insulting, he's very attractive, I'm just not…I don't… I'm unattached," she finally said, landing on the statement.

"Unattached?" Toni looked surprised. "That's strange, a pretty girl like you, and a musician too. I should think the boys would be just abuzz around you."

Truly sat back down at the typewriter, avoiding eye contact.

"Well, I'm really busy with Betty and the band, you know, and…"

"Ah, I see. Yes, that makes sense."

Something in Toni's tone made Truly's heart leap with fear.

"What makes sense?

"Just as you say, you're busy with Betty…and the band. You know," Toni went on, confidentially, "I've been all over the world, and I never thought the most fascinating people I would ever meet would all gather in one little café on Laguna Beach. It's perfectly marvelous. And thank you," she added. "For being willing to share with me. I like getting to know people, though I'm afraid I'm sometimes a bit…overwhelming."

"That's all right," said Truly, feeling slightly more relaxed. "Anyway, what's next?"

Toni plunked another full file in front of her.

"More transposing I'm afraid."

Truly cracked her fingers in front of her and set them on the typewriter keys.

"It's all just music to me, Professor."

When Frannie finally came back in, her head was a bit clearer. Saul was still entirely in the wrong—but he wasn't entirely wrong. She had been talking very openly (maybe loudly) about magic right in the middle of the café, and though it hadn't been even remotely busy, it still wasn't the place. But Toni knew things, things that Frannie hungered to know herself, and she was tired of crumbs and snatched information. If Saul wasn't going to tell her what she needed to know, she'd get it from Toni.

She set her board inside Hooky's hut and shook the ocean out of her hair. On the wide spread of level beach in front of Gogo's board shack, several of the Legionnaires were scooping buckets and shovelfuls of sand away to create two deep troughs. It took Frannie nearly a full minute to figure out what it was they were for, and she silently cursed herself.

The Luau. It was tomorrow. Go-Go and the boys would be setting up the coals soon and working on getting the hogs ready to roast. She looked around, and sure enough saw Newp, giving orders and working alongside the Legionnaires. Just as she should have been.

Chagrined, she made her way to Go-Go's hut. Instead, she found Brainiac, tongue sticking out of the corner of his mouth in concentration, as he painted a hibiscus flower on a 'Luau To-Nite' banner. It was surprisingly good, and Frannie took a long look at Brainiac. Good with kids, secretly an artist, decent surf teacher…if he could just keep his mouth shut and his hands to himself, Brainiac could have quite the future ahead of him.

He looked up at her and grinned in a slightly sleazy way that made her shake her head and sigh. Maybe someday Brainiac's maturity ship would come in, but it wasn't today.

"Admiring the view, Fran?"

"Admiring the hibiscus. You're a surprisingly good artist."

"I have good hands" he said, wiggling his eyebrows suggestively.

"Shut up Brainiac."

He grinned wider. "Got it, boss lady."

"Speaking of boss, where is Newp?"

"Dressing the hogs with some of the other guys. You need something ol' Brainiac can help you with?"

"Just wanted to know if there was something I could do to help with the luau before I headed up for my shift."

Brainiac offered her a paintbrush like a sword, and she laughed and shook her head. "My flowers would look like blobs. Yours actually look like flowers."

He nodded and turned uncharacteristically serious. "Maybe tell me if there's something we really need to worry about? Newp's got us watching the beach like hawks and Go-Go says keep people away from the Pirate Tower. We're all kinda spooked. What's the beef?"

Frannie hesitated. She wasn't sure how to answer him. If this was how leadership really felt, she wasn't sure she liked it.

"There's been some trouble up at the café and the university with a weird...gang. They wear trench coats and maybe walk a little funny. And there were the bikers. And the girl who drowned last week. I guess..." she shifted her feet in the sand and struggled to meet his eyes. "I guess just keep doing what you're doing and keep eyes out. There's things to worry about, and I wish I had more to tell you, but I don't. Just stay wary. And stay safe, okay Brainiac?"

He nodded sagely. "You too, Frannie. We know you're some kind of...something, and one bad dame to boot, but we've got your back too you know?"

"Thanks, Brainiac."

He waved the paintbrush at her and she headed up the stairs, not feeling less guilty...but a little comforted. She was surprised to find a familiar face at the top of the stairs.

"Professor!"

"Hi Frannie. I just checked on Michael and thought as long as I was here, I might practice my surfing. You said it was the best thing you knew for clearing the mind."

"It is—is your mind having troubles?"

Toni smiled sadly and nodded. "I feel responsible for all this. And for the argument with your uncle this morning. I've brought you a lot of trouble, and I'm sorry."

"No, no, not at all," Frannie protested. To think that Toni was apologizing to her, after all the amazing things she had done for Betty and Truly and the rest of them was beyond the pale. "It's not your fault in the least."

"But Saul—"

"Isn't always right," said Frannie hotly, her temper coming back. "And it's not fair how suspicious he's being of you. You know what?" she said, her pulse quickening. "Give me just a minute, I'll meet you in Hooky's hut."

Toni looked surprised as Frannie jogged back to the café. Her luck was in—Kurt was behind the bar and paid her no notice as she walked to the door that marked the bookshop. She reached up to the shelf above the door, grabbed the nearest Blank, and stuffed it in her suit, under her oversized button up shirt. She grabbed a beaten-up Louis L'amour and waved it at him as she made her way out the door. She ran back across the highway and made her way down to Hooky's hut. She found Toni outside, admiring the view of the ocean.

"Come on," said Frannie, holding open the door curtain. "I have something to show you."

They sat on the cot, and Frannie pulled out the Blank. Toni's eyes widened. "Is that a…"

"Yeah. This is my call, I'm making it. Go ahead, open it."

"Are you sure?"

"I'm sure. I don't know what it will show you, or me, but I think you've earned the right to look at least."

Toni looked at Frannie carefully, then at the plain black cover. "It looks like a notebook. What's inside it?"

"Let's find out."

Toni froze as she saw the empty pages. Frannie felt the throb of the book as words began to fill in, and suddenly Toni was floating, and Frannie was floating, and they were in the South Pacific.

CHAPTER 23

IT IS 1945 AND TONI is covered in blood. There is no time to deal with the wounded who are coming in. All Toni can do is move from cot to cot and say, "Everything will be fine. You're going to get home to your mother," and she knows that to these bleeding men, she is their mother. Even if they were flirting with her yesterday, even if on any other day they would want to date her, right now she is their mother, and she holds their hand, and she watches them die.

"Incoming wounded!" Somebody shouts over the intercom. And more litter carriers come in, more and more sailors and soldiers.

It is agony. The people who die on a ship that is torpedoed die agonizingly but quickly as they drown. But those who do not drown are burned and maimed, and they come here. And her job is to try to stitch them together.

In Frannie's hands, the book is growing strangely warm. She ignores it, swimming back to Toni's story through the river of stars.

Toni Sutcliffe of Tulsa, Oklahoma, tries in every way to remain an optimist. As her white uniform is covered with blood, she tries to remember all the things that she has learned from all of her books. She tries to remember all the wisdom of how to win friends and influence people and the power of positive thinking. She knows firsthand the power of true belief, and if she can make even one of these boys believe that they can live, then they will. But there is no positive thinking here. There is only agony and palm trees. There is only death and then pretending that death is not around the corner. There is only death and then weeks and even months of beauty as though all of the death is far away and never to return. And yet it always does.

The stars burn brighter, the book grows warmer. This has never happened before, and Frannie is struggling to ignore it. She needs to know what happens to Toni. She wants to understand—because she fears the parallels already.

There is a man she has been seeing, somebody that she has thrown over her own fiancé back home for, a beautiful older French plantation owner.

Her problems with him are pedestrian. She is having a hard time getting over the fact that he has children with dark skin. And she is revolted that he would touch someone like that, much less have children with them, but she has begun to see the goodness of the man. And she thinks maybe just possibly she could learn to love his children after all. Maybe even live with them. She would be willing to do that. Anything is possible in the weeks and months between the returns of death.

And then he is brought in. He has been doing a job for the Americans, he has stupidly decided to get involved in their work. and his leg has been blown off above the knee. His arm has been torn away, so far into the shoulder that she has no idea how in the world they're going to close the wound. And of course, they're not going to close the wound. What they're going to do is give him so much morphine that he will not know when he dies.

When he arrives, she recognizes him instantly on the gurney, even though his face is drenched in blood. He is spitting and grasping for her.

Toni Sutcliffe is an optimist. There is going to be a way to overcome all of this. Even if she asked to rewrite the rules entirely. And she doesn't care what the cost to herself is. She is going to make men better than this. She is going to find a way.

She goes back to the states, and she does not bother to look up her fiancé. She gets a Ph. D. in anthropology and a doctorate in psychology, and she begins to travel the world, studying cultures, and secretly studying their magic. Until finally in a library in Australia, she discovers a book that mentions the Delta of Enoch. She begins her search.

With a cry, Frannie and Toni both dropped the Blank, the heat becoming too much for their hands to bear. It smoked in the sand, before bursting into a bright blue and purple flame, vanishing into ash faster than either could believe. The women stared at each other, shocked.

"Has that ever happened before?" asked Toni.

"N—nope," Frannie replied, shaken.

"Did I break it?"

"I don't know…I don't think so. Usually it shows you other paths, other potentialities, but…" Frannie searched herself for an explanation. "If you don't have another path, if this just is your course through life, then maybe this is what happens."

"We had a path. A life. It was stolen from us. Stolen from us by war, by fools with guns, by more fools who controlled them. Our path forward was stolen. And there's no one to bring us justice for it."

"I know. I'm so sorry, Toni. I wish I could bring it all back for you."

"I will. The Delta will. I'm going to get that life back."

"And I want to help you, I do."

They sat in silence, the emotion thick and heavy in the air between them. Had Hooky's hut always been such a place of grief?

Finally, Toni broke the silence.

"Are you going to tell Saul?"

Frannie hesitated. Then her voice hardened.

"No. Because I was right to show you that blank. I understand you, and I understand why you want the Delta. I would want it for the same reason. There was a… a monster, a monster that ate Blanks, and he showed me that there's a war coming, just like your war, and that I was there the same way you're there, and it's all the same, it's all so terribly the same. There has to be a way to stop it, or at least prepare for it."

"A Collector. That monster must have been one of the Collectors. They eat magic."

Frannie threw her hands in the air "See!? THIS is what I'm talking about! I need to know these things! A Collector. Saul used that word, too, but hasn't given me more. Are there lots of them? What do they do? Are they all really powerful?"

"I'll lend you my book and you can read all about them."

"Really?"

"Really. And you're right—we have to stop it. Stop the madness once and for all."

Frannie nodded, and the two women understood each other.

"But it'll have to be later," said Toni, looking at her watch. "Because it's almost time for your shift and my night class."

On the sand between them, the thin ashes of the burned Blank blew off into the breeze.

The café was starting to buzz as the girls warmed up and the tables slowly filled. There were no families tonight, which was a little bit of a surprise, but there were certainly a lot of new faces in Frannie's age range. She hoped they were there because of the impending luau, and secretly crossed her fingers that the night would just build interest and energy for the next day's party. Burgers, baskets of fries, milkshakes and the odd BLT flowed evenly out of the kitchen and onto tables, and the rhythm of the evening felt good and comfortable. But the burned Blank weighed on her mind, and the guilt of it tarnished the otherwise happy atmosphere.

Newp came in around 8:30, shaking off sand and throwing on an apron. He locked eyes with Frannie only once, and the moment was a bump in the smooth road of the shift. The guilty feeling doubled down, and her own words echoed hauntingly in her mind—I don't have time to worry about

Newp's feelings…

The band's first half closer was always Sloop John B. Halfway through the night, and she still hadn't shaken off the feeling that something was wrong. Very wrong. Was it Michael? Hooky was down at the tower watching him and bringing him food now that darkness had settled in—if something was amiss in that direction they would surely know by now. So, what was it?

The song ended, the clapping started—and then did not stop.

People slowly started to realize that the clapping had not let up with the general tapering of the applause and turned to look. Spread throughout the café were young men and women, smirking, clapping, and beginning to rise. Moving toward the center of the room in a powder blue suit and slicked back hair was a medium sized young man, his eyes locked on Betty. Frannie's stomach dropped. The clapping stopped, as though on cue.

"Hey, beautiful. I liked that set. I like the new nightgown."

Truly got up from behind the piano, her face ashen, as Betty started to back away from the microphone.

"Oh, stay," said the young man, opening his arms wide. "Stay and talk to me, Betty. Because you know how I feel. You know how I like you."

On silent command, the other clappers started advancing on the stage, forming a semicircle behind the blue suit.

"And when Eric likes someone—"

"T-they s-stay liked." Betty gasped into the microphone, on the verge of a scream.

With a sinking heart, Frannie started to recognize the faces of the biker gang. They had been clever, dressing like average beach bums or girls out for the night. She would never have recognized Eric and the Phantoms dressed as they were. And now it was too late. She cast her glance toward the booth where Mutt and Jeff usually sat, even though she knew it was far too early to hope to see them in it. From the stage came another commotion as Truly marched down in front of Eric.

"This is private property, and you got kicked out of it. Get your ass out that door before we call the police and have it thrown out."

Eric stepped forward, toe to toe with Truly, and smirked. "Your pet cops don't scare me. And I still don't like you. That's gonna mean bad things for your smart mouth."

"Go to Hell, you stupid—"

Several things happened at once. Betty screamed, long and loud into the microphone, causing people to flinch and cover their ears. Newp and Saul came racing out through the kitchen doors, Newp leaping over the bar to get to the semicircle of bikers. Frannie rushed toward Truly and Eric through the crowd, just in time to see Eric's wrist flick outwards and an arc of red cut through the stage lights to spatter against the rise of the stage and the floor. Betty's scream deepened as Truly stumbled into a small table, collapsing into a chair. Eric turned and stared into Frannie's eyes, a grin of triumph and bloodlust cutting across his face in a sickening smear.

For the first time since discovering her abilities, Frannie felt frozen. This wasn't magic, this was a crazy with a knife. There was blood on the floor, staining Truly's dress, the switchblade, tiny drips and speckles coloring the hem of Eric's pants and the white cuff of his sleeve. This was no otherworldly creature, no strange other that she could shrug at and begin to fight. It was nothing more, nor less monstrous, than a man with a weapon in his hand and madness in his eyes. For the first time, Frannie Cohn choked.

Newp threw himself at the rest of the bikers, trying to break through the line of them to get at Eric. Eric laughed and hopped up on the stage next to Betty, who stumbled and shrank away. She tripped over the hem of her nightgown, tonight a deep cobalt blue, and lay sprawled out along the edge of the stage. Her scream cut out as the breath knocked out of her, and the sudden lack of the sound finally snapped Frannie back into reality. She started racing toward Truly, only to be grabbed by the wrist by a large member of the group and hauled back against the thick weight of his chest. She threw her free fist out with an enraged scream, only to find it caught and pulled backwards against her own back. Her arm lit up in pain and her cry of anger changed tone to one of agony. Saul was yelling at someone to call the police, Newp was calling out her name, and Eric had taken the microphone.

"Listen up, Café Monstro. You kicked us out of your little club…okay. Maybe you got something against bikers. Maybe your mothers didn't love you enough. We like the Café Monstro. When we like something, it stays liked. But it also becomes ours."

Beyond the pain, Frannie could hear Saul bellowing. "This is private property! This is my café! The police are on their way right now and you can bet your ass I'm pressing charges you sawed off little shlemiel, you're going to see in the inside of a cell so fast—"

"Oh, it is private property, sure, sure," said Eric, all smiles and pleasantries. "But Laguna Beach, well, that's public property."

He held up one of Newp's fliers, and neatly sliced it in half with the switchblade. "So, you. Can't. Stop. Us."

The knife flicked closed, flashing in the light, and disappeared into a pocket. On the ground, two of the gang holding Newp turned him to face their leader as he stepped down from the stage. Eric crumpled the remaining half of the paper and threw it in Newp's face.

"See you at the Luau. Can't wait to make Laguna Beach my new turf. Ha! Surf and turf."

With uncanny speed, Eric landed a sucker punch to Newp's stomach, winding him and putting him on his knees. He walked back to the stage, where Betty had gotten to her knees, and wrapped a hand around her long blonde hair, falling out of its pins across her shoulders. Gently he caressed her cheek, running a finger down her neck.

"Oh, I do like you Betty. I like how you look, how you sound. I'm sure I'm going to love how you taste. Can't wait to find out."

Betty tried to scream, but only a hoarse sob came out as he planted a thick and sucking kiss at the base of her throat.

"Next time. Phantoms, disappear!"

Frannie felt herself released, and she turned, trying to gather the strength, the courage, the power. "You bastards," she screamed. "Got zol im bentshn mit dray mentshn: eyner zol im haltn, der tsveyter zol im shpaltn under driter zol im ba'haltn."

She threw the curse, felt something move along her arm that was more than the pain, but was it enough? The bikers just laughed and departed into the night. Many patrons yelled and some cried, most leaving, though some kindly souls stayed to help Truly and sit Betty down with a glass of ice water.

Truly. Frannie stumbled over in a panic. By the time she made it to Truly's side, Toni had joined her.

"I'm sorry," she gasped "I was upstairs looking at the research, what is it, what happened?"

Frannie explained as quickly as she could while Toni spoke gently to Truly, easing her back in the chair.

"It's all right," said Toni, and called for a first aid kit. "It's shallow, just long. Truly, you're probably feeling a little bit of shock right now, can you stay with me? I need you to not fall asleep. Whatever you do, don't fall asleep."

Betty, sobbing, was brought gently to Truly's side. "Tru! Tru, I'm going to talk to you, and you have to talk to me, okay? Okay?"

"Betty?" said Truly, working hard to pull her head up. "God it hurts. Betty are you okay?"

"I will be if you just talk to me," said Betty, trying to get her voice under control.

"Good," said Toni. "Keep her talking, don't let her fall asleep."

The first aid kit arrived, and Frannie felt herself pushed backwards, as though in a fog or a dream. Hazily she watched Toni move like clockwork, cleaning and patching and administering to the long, thin cut that crossed from Truly's lower left hip to just under her right breast. Her beautiful green sequined dress was starting to unravel and lose sequins, like tiny leaves falling from a dying tree.

"My dress—" started Truly.

"Saved your life," said Toni, with a hint of a chuckle. "Even with a sharp knife, it's hard to cut through sequins. You're going to be just fine my dear, just fine."

The sirens sounded then, as the cops began to arrive. In a daze, Frannie walked among the people and the overturned tables and chairs left in the wake of the gang. She heard Saul making a statement, Newp yelling something obscene, Kurt trying to calm him down. She walked to the door and out into the night to stand beside the statue of Kronos.

She had failed. Her friends were hurt. She had frozen; she had done nothing. Why? Why?

Because she didn't even know if there was anything she could do. She had never fought anyone...normal. Just the supernatural. Would the curse she had thrown at Eric's retreating form even work?

It had been the worst curse she could think of. God should bless him with three people: one should grab him, the second should stab him and the third should hide him.

Would it even work?

Frannie leaned against the statue, bewildered, powerless, and afraid.

CHAPTER 24

TRULY WAS FURIOUS.

"You aren't canceling a damn thing," she shouted at Newp a half hour later. The cops, and indeed the rest of the patrons, had left. Toni was carefully applying gauze and tape to Truly's midsection, tsk tsking as Truly vented her frustration.

"He tried to kill you, Truly!" cried Newp. Betty burst into tears, and Saul wrapped his arms around the shaking girl. "He tried to kill you, God knows what he wants to do to Betty, and he's declared open war against the Legionnaires. We're just a bunch of goofy surfer guys; we aren't fighters. I think the only one of us who even owns anything sharp is Go-Go and his board knives, and the only person who knew anything about fighting was Hooky."

Frannie kept her mouth shut. Normally she'd be leaping into the verbal fray, but the shame of the evening hung thickly on her like a black veil. Newp was right. Monsters, mannequins, those they could fight. But garden variety monsters like Eric and the Phantoms? Apparently, not so much.

"Mutt and Jeff will have cops there. The Legionnaires will be there. You were already trying to get the local news down there. You really think they're going to come start some kind of street fight on Laguna Beach? No! They know the cops will be there. They want to scare you. They want to see if you'll fold. And if you do, then Laguna and the café may as well be theirs, because they'll know you won't stand up to them again. You gotta call their bluff. Shinola, you don't know anything about turf wars do you?"

"I'll be there," said Toni quietly. "For what it's worth."

"See?" said Truly. "The Professor is coming. She beat his ass in the first place. He tried to lay claim to Café Monstro. Well, it's not his, it's ours, and I'm going to fight for it."

"Technically it's Saul's," sniffled Betty, and Saul kissed the top of her head.

"Bless you sweetheart, but no. It is yours. All of yours. It was meant to be a home for oddballs like us, and that's exactly what it is."

"Besides," said Truly, "We have Frannie and Saul with their hoo-doo."

Frannie felt herself pale and shook her head.

"Some good it did just now," she said. "I just froze. I didn't do anything. I couldn't—" she felt tears threatening and broke off.

"It's fine," said Betty, patting her arm. "You did what you could. That's what counts. I saw you trying to help me. It's okay."

"It's not okay," snapped Newp. "What happens if you're wrong? What happens if they show up tomorrow night? What if they are crazy enough to pick a fight with the cops around? What then?"

"Then you fight," shrugged Toni. "Truly is right. She'd make a great sociologist. They want to know what you're willing to put up with. They're taking your measure."

It was Newp's turn to storm off, his face a mask of fury. Toni sighed, then checked Truly's bandages.

"Take two aspirin and call me in the morning?" she said, trying to lighten the mood.

"Really, I'm fine," said Truly.

"Of course, you are. Just take it easy. Try not to move around too much. I've got some good home remedies also that we can use, I'll bring some to work tomorrow. But if you're not feeling up to it, you just call me, all right? You don't need to be there if you're feeling pain."

Truly nodded gratefully and turned to Betty. "Come on, why don't you take me home, Newp can take care of himself. Don't worry, Bets, it's okay. I'm okay."

Betty nodded wordlessly and slipped an arm around Truly. While Saul walked them out of the café, Toni turned to Frannie.

"You all right?"

Frannie shook her head. "I couldn't do…anything. Why?"

"Sometimes we can't. It happens in fights, in war. Sometimes you freeze, and there's no shame in it."

"I've never been in a fight," said Frannie. "I mean, I have but, not one with…just people. They're just people. They're not monsters, or magic."

Toni nodded thoughtfully "No, they're not. And even with everything I do know, I don't know enough about all the different kinds of magic and practitioners to tell you if you even could have done anything. I just don't. But you do your best. You do what you believe is right. You believe in yourself and your friends. That will be enough."

Saul returned, and wordlessly wrapped his arms around Frannie. Over her head, he leveled teary eyes at Toni.

"Thank you for patching up our girl, professor. I'm grateful. I grant you the freedom of the café, as thanks."

Frannie felt something tingle and shift, and Toni relaxed a little. She wasn't sure what had happened—had Saul lifted some ward?

"I am very honored, Saul. Thank you. If no one minds, I think I'll get home and get to bed. Tomorrow promises to be a little too exciting not to face it without a good night's sleep. Rest well, you two."

Alone, Saul and Frannie stood for a moment, embraced. She felt his grip tighten gently before he released her.

"You're angry because you didn't do anything, huh? What is it you thought you were gonna do, square up with a guy twice your size and armed with a knife?"

"I have magic, Uncle Saul. I could have—"

"Nothing. You could have nothing. That's where things get dark and blurry. Look, magic...has rules. And I'm not saying I know all the rules, I don't. But I've figured out that it calls like unto like. The Book Man was magic, so we fought him with magic. Magic things, you can do magic on. But just normal, everyday people?" He shook his head.

"What, I can't curse him? Make him fall down? I can't hit him with my staff and make his bones cry?"

"Oh, the hitting you can, absolutely. But the magic?" he shrugged. "It depends on how much he believes. Superstitious people, sometimes you can manage something. But cursing people? That's black magic. That's a dark path. And there are prices you pay for that. Heavy ones."

Frannie's head hung low. All this power and ability, just to be brought down by one goon with a switchblade. What the hell kind of cosmic joke was this?

"Everything has a balance," said Saul. "This is one way the universe balances. I can't explain it, I can only tell you what I know."

"And what else do you know?" she asked, the exhaustion and despair creeping into her voice.

He pulled her into his arms again. "Not much," he said, stroking her back as though she were a tiny child again. "I know that I love you to pieces and it would be the death of me if anything happened to you."

Saul sighed and pulled her back to arm's length. "But I also know that you're a woman now, and that the world is coming. I've taught you almost everything I know about magic, honestly I have. I just haven't taught you what I know about the other people that use it. I hoped...I hoped that you might get to have a life like mine, where you tend the Blanks and mostly don't have to worry about the politics and the intrigue and the backstabbing bastards of the Hidden World. But I also know that time isn't endless, and neither am I. It's late," he added, rubbing one eye with the heel of his hand. "And I'm exhausted, and so are you. I promise I'll tell you everything I know in the coming days. It's clear that my hope of keeping your world smaller and safer is an old man's dream. For tonight," he waved his hand at the empty café. "We rest and strengthen ourselves for tomorrow."

"After we clean the blood off the floor."

He sighed. "After we clean the blood off the floor."

In the executive suite at the top of the Hotel Riviera, they waited. They had waited for years—they would not have to wait any longer. On the floor of the room, a clear space had been made. The whirling circles of sand that patterned the mint green tile glittered like diamond dust in the bright light of the ceiling fixture. They were getting closer to the goal every day.

In the corner, the mannequins leaned against the wall. In the second room, piles of mannequins littered every surface, tossed haphazardly about, waiting. Empty vessels, awaiting the spirits that would animate them. Who would come and fill them? When?

Half of a luau flyer tumbled to the desk. Tomorrow, it read.

Tomorrow.

CHAPTER 25

SAUL DROVE HER HOME, HUGGED her parents, and commiserated that her job at the café kept her so late these days. "Business is too good," he joked with his brother. "May I always be so cursed!"

Sally had taken one look at her daughter and disappeared to draw a hot bath. Frannie was too tired and disheartened to protest. Her mother gently pushed her into the steamy bathroom and went to fetch a nightgown and robe. Frannie stepped into the tub and felt everything melt away. She didn't know what her mother put in the tub with the water, but it was a mellow and deep fragrance, and she felt the ache of her failure loosen a little bit more. By the time Sally knocked on the bathroom, Frannie wondered if her jelly-like limbs would let her up. A few minutes later she was wearing a fresh clean nightgown and felt like she might just float off the world.

"Franneleh," said Sally softly. "Can I tuck you in?"

Frannie nodded dimly, and Sally lead her daughter down the hall.

"You know," said Sally, pulling the counterpane up and arranging it gently around Frannie's shoulders. "Your battles, they are different than mine, I know. But I have fought my own. Sometime, maybe, we should compare war stories."

Had she still been awake, Frannie would have been surprised to hear such a thing from her mother. But she was already fast asleep. Sally kissed her hair, brushing it away from her sun bronzed cheek, and returned to her husband.

"Just like your mother," she said. He nodded.

"It scares me."

"Me too."

She slept longer than she had intended. By the time she stumbled down the stairs, both her parents were long gone for work. There was a note on the table telling her to have fun at the luau, and that they expected her home Saturday night for Shabbat. I should live so long, she thought.

Scrounging herself a quick breakfast, she headed out the door to her bike. It leaned against the garden fence, looking forlorn and forgotten. "Sorry baby," she murmured, hopping on.

By the time she got to the beach, the preparations for the luau were in full swing. She was glad that Newp had decided to go on with the party, but her guts were a slowly writhing ball of worry. She parked the bike at the top of the steps and started down.

"Frannie!" called Catscratch. She jogged down the beach to join him by Go-Go's hut.

"Hey, is it true, about the fight last night? Is Truly okay?"

"Yeah, she is, it was a shallow cut. The Professor patched her up really well."

Catscratch's already thin expression narrowed in anger. "So, he did cut her. Newp wouldn't give us a lot of details. Just told us that one of them had a knife and they weren't afraid to fight dirty. Now it's personal. No one touches our people and gets away with it."

Frannie shook her head. "We'll cross that bridge when we come to it. Don't go looking for trouble tonight, okay? Let's just have a good time and if they show up, we'll let the cops handle it."

Catscratch grumbled something that sounded like assent and pointed her toward the group that were working on setting up tables and decorations. She went to it with a will—maybe the work would keep her mind off her worries about the night ahead.

The work was not keeping her mind off the night before. Truly shifted uncomfortably, trying to find a position in the typing chair that didn't ache. She sighed and picked up another article clipping. Salton, Salton, Salton. This was the fifth article about a talking, haunted jawbone in Salton that she had read. She typed up a quick summary of the article, which was much like the others—voice of child lost to smallpox says final goodbye through jawbone. She wrote down the names, the time of year, the pertinent details. She sighed and very carefully rolled her shoulders, wincing as she felt the gauze and tape pull at her skin painfully.

Suddenly, a tall glass of something white and slightly cloudy appeared in front of her. Toni frowned at her assistant.

"Drink this. You really shouldn't have come in; it's clear you're uncomfortable."

"I'm fine," she replied, an edge of temper to her voice. "It's no problem. You paid me in advance, and you're going to get your value out of the investment, I promise."

Toni softened and nudged the glass toward her. "You're a strong woman, Truly, but even strong women need to take their medicine sometimes. Go on, I promise it doesn't taste terrible. It's coconut milk and a few special extracts I brought back from the Andes."

Truly sighed but did as she was told.

"You're right, it's not terrible. This is delicious! Coconut milk, huh?"

"Mm-hmm."

"Well, I'm hooked, this is great. Thank you, Professor."

"Now will you go home and get some rest? I won't need you for the rest of the day anyway, I'm just going to work on the Delta piece."

Truly hastily took another sip and set down the glass, tugging the page out of the typewriter and handing it to Toni. "This is what I've found so far. It never mentions the name of the preacher, or often even people, just general stuff like 'dead boy talks to mother, says farewell.'"

Toni took the page and frowned. "That's not surprising, sadly. Talking to the dead is one of the oldest spookshow tricks. Carnies and revival preachers alike have used it for decades. It's really only notable because it isn't connected to a traveling show. It would actually be much easier to track if it were. Still in Salton?"

Truly nodded. "Is that something at least, that it seems to have stopped there?"

"Too early to tell. I suppose we'll find out sooner or later."

It was too early to head up to the café yet, but most of the work for the luau had been completed. Flowers and tiki torches festooned two long tables, and the smell of roasting pork and fruit was beginning to luxuriate in the air. Coolers and bags of ice were being brought down the staircase, and the big banner had been raised half an hour ago, covered in Brainiac's beautiful hibiscus flowers. Left with nothing more to do, Legionnaires began to hit the waves, Newp among them. Frannie imagined he was trying to let off some steam before the big fi—party. The party. There would be no fight. Mutt and Jeff had cops at the ready. The boys were on high alert. Hooky would be nearby in the woods near the tower just in case. Kurt had fitted him with a pair of articulated hands he had found at a flea market, a development that had made everyone a lot happier with Hooky's…situation. I'm going to fix it, she swore to herself. I swear I am going to find a way to fix Hooky's body, I have to. How? Well… she wasn't sure, of course. But the more she learned about other kinds of magic, the surer she became that there had to be a way. His spirit had been placed in a vessel, after all. Couldn't it be placed back in a body somehow? Not that she had any idea where she was going to get a body. She glanced up the beach, wondering if he was there now.

The tower. Frannie looked down toward the curve in the beach. She had spent a great deal of time and effort (most of it unsuccessful) not thinking about Michael Landry. She hadn't seen him since the day—was it really only two days ago?—she and Toni had trapped him in the tower. Hooky had taken over care and keeping of the werewolf, since he himself couldn't be killed or turned into a werewolf, and the only other person who had checked on him was Toni. He must be lonely.

How strange it was to fear and distrust, and yet feel so drawn to someone. It was uncomfortable…and she had to admit, a little exciting. She looked back over her shoulder at the luau. It was still plenty light out. Loads of time before she needed to be up at the café to bring food and drinks and equipment down to the luau.

She would just go for a walk.

The tower loomed large in her vision as she neared it, and she began to doubt her decision. What would she even say? Hey Michael, looks like you're in a hairy situation! Hi Michael, sorry I haven't visited, I would bring you lunch if you didn't want to make me lunch. Good afternoon, Michael, I—

"Frannie." A thick, brush-filled growl came from beyond the tower door. Michael stood, shifting slightly in the shadows. She could make out his tall, burly form, but did not miss the yellow glint in his usually soft brown eyes. She thought about waving but decided against it. Near the door was a long thick log, possibly a piece that had drifted down from Canada, and she took a wary seat.

"Hi Michael. Are you…doing okay?"

She couldn't tell if his response was a growl or a bark. "All the comforts of home. Your friend Hooky, he's been very kind. Even brought me some magazines."

Shame swept her, but there simply hadn't been another choice. "I'm sorry, Michael, if there were some other option—"

"No," he said softly. "It's fine. It's the best thing you could have done, besides just shoot me."

"Don't talk like that," she cried, standing. "No one is going to shoot you. We're working on finding the Delta, and—"

"And having a cookout. I can smell the pork from here. Don't forget to bring me a plate, huh?"

She felt the rancor in his words and stepped closer to the door. "Michael, you could have killed us. It's all we could think to do. I thought it would be temporary—aren't you supposed to go back to normal in the morning?"

He stepped toward the door then, and she saw the fur along his jawline, spilling out of his collar, a long dark tail swishing slowly behind him. She saw the long, dark claws, and shivered to think of them tearing into skin. He crossed his arms self-consciously to hide them.

"That's how it's been before. I don't know how it works; I haven't exactly been this way long. But yeah, I should've gone back to normal by now, I think. Anyway, enough about me. Are you okay? Hooky said that there was trouble last night, and that one of those biker assholes pulled a knife on your singer friend. Is she okay?"

"She will be. It was a shallow cut, but it was long. They threatened to crash the luau tonight...but it's going to be okay. The police will be there, Hooky will be watching, Saul and Kurt too."

"And you, with all your big magic."

She flushed with yet more shame. Maybe this had been a bad idea.

He shuddered, and she resisted the urge to reach through the wide bars and touch his arm. Unconsciously they stepped closer to each other, the door between them.

"What's wrong?"

"The wolf. We fight. I always lose."

"Why? What's happening?"

"I think...I think, Frannie, maybe some of it is you."

She started, shocked. "Me? What did I do?"

"Nothing. You're just...you. Beautiful and friendly and powerful. The man in me, he wants to kiss you."

Her heart leapt into her throat. He wanted to kiss her? She had thought it was idle flirtation just to get a rise out of her. She started to speak when he continued. "But the wolf, Frannie..." he shuddered again, and Frannie stepped back slightly. Fangs, long and white and terrible, slipped from Michael's lips, and his voice dropped down a long dark well of horror. "He wants your throat between his teeth, and your blood pouring down his jaws. He wants you—your life—"

Without warning, he slammed himself against the bars, and Frannie stumbled backward in the sand, tripping over the log and landing behind it. "Run!" he shouted, even as he tore at the bars. "Run, damn you and don't look back! Run, Fran!"

She ran.

She didn't look back.

CHAPTER 26

THE TORCHES FLICKERED, THE TABLES were laid, and the music had just begun. Truly had moved a little stiffly at first but swore up and down that she was able to play. The long taped up wound was covered by a bright floral Hawaiian style dress, and her hair was filled with tropical flowers. Betty too had a luau look, in a bright pink baby doll flannel number that showed off her long trim legs with flowers wrapped around each ankle. The bright sound of their music lightened the night as Legionnaires, their dates, and what Newp forcefully reminded them all were 'potential clients' began to arrive.

Frannie leaned on her staff at the edge of the firelight, keeping watch. Down by the tower, where the curve began, she knew Hooky was watching also. After the incident with Michael earlier, she was even more wary than ever. At the top of the hill, overlooking the party, Mutt and Jeff's squad car sat, a visible reminder that the police were on the scene. Kurt and Saul were over at the party tables, helping to serve, while Newp ran around like a man on a mission, solving problems before they even started and making sure everyone was having a good time. She really was proud of him when she thought about it. He would do an amazing job helping Saul run the café.

They would be fine without her.

Her. Her and her stick. She sighed and swung it halfheartedly. She really did need to learn how to use it properly. Saul had said there was a book in the shop on Bartitsu, but she'd yet to crack it. It wasn't as though she had a lot of spare time these days. Ah well. If Eric and the Phantoms did show up, she could at least whack them with her stick.

She swung it again, lightly, just testing it against the breeze, and found it caught in someone's hand. She turned, startled, to see Newp. He grinned and let it go, and she gave him a playful whack in the shoulder for his troubles.

"You look like some kind of wild pissed off ocean goddess," he joked, and she found herself relaxing a little bit.

"Who says I'm not? Watch your tuches, or I'll sic an octopus on you!"

They grinned at each other like the kids they still secretly were, and Newp put his hands up in mock compliance.

"I'm sorry, your high majesty, please forgive this poor unworthy surfer!"

He bowed playfully, like they used to do for Hooky, and they both sombered a bit.

"In all seriousness, Frannie...I really am sorry. I'm sorry about the way things have been lately. I'm sorry about how I've been. There's just so much happening, you know? For you, too."

"Yeah. It's been a lot."

They fell silent for a minute, watching the party start to swing. It was really picking up—there were at least fifty people in attendance who weren't connected to the Legionnaires, and there was a solid line of boys, girls, young men and young women in front of Go-Go's hut, looking to sign up for surfing lessons. Only an hour in, and it could be said that the luau was already quite a success.

"Truly sounds good. She looks good too. Said the professor gave her some elixir that made her feel better. She's something, your professor," said Newp, standing companionably beside her.

"Truly does look good. And yeah, I need to talk to the professor. There's a lot of magic stuff that Saul promises to tell me, but I have a feeling she'll tell me stuff he won't. If there's more of this mishegoss out there, I want to be ready for it."

"You will. You're always ready for anything. Well, almost anything."

She cast him a sideways glance. "What is that supposed to mean, exactly?"

Newp shifted uncomfortably, then stood his ground and faced her. "When are you going to be ready for me? For us? You know we're good together, you know we could make this a life. Come on, Frannie, what is it?"

She gaped at him, and then without thinking hauled off and hit him with the stick.

"Ow!"

"Stop. Deciding. My. Life!" She shouted, emphasizing each word with a swing of her stick into the sand. "It is not about being ready, it has never been about being ready, I have bigger things to worry about."

"Like what?! Like this nursing thing you want to do? So go do it, I'll still be here, I'll wait."

She growled in frustration, throwing her arms in the air. "I don't need you to wait! Why do you not understand that I might not come back? I'm not going to make some promise that I can't keep! And no, it's not just nursing, there is a war coming, the world is going to lose its mind again, and I have to be ready for it. Hooky—"

It was Newp's turn to throw his hands in the air, defeated and disgusted. "You're still hung up on Hooky!"

This was the third time tonight that she had been absolutely stunned by the men in her life. She was getting fed up with it. "Me? I'm hung up on Hooky? You're the one who is always bringing his ghost in between us. I don't summon him, you do. So, who is the hung up one?"

"You are, you hero worship him, you always did!"

"Yeah, because he was a hero, and that's what you do with heroes."

Newp spun, and she was taken aback by a fury in his eyes she had never seen before. "Well, I'm a hero too, aren't I? Who jumped out of a helicopter with you and rode the surf to kill the Book Man? Who ran around with you into God knows what, who fought whatever that thing was in the water with you, aren't I a hero too? Maybe I'm not some crazy surf mystic like you are, Frannie, maybe I don't have your hoodoo or whatever, but I'm here, and I'm fighting too. Doesn't that make me a hero?"

She looked at him coolly, levelly, the downward look of a growing woman to an angry boy.

"Heroes know what they are. They don't have to ask. And they don't like to tell. So, here's a question for you, Newp. What did you do all that stuff for?"

He stared at her, his broken heart in his eyes. "Christ, Frannie, I did it for you!"

Her own heart hurt as she realized, with the quick and cold understanding of unsought maturity, that what she had to say next was the truth. "That's the wrong answer."

She turned, and with unshed tears in her eyes, made her way to Hooky's hut.

That's when the shouting started.

No one had taken much notice of the little boat when it first appeared—it was a fine night after all, and everyone was in good spirits. Tombo had been waving at the driver and the small party aboard, and the boat had turned its course and looked to be joining the luau. They dropped anchor about fifty yards out, and young men and women had jumped out, making their way toward the shore. It wasn't until they were a bit closer that in the fading light, Brainiac noticed they were dressed all in black.

"What the…"

Brainiac shook his head as though to reset his vision. Something was wrong here. Who were these boat people?

He heard a loud crack, and a small explosion of sand went up at his feet.

"Run!" he cried, scooping up the nearest kids and making for the stairs. "Run!"

Like a ripple, the cry spread, taking almost too long to be heard over the music. Another crack, and this time there was a large splash of water and a curse from the boat people. They were only a few hundred feet from shore now, wading hastily through the water. Tombo cursed himself for not wearing his glasses—he thought they made him look like a Poindexter, and he was hoping to make the acquaintance of one of the girls at the luau. Instead, he was unable to clearly make out the threat from the boat people until they were nearly upon him.

"Newp!" He yelled, trying to splash backward in the surf and get back to the beach "It's the—"

Crack. Tombo's shoulder exploded outward in a mess of blood and torn muscle, and he fell screaming into the surf.

A shrill scream went up from the party, and the music stopped. There was mass confusion as people stumbled in the shifting sand this way and that, running toward the stairs. Frannie bolted out of the hut, taking in the scene. Mutt and Jeff were stuck at the top of the hill, the stairway acting as a bottleneck for the escaping party goers. One of them threw the car lights on, flooding the beach with red and white spinning light, making the chaos even harder to see. Through flashes of red she could make out the Phantoms, now nearly on the beach, and she watched in horror as one of them raised an arm as though they were holding a pistol. She couldn't see a gun, but she heard another crack, and a piece of Hooky's hut flew off into the darkness, leaving splintered wood in its wake.

She grabbed her staff and ran toward where Tombo had fallen, catching up to Newp and matching him pace for pace as they ran toward the fallen Surfer. One of the Phantoms was almost on Tombo when they got there, and Frannie swung her staff as she leapt forward in the shallow water. The staff made its own wooden crack as it connected with his face, and in a flash of red light she could see that she had made contact with his nose before he dropped to his knees with a screech. She whirled away from him to see Newp scoop

Tombo up onto his shoulder fireman-style and started working his way back to shore as quickly as he could with the unconscious Legionnaire. Frannie looked behind them—it wasn't going to be fast enough. Three more were nearly upon them, as she swung her staff menacingly and put herself between Newp and the Phantoms. She saw another one raise a rifle and take aim.

This can't be how I die, she thought, thinking of the visions the Book Man had shown her. Another thought, a deeper one, was waiting to betray her, and dropped like a stone into her consciousness. But it might be how Newp does.

She braced herself for the crack and splat, ready to jump between Newp and the firearm, when a figure moving stiffly but fast loomed out of the darkness. She heard the crack and then saw the wood splinters fly as Hooky leapt into the fray.

"Zip guns!" roared the mannequin man. Cheap guns, in other words. Often cobbled together. A hoodlum treasure. "Get them out, angel!"

She heard rather than saw the way the wooden limbs struck out madly at the three, bones crunching and cries of pain. Newp was at the beach now, but there was no way he was going to get Tombo up the clogged stairs, and already five of the Phantoms, three male and two female, had made it to shore. She could see knives and chains glinting crimson in the police lights, and she could hear Mutt and Jeff and the patrol officers yelling at everyone to clear a path, but the panicked mob only scrambled to make their way up the steps, every man for himself. Go-Go, Brainiac, Catscratch and Mason had climbed most of the rocky, grass riddled hill and were passing younger kids up like a fire bucket line to a police officer at the top. Frannie's gut clenched as she realized the other six Legionnaires, unarmed and overconfident, had lined up on the beach to face the attackers.

There was no way out. It was going to be a bloodbath.

The wolf woke, smelling the blood on the air. It leapt at the bars, hungry, angry. A piece of paper was held in front of it, and he heard the master speak.

"Get the scent."

The wolf breathed deeply, every sliver of smell left on the paper flashing through its primordial brain. A male. An Alpha Male. It smelled the challenge on the paper, the arrogance in the oils of the fingerprints. A challenger. An opponent. It smelled the fear of countless others, it smelled blood in the air.

The door slowly swung open, and the wolf ached to be loose, to chase, to kill.

"Sic 'em," said the Master.

The wolf disappeared down the beach toward the sound of screams.

At the top of the stairs, Saul held up traffic as feeling partygoers ran across the street and scattered into cars and vans, disappearing into the night. Kurt was in the café gathering first aid supplies as fast as he could, waiting for the inevitable victims from below. "Where the hell is the professor?!" he yelled at Saul, "We need a medic!"

"Stuck down on the beach with the others I think," yelled Saul. "Call an ambulance, we'll do our best!"

Brainiac's head popped up above the hill as he handed another gangly teen girl up to Jeff. "They're squaring up with the Legionnaires, Newp's down there with Tombo over his shoulder, they're covered in blood."

"Zip guns," said Jeff grimly. "Lousy punks, help us down there! If you can lift them up you can swing us down!"

Mutt swung a khaki clad leg over the railing and followed his companion down. The Legionnaires moved in reverse, as quickly and carefully as they could, slipping and sliding the cops down the hill.

They were halfway down when the wolf took down the chain wielding Phantom from behind, snapping his neck with a twist of its powerful jaws on the young man's nape. One of the Phantom girls screamed, as the wolf lunged for the line of Legionnaires, in search of its true prey.

"Scheisse, Newp faster, Michael is out!"

Frannie scrambled between them, as the werewolf closed its jaws on a Legionnaire's leg, and she heard the snap and gush under the screaming as the femur broke.

"Shteyner af zayne beyner." she cried, swinging the glowing staff and cracking it down on the werewolf's head. It whined and let go, staggering to its knees, struggling against the power of the curse. She could hear the Legionnaires and the Phantoms closing on each other, heard Mutt and Jeff shouting, firing their guns into the air as they ran toward the fray. None of it mattered. She had to keep Michael off of Newp and Tombo. She couldn't even be sure Tombo was breathing. She had to stop Michael.

The werewolf snarled through the blood on its snout, the air bubbling up under the thick crimson layer. She swung the staff in an arc in front of her, desperately sorting through spells and curses in her head. What did you hit a werewolf with? Stones on his bones had slowed it down, but it was still struggling toward her, advancing, and she felt her mouth dry with fear.

But the wolf, Frannie... He wants your throat between his teeth...

Screams and punches flew. Knives flashed. Gunshots fired into the summer night. But there was nothing in Frannie's world but the crouched and snarling form of the wolf about to pounce.

It leapt, slowly, ponderously through the air. She felt the staff swinging in response, felt it burning in her hands. Her vision slowly faded into white, and the gilded lettering whorled gently into her line of sight. She knew without thinking what to say, and let the words flow out of her and through the staff, a blinding golden arch of light.

"Zol er krenken un gedenken. Let him suffer and remember."

The staff shuddered in her hands as it struck the thick fur of its shoulder, and she felt her body moving, lunging to the right as the strike shoved the wolf to the left. In the flashing red light, the wolf seemed to morph from beast to man to beast again, and a shocking cry of anguish forced itself out of the wolf's throat. It crumpled to the ground, and Frannie felt herself drained and panting, trying to get herself upright for the next attack.

It didn't come. The wolf lay, dazed, and Frannie stole the precious moment to take in the rest of the scene.

She saw Mutt with a bloodied nose grappling with a black clad Phantom.

Two Legionnaires had grabbed a Phantom girl and were dragging her towards the stairs. Two more had picked up Jumper, the new boy with the now broken leg, and were basket carrying him to the stairs. The lights of the cop cars were now joined by the lights of an ambulance, and she could see someone she thought was Jeff sprawled face down on the sand. Two more Phantoms were struggling with four other Legionnaires, and she could see blood from knife wounds rolling down more than one arm. Something wasn't adding up. Here were all the pawns—where was the King?

The answer came with the sound of a pistol cocking from the shoreline.

"Laguna Beach is mine," Eric howled, laughing in his madness. From the stairs, Newp, Brainiac, Go-Go and Catscratch were running toward the fray. From the waterline, Eric lifted a long gun that glinted red and silver in the fire and moonlight. I can't get there in time, her mind screamed at her. I can't—

A shot went off, and the sand to the left of Newp exploded. Eric swore and balanced the gun on his arm, taking new aim. Frannie started to run toward him, hoping he hadn't noticed her in the darkness and confusion, as he pulled off another shot. She heard Go-Go cry out and swear. I can't get there in time. Eric swung his arm slightly to the left, closing one eye to narrow in on Newp.

NO!

From the water behind Eric rose three stiff and familiar figures, the blazing green eyes an eerie counterpoint to the sirens and torches. She watched numbly as one of the Mannequins, this one slightly smaller and rounded, wrapped its wooden arms around Eric's torso, lifting him bodily from the ground. He screamed in shock and pain, and another mannequin slammed its wooden fist into the forearm that held the gun, knocking it to the water. The smaller one disappeared into the waves, taking Eric with it, and the screams disappeared into gurgles beneath the water. The other two mannequins made a beeline for the shore, knocking people to the ground left and right, seemingly without notice. Frannie returned her gaze to Michael, but the wolf had disappeared, a limping pattern of prints trailing off into the surf and disappearing.

Newp plowed a shoulder into the back of one of the knife-wielding Phantoms, knocking him to the sand, while Brainiac grabbed a chain out of the sand and began to swing it, preparing to nail the Phantom locked together with Mutt. Go-Go suddenly stopped running, yelling and pointing.

"What the HELL is that?!"

The other two mannequins closed on a Phantom each, one male and one female, and dragged them screaming away into the surf. All fighting stopped as everyone watched in horror as the mannequins and the Phantoms disappeared beneath the surface...and did not resurface.

Brainiac took advantage of the lull to tackle the Phantom off of Mutt, and there was a wet smack as Frannie used her staff to take the wind out of the remaining female phantom. The eerie silence that followed all the chaos was broken by the moans of the injured. Mutt stood, panting, and shaking his head.

"What the actual fuck just happened?"

Frannie turned, her voice breaking hysterically, somewhere between laughter and weeping.

"It's summer on Laguna Beach."

CHAPTER 27

"BETTY AND TRULY," NEWP BELLOWED. "Where are the girls?"

After a short search, Catscratch found them hiding in Hooky's tent. Betty threw her arms around her brother, as Frannie scooped Truly in for a gentle hug.

"I couldn't think of anything else to do," sobbed Betty. "They would've killed Truly, they would've!!"

Frannie helped Truly up the steps while Newp comforted and guided Betty. It was surreal to her how quickly the aftermath of the fighting had cleared, how quickly people had been bundled into squad cars and ambulances. By the time they made it to the café, there were cups of coffee being handed out as Kurt, Saul and Toni tended wounds and bandaged hurts. Jeff sat at the bar, an ice pack against the back of his head, and Toni knelt in front of him checking his eyes with a penlight. Brainiac appeared, looking somber, a white bandaged wrapped around his upper left arm and splotches of blood freckling his suntanned face.

"Newp, Frannie, it's pretty bad. Tombo wasn't breathing, but they got him going again in the ambulance. Jumper, the new kid, he lost a lot of blood, and the leg is broken. One of the Phantoms is dead, and the others—"

He shook his head, trying to work past the emotion. Newp put a hand on his good shoulder, pulling his eye contact.

"Just tell us what you know."

"It's what I don't know, Newp. Mutt and the cops arrested the three who were left, but the others...and what the hell was that mad dog, that's what killed the Phantom and busted up Jumper, I saw it go for Frannie and then I don't remember much, except running and fighting..."

"It's okay, Brainiac," said Frannie, quietly. "I'm all right, and you're all right, and you were a hero getting the kids out like you did. The Legionnaires did everyone proud tonight."

"You're damn right, they did," said Jeff, wincing. "I'm putting every last one of you up for commendations. You fought those bastards unarmed and kept citizens safe until we could get down there. Goddamn heroes."

Heroes. Where was Hooky? Frannie turned to Newp wide eyed as she realized he was missing, and Newp nodded, receiving the message.

"Let's get everyone bandaged up and get them home. Frannie why don't you check upstairs for extra bandages or some cloths okay?"

Frannie nodded, grateful for the excuse, and ran up the stairs to look for Hooky. To her relief, she found him in Kurt's workshop, where he and the artist were taking stock of the mannequins 'injuries.' The unsettling painted eyes blazed with blue fire, as Kurt measured a sizeable hole in Hooky's torso.

"It's patchable," said Kurt thoughtfully. "Or I could cut out a chunk and make you a little door and you could store things in there. It's not the worst idea."

"Goddamn punks with zip guns. They can just make homemade guns and blow people away. The little—"

They both stopped at Frannie's gasp from the doorway.

"It's fine Angel," said Hooky. "It doesn't hurt. I don't feel anything, remember? Anyway, what's the damage, is everyone okay?"

She shook her head, and filled them in. Both men swore softly to themselves and looked at each other grimly.

"So, the Phantoms are no longer a threat," said Kurt. "But now we have a werewolf on the loose."

"Oy," said Frannie, as realization dawned. "Doesn't that mean...doesn't that mean Jumper is cursed now too? A werewolf bit him—"

"No," said Hooky. "You only get cursed if you get bitten on the full moon. He'll have some weird cravings for a while, from what I've read, but he should be fine."

"From what you've read?"

Hooky waved a slightly splintery hand at himself. "I can't exactly go out during the day. And I don't sleep. Figured I would make myself useful and do some research. What, you think a washout army bum like me can't take notes?"

She gestured wordlessly at his carved wooden hands.

"You know what I meant."

"The solution to that is coming in tomorrow morning, I found a pair of articulated ones in an art catalog that should fit you, you'll be able to write and hold things soon," said Kurt, sharpening a pencil.

"You're a real pal, Kurt. I owe you one."

Kurt just shook his head, and started sketching on Hooky's body, muttering something about hinges and a latch.

Frannie stood, feeling useless again. What now? What should they do? Hooky read her face easily—Frannie had never been much mystery to him.

"You should get everybody together who's still okay and make a plan for keeping everybody safe while we solve this werewolf thing. Which I guess is also this Delta thing. I have some thoughts about that. We're gonna figure this out Angel. You don't have to carry all this yourself. You've got Saul, and Kurt, and Newp, and your friends. And a version of the Tin Man."

Kurt finished his sketching and picked up a small hacksaw, talking absently to Frannie.

"He's right. Get the... uninvolved out of here. I'll make some coffee."

It was easier said than done, but an hour later Jeff was off to the hospital to talk to the families of Jumper and Tombo, and Mutt had left with the rest of the cops, complaining loudly about the amount of paperwork this was all going to be. Brainiac, Go-Go and Catscratch were the hardest to convince to go.

"We can't just leave," said Catscratch, his brow furrowing. "What were those things? What if they come back? I'm going to have nightmares for weeks."

"Maybe we're not the only ones the Phantoms pissed off. Maybe they had beef with a gang who wore fancy diving suits. That would explain it," said Brainiac, picking at the bandage on his arm where the bullet had grazed it. Now that things had calmed down, he was looking more than a little pleased about his wound. On any other day Frannie would have rolled her eyes, but this time, Brainiac had earned some bragging rights. He had really shone bravely on the beach.

Go-Go, ever the voice of reason, talked them down. "Yeah, that would explain it. But listen. Frannie is right, we need to get back to the barracks. We need to rest, and we need to make a rota for visiting Jumper and Tombo in the hospital, and another for being lookout on the beach in case those things come back. If Laguna Beach is ours," he said, slowly and with gravitas, "then we're responsible for what happens on it."

The others nodded, and Frannie sent up a prayer of thanks for Go-Go and his calm and quiet ways. It was no wonder the board-maker was Newp's right hand man.

A short time later, there was a hot cup of coffee in the hands of everyone who wanted one. They had pushed two round tables together and sat quietly. Frannie looked at her friends. Newp, Betty and Truly sat together, Newp with his arm around each of the girls, the girls holding tightly to each other's hands. Saul and Kurt took the other side of the figure eight, Saul looking pale as death next to the normally paler Kurt. Toni had taken the opposite end of the table from Frannie, between Truly and Kurt. Her eyes widened with surprise and alarm when Hooky appeared to stand behind Saul, but she said nothing, turning her gaze to Frannie with a raised eyebrow. When they were all assembled, Saul stood.

"It's like the round table, this," Saul said, looking at them. "But I'm no Arthur. And I'm not sure what to tell you. I started Café Monstro because I wanted a place to finally escape such things as tonight. I've seen enough death and suffering. I've seen enough war. And I've seen enough of the Hidden World to last lifetimes. I wanted this to be a safe place. And it's not your fault that it isn't—it's mine. I'm a Blankguard. I can't change that—the books appear, and I tend them. That magic draws magic—like draws like. Magic brings trouble. So here we are, in trouble again. It all comes to the café and everyone in it."

"You didn't start the trouble with the Phantoms," said Betty quietly from Newp's shoulder. "People like that, they just exist. It's scary and awful but it's nobody's fault."

"You gave us a stage where no-one else would," said Truly. "You give people a chance. Don't you even dare think about closing this place down because some whack jobs decided to get wild."

"No one is shutting down the café," said Newp, the steel in his voice surprising everyone. "This is home. You don't abandon your home just because it gets threatened some. You stay and fight."

"And I brought this trouble on you," said Toni, firmly. "I'm the one who brought Michael and the Delta and the mess with the mannequins. I'm the one who needs to go and take this trouble off of you."

Frannie shook her head. "Michael was called by a Blank. We became friends. We'd still be in this; we don't abandon friends."

Newp flinched at her words but didn't meet her eyes.

"Besides," said Hooky, in the strange, displaced voice. "If you hadn't, I wouldn't be reunited with everyone. Though I gotta tell you, as far as an existence goes, this is pretty wild and not the most comfortable."

"We're going to get your body back," said Frannie fiercely.

"I'm not worried about it right, now Angel, we have bigger problems."

"Yeah," said Newp, his voice bitter. "We have a werewolf on the loose and those mannequin things are still out there, and we have no idea what they want."

"They want the Delta," replied Toni. "All three pieces, it's full power."

"They won't be getting the one at the University," said Saul. "I warded it when they first attacked. They're not human, so they can't touch it."

Betty looked up, curious. "Why would you ever need something like that? I mean, like, that's just animals, right?"

"It's really useful when you're camping, and you don't want raccoons taking off with your picnic basket."

Newp turned to Toni. "So, what exactly does this Delta do? Why do they want it?"

To everyone's surprise, it was Truly who answered.

"It moves souls. If you have one piece, you can put a soul into an object, and it can talk to you. If you have two pieces, you can move souls from body to body. If you have three pieces, you can make something called a homunculus—a body with no soul in it."

They were all silent for a moment.

"That's...scary." said Saul.

"Why?" said Frannie, a little more sharply than she intended. "That's not scary, that's amazing. You could bring people back from the dead, you could make new bodies for them. If we had all three pieces, Hooky could really be alive again. No offense."

"None taken."

"That's how you would cure Michael," she continued. "Take his soul and put it in a homunculus that isn't a werewolf."

"It was one idea," said Toni. "Even with just one piece, I could take his soul out of his body and store it in a vessel so that he couldn't attack anyone at the full moon. A body without a soul is generally paralyzed."

Hooky broke in. "Yeah, it's amazing. It's amazing being trapped in a wooden body and feeling nothing and never sleeping. And how amazing will it be when the wrong people get their hands on it, and suddenly have an army of humo-whatsits that they can create and order around? I mean…this stuff is real, right? I'm proof. Hitler was after stuff like this. Imagine what he could have done with a full Delta. Imagine what he could have done with the souls of everyone he murdered. Amazing," he said scornfully, and Frannie's cheeks grew hot.

"So, we don't let it fall into the wrong hands! So, we get to it first! And we make sure no one can ever use it like that."

"Yeah? Look how well that worked out with nuclear weapons."

"Then what it needs to be is destroyed," said Newp. "No one should have that kind of power. That must be the reason it got broken up in the first place."

Toni paled but said nothing. "You can't destroy it!" cried Frannie, "it's our only chance of getting Hooky a body again, and saving Michael, and think of all the other people it could save!"

"We don't have to destroy it," said Saul. "We can just split it up again and give it to people who would never give it to each other. Give a piece to the Vatican, and another piece to the Polidorium, and the third piece is still lost so we don't have to worry about that."

Kurt raised a hand. "Not the point. We can only solve the problems in front of us. Problem one, werewolf. Problem two, can't let the mannequins get the Delta. What do we do about werewolf?"

"I'm going to put a ward around the café grounds," said Saul. "Same ward against non-humans. That'll keep him out of here, at least. And the mannequins too. Like a magic fence."

"A magic fence they can't climb?" asked Betty.

"Unless they can jump 20 feet in the air, and I don't see either party doing that."

"That just keeps him out," said Frannie. "That means everyone in the area is at risk unless they're in here."

Hooky shook his head. "The books said that most werewolves will have a prey focus. If it's a male werewolf, they tend to focus on a specific female. They'll go for that target. It's part of the hunting instinct."

"He's right," said Toni. "You've really done your homework."

"Me," said Frannie, softly. "It's me." Quickly, she told them about her last encounter with Michael at the Tower. Many heads shook.

"Just like in that movie," chimed Betty.

"Just like," said Newp, his face a thunderstorm of anger.

"Okay…well, it's not good news, but it's news." said Saul. "We just keep Frannie in here, easy peasy. He can't come in, she doesn't go out, we set a trap for him when he comes around and then try to help the poor kid as best we can."

"He's not a poor kid," snapped Newp. "He's the reason Jumper is in the hospital."

"Newp."

Hooky shook his head, and Newp shut his mouth. Dead or not, Hooky was still the Hookeleh.

"Second problem," prompted Kurt, sipping his coffee.

"One Delta piece is at the University, safe," said Toni. "The second—"

"Dead ends at Salton," said Truly, and Toni nodded.

"That's where the newspaper clippings end. Always a mention of Salton, and a preacher who could call spirits into donkey's jawbone. It's the best lead we have, but I don't know where to go with it."

"The Salton Sea is just a tourist trap," said Newp. "Mom and dad have taken us there loads of times. It's just a nice beach and some casinos and little giftshops. There's nothing there that's really old, not even a museum."

Betty raised her hand as though she were in class. They looked at her, and then Saul chuckled. "Yes, Betty?"

"I'm sorry if this is stupid, but…why don't you ask someone?"

Blank stares.

"Ask someone what, Bets?"

Her cheeks flushed as she rushed to explain herself. "Ask a dead person. I mean, we know where one Delta piece is, and you have all those newspaper clippings. Why don't you find a name, and use the Delta at the University to put them in a candlestick or something, and ask them who it was that had the jawbone, or what happened to it, or something?"

This time the blank stares were joined by stunned silence.

"I can't believe I never thought of that," said Toni. "The first piece has been right in front of me this whole time, and I never thought of that. Betty, you are a wonder."

"Okay," said Frannie. "So, the plan is, go get the University piece, bring it here, use it to find the second piece, trap Michael, get him out of his werewolf body until we can find a better solution?"

Nods.

"Then what are we waiting for?"

Saul answered for all of them.

"To finish our coffee first."

CHAPTER 28

NO AMOUNT OF ARGUING, HASSLING, threatening, or cajoling would convince anyone to let Frannie leave the safety of the café.

"I faced him! On the beach, by myself, when he was the wolf. I'll be fine!"

"Sure, you'll be fine," said Saul. "Because you'll be here, behind the wards. Hooky, the professor, and I are more than capable of getting the Delta and bringing it back here."

"How come you're going?!"

"Because I, little smarty pants, set the ward, so I have to take it down. Professor lets us in with her keys, I take down the ward, Hooky does a smash and grab, badda bing, badda boom. We'll be back in an hour. You little shaygetz, however, are going to stay here with Kurt and grab a catnap. Got it?"

The others nodded, while Frannie bit her tongue. The three disappeared in Saul's car, and Kurt turned to them.

"I have work to do. You four get some sleep in the spare room."

They nodded like obedient children, as Kurt disappeared up the stairs into his workshop. Truly was the first to speak.

"I'm too wired to sleep. Let's start looking through those notes so when they come back, we have some names for them to call on."

The idea was a good one. Newp stayed in the kitchen to fix sandwiches while the girls started pouring through the papers—coffee on empty and frightened stomachs had done no one any favors, he correctly claimed. Frannie could acknowledge from her own experience that not feeling hungry and not needing food were two very different things, especially in a crisis.

While the girls hunted for names, Kurt had pulled out a serrated knife and some wire. He made his way down the stairs, across the café, to the great papier-mâché Frankenstein on his enormous wooden cross. He got out a ladder, angling it carefully beneath the sculpture, and with knife and wire in hand began to climb. When he came to the floor again, Newp was holding out a sandwich and a soda.

"You hinged it's jaw," said Newp. "So, it can talk to us?"

Kurt nodded. "It's affixed to the wall. It can talk to all of us at once, easy to see and hear, but it isn't going anywhere. Seemed safest."

It took slightly more than an hour and a half, but all five were waiting when Hooky, Saul and the professor reappeared with the Delta, wrapped in a cloth. It shone softly in the light and sat in the middle of a round table. Saul nodded at the sculpture.

"A very good idea. Who is going to do the honors?"

"I will," said Toni, standing. Truly handed her the list, and she picked up the Delta.

"I call upon Jessica Simmonds," she intoned, looking at the Frankenstein sculpture. "Return to this dust, for all is dust, and speak to us, for all speech is meaning."

They waited, breaths held. Frannie could feel a faint humming from the delta deep in her bones. Then it faded.

Nothing.

"Try a different name," said Betty.

Toni squared her shoulders, letting out a slow breath. "All right. Ah...I call upon Samuel Stanford. Return to this dust, for all is dust, and speak to us."

This time, a breeze blew through the café. It lifted the curls at Frannie's neck and seemed to pour into the waiting mouth of the sculpture. The eyes filled with a strange grey light, as though slowly filling with liquid. Slowly, in an uncanny jerk that made Frannie shudder, the large head turned, and the jaw swung on its wire hinge. A deep, dark voice broke out.

"What the hell is this? Where am I?"

"At the Café Monstro," said Toni. "We are sorry to disturb your spirit, we need to ask a question."

The head turned, the silver eyes blazing. "I'm dead, aren't I?"

"I'm afraid so," said Saul, after an awkward moment.

"Figures," said the voice, with a weary note. "Just my luck."

"We wanted to ask you," said Toni, clearing her throat. "About something you witnessed. A preacher, who would talk to a jawbone?"

"You called me from my grave to ask about some revival tent charlatan? You don't have something more important to ask me?"

"It is important, we promise you," said Frannie. "It was very difficult to call you up, it isn't an idle question. We are trying to find another piece of this," she said, pointing to the Delta in Toni's hands. "We think the preacher may have had it, but the trail goes cold at Salton."

Frankenstein laughed, bitterly. "Of course, it does, everything goes cold at Salton. They screwed up diverting the river. Salton's under a lake now, whole town has been underwater for two years. Well, longer, I imagine. What year is this?"

"1959."

"No kidding."

"What?" said Newp. "There's a town under that lake?"

"Town of Salton," said Samuel Stanford through the monster. "Population zero. If you don't count the fish."

"What was the preacher's name?" said Toni, sharply, and Frannie looked at her. Holding the Delta seemed like it was straining the professor.

"Jesus, I don't know…that was a long time ago, my last wife made me go…her name was Kitty. I miss her…"

"Please, try to think back, can you recall his name?"

"Kitty wanted to see him because of the talking jawbone. It was her birthday; she was so excited. Pretty Kitty, I miss you…Clemens. Dr. Thomas Clemens." Frankenstein said triumphantly. "That was his name. He wore something that looked kinda like that doohickey she's holding around his neck. Spooky thing… I didn't like it. Or him."

"Thank you," said Toni, with a sigh. "I release you to the cosmos."

The silvery light faded, and the sculpture dropped its head to its chest. The silence was uncomfortable, and Betty shook her head. "This is spooky. I didn't like that. Poor man."

Toni dropped the Delta gently to the table and slid it over to Frannie. "Can you do this one? I'm not sure I can hold the connection again."

Frannie nodded, picking it up. It was warm and heavy in her hand and felt slightly oily to the touch. She didn't like it. She closed her eyes and reached out into the magic.

"I call upon Thomas Clemens, return to this dust, for all is dust, and speak to us."

This time a full wind kicked up, and the eyes were brown and sparked like topaz. The Frankenstein's face took on an aura of surprise, before a thin and reedy male voice spoke.

"What have you done? What have you done? This is an abomination! Release me at once!"

The sculpture began to shake as Frankenstein tried to escape his artistic crucifixion, but the wire and paint and nails held tight.

"Please, Dr. Clemens," said Frannie through gritted teeth. She understood now, it was hard work to be the conduit—she felt a heavy power flowing through her, sluggish like molten lead. "We just need to know one thing.

Where is the other piece that looks like this?" She held up the Delta, and the eyes of Frankenstein widened.

"Where did you get that?"

"There are three. We need to know where your piece is. Before they fall into the wrong hands," said Saul.

"It's cursed!" cried the Monster, and Frannie felt as though the spirit were bucking in her grip. "Please, leave it lie, leave it under the water, it brings no good to anybody."

"We need it," said Frannie firmly. "We need it to save our friend, and to save others. Then we plan to bury it where it will not be seen again. Please, where is it?"

"In the holiest place in Salton, never to be seen again. Beneath the cross, beneath the sacraments. Let me go," it wailed. "I want no part of it. Let me go!"

"I release you to the cosmos," said Frannie, panting. The light in the eyes of the sculpture winked out.

"That was worse," said Betty.

Toni held out her hand for the Delta, to wrap it in the cloth. Frannie handed it over, wearily. "That was rough," she said. "I'm so ti—"

Her sentence stopped dead in her throat. Under the cloth, was a long silver gun barrel. She recognized it from the beach.

"I'm sorry, everyone," said Toni, backing toward the door. "But I'm afraid this part of the adventure is mine alone. Stay back!" she cried, as Newp started to move toward her. "You are all truly dear, you are, but I can't let you break up the Delta. I know exactly who you are," she said to Saul, and more cryptically "and who your mother is. Too many strange coincidences. So, everyone will kindly sit tight right here, until I'm well away. Do you understa—"

It was strange how silently Hooky could move, given that he was made of wood. He stepped neatly in from the side, like a suitor cutting into a dance, and swung downward with both his wooden hands. The gun and the Delta both went spinning to the floor, as Toni shrieked. She ran for the door and shouted a curse that made Frannie feel dizzy.

"It's okay," said Saul, starting to sweat. "The wards are up; nothing can get in here."

Which is precisely when the first Mannequin crashed through the roof.

On the roof of the Hotel Riviera, the mannequins clasped hands. There were ten of them now, and soon there would be more, if it was willed. But for now, the instruction was simple. Two mannequins clasped arms, and one began to spin. Spin, spin, faster and faster, letting the weight of the partner, the centrifugal force, lift the other from the ground. Like some kind of evil hammer throw, the spinning mannequin released, sending the other flying through the air, onto the roof of the Café Monstro. Only one had landed headfirst in the sand on the beach before they had their aim corrected.

Frannie looked up and heard another wooden man flew across the sky and land, wham, out of sight on the roof of the café. It appeared in the hole, and then dropped through to land next to its brother, their wooden jaws clacking excitedly. Another flew next to it and landed less elegantly, catching itself on the edge of the roof. An arm went skidding across the café floor as it landed sideways between shoulder and neck, the wooden head bouncing haphazardly off the torso and onto the stage. Clack clack, went its jaw, as the body flailed helplessly on the ground. Clack clack clack they said to one another, and another one landed nearby.

Frannie reached for her staff and froze. She had left it in the spare room.

Truly picked up the gun, holding it out in front of herself and Betty. Newp had scooped up the Delta and was making a solid run for the back door. Saul bellowed a spell, something Frannie didn't have time to identify, as she raced for the stairs.

Stupid, stupid! She chided herself. Never leave your weapon again you idiot. Downstairs she heard shouting and crashing and said a quick thanks that she heard no gunshots, but the crack of wood on wood was clear to her even from the second floor.

She grabbed her staff, rushing back toward the narrow hallway, when a sound made her stop. There was an access door to the roof at the end of the hall, so that you could go up and work on the chimney if you needed to or any of the other stuff that was up there. There was even an aerial antenna, not that they ever used it because Saul hadn't bothered to put a TV in the café.

That door wasn't locked. It was never locked. Why would it be? Not that it would matter—a mannequin tore the metal door off its hinges and tromped into the hallway. She saw it standing there and saw its reflection in the vanity mirror, and for a moment she remembered looking at herself in a dress that she wore to a party on the night that Hooky died. All is vanity, Emmet had said. The golem had been right then, and he was still right.

She ran towards the mannequin, swinging her staff, and hit it with the stone curse. The curse may have worked, but the momentum of the automaton was unstoppable, and it nearly crushed her foot as it tumbled away down the stairs to the café. She felt her own energy dissipate. It would be a while before she could do that again. There was nothing she could do about the access door but hope that was the last of the mannequins.

Frannie flew down the stairs and saw where the mannequin she had just cursed lay on its side, struggling to get up. She put a foot on its chest, and with the other gave its head a sharp kick with the sole of her sneaker. With a soft pop, the head went rolling into the kitchen, clack clack clacking all the way. The body however, stilled, and she hoped it would stay that way until she had the energy to release that soul. Whoever it was. The thought made her sick to her stomach.

Coming out from behind the bar, Frannie witnessed chaos. Newp and Kurt were playing a dangerous game of keep-away, tossing the Delta back and forth between them. In the center of the room was Saul, a short stick that looked a lot like Frannie's staff in either hand. He smashed at the mannequins as they came, shouting curses left and right, sweat pouring down his face. The headless mannequin appeared to be crawling about looking for its head. Frannie grabbed it by the waist and tossed it into the supply closet, shutting the door. Get out of that with no opposable thumbs, she thought grimly.

"Newp!" cried Betty, arms raised, and he flung the Delta to her. She caught it triumphantly, using her nightgown as a makeshift net, then grabbed it and tossed it to Kurt. He snatched it out of the air, taunting the mannequins to come closer, before slinging it over to Newp. While the effect of the mannequins slowly turning in circles to follow the Delta's path was comical, Frannie knew they couldn't keep it up forever. She ran to Saul's side and leaned against his back.

"We have to unbind them. All of them. Can we do it?"

Saul glanced around, counting "Three?"

"Five"

Saul swore. "Yeah but don't expect to wake up without a headache. Or for a while."

"Chance I'll take. They can't get the Delta. Ready?"

As though all of this were an old dance she had known from birth, Frannie held out her staff horizontal to the ground. Saul reached with his own weapons and touched the ends of the staff with them, closing the circle.

This was going to hurt.

Frannie closed her eyes. She could hear Truly laugh darkly, heard the thud and the sound of wind being knocked from lungs in Newp's direction, heard the clatter of something heavy fall to the floor. She felt Kurt fly past her, and she took a deep breath, letting it all go.

All is vanity. Let go of trying, and just do. Believe.

They began to chant as they had in the upper room. The golden glow flowed down the staff, down the sticks, creating two brilliant points of shining light at each end. They chanted faster, the intensity rising, the effort climbing, as the light grew brighter and brighter. Even with her eyes closed, the light was creating flashing and twisting patterns behind her eyelids, brown and grey and shifting noiselessly across her vision. Almost there. Almost to the tearing point. She braced herself for the pain.

"Che'rut. Cho'fesh. Amen."

The points of light slid together as one, and then exploded outwards. She felt her heart convulse, felt lighting rip through fillings in her teeth, felt time itself slice into her very soul like a knife of fire. She felt her skin peel away in thick, wet layers of raw nerve as she screamed and screamed and screamed.

And then she knew no more.

CHAPTER 29

WHEN SHE AWOKE, SHE WAS in the bed of a truck, barreling down the highway. The first pale rays of dawn were creeping past the trees, and the wind whipped through her hair. Beside her, expressionless as ever, was Hooky. Behind them, hitched to the truck, was a very beautiful boat.

She leaned over the side of the truck and threw up.

Stomach empty, she leaned back against the cab, pressing her palms to either side of her head in an attempt to hold her brains in. She did not want to be in this truck, an opinion which she made known.

"Sorry, Angel," said Hooky, handing her two aspirin and a canteen. "This was the best plan we could come up with, given the circumstances." His voice cut through the wind as though the wind weren't even there, and she could hear him plain as day.

She winced, swallowed, and winced again. "Where is Saul?" she called above the roar of the wind. "Is he all right?"

Hooky didn't hesitate. "He's in the safest place he can be right now. Kurt is with him. We thought we'd let you sleep. It's a two-hour drive to Salton at best, maybe three hours, and the professor already has a head start on us.

Our advantage is, you and Saul took out five of those goons. I was lucky, I was outside chasing her when you did that, or you might have blown me away too."

She hadn't even thought of that. The idea made her feel nauseated again, and her stomach obliged by sending her to the side of the truck again. Hooky just handed her another two aspirin and the canteen again.

"Relax. We're almost to Salton. She may have a little bit of a head start, but we have something she doesn't."

He gestured with an articulated wooden hand to the boat, and she gasped at the movement of his wooden fingers. She heard the grin in his voice. "Pretty neat, yeah? Kurt's a real tool-head. Took him five minutes to put them on. He said they weren't ready yet, but we were going to need them, so he put 'em on anyway."

It was all too much. She wrapped her arms around Hooky's wooden torso and held on for all she was worth. She was tired, and frightened, and her head ached beyond all comparison to any other headache she'd had before. Hooky wrapped one wooden arm around her as the truck began to turn, and then with the other handed her the staff.

"Almost there, Frannie. Can't give up yet. Hang on."

The air started to turn dry, so much that Frannie could feel it, and it reminded her of the places where she used to ride her bike with her friend Noreen. It was 9:00 o'clock in the morning when they finally reached the new town of Salton, California, which in the morning light was lit up in a crazy quilt of colors. They moved along new roads with wide sidewalks on either side where men in hats and women and pretty dresses got out of enormous cars, moving in and out of casinos.

They passed an enormous band hall called the Salton Sultan, where a blazing marquee said Frank Sinatra tonight.

"Sinatra?" said Frannie, not straining to yell now that the truck had slowed.

"I guess this place is a bigger deal than we thought," said Hooky. He began to wrap his face, mummy style, in a bandage. "If anyone asks, I'm a burn victim from the war."

"Which war?"

"Does it matter?"

A few minutes later, and Newp was backing the boat into the water at the public launch. Hooky helped, while Frannie and the girls gathered. Betty handed Frannie a slightly stale Danish to eat, as Truly jumped into the plan.

"We need to get to the public library and find a map of the old town of Salton, so we don't waste time driving the boat around hunting for it or swimming around looking for the church. So, while the boys do this, let's get hunting."

Together they marched off into town. Truly made a quick stop to grab a 'Salton Sight-Sea-ing' brochure, complete with a map of the lake. Moments later they were headed in the right direction. A man in a light green sport coat and a hat was unlocking the door of the small stone building, the white painted word Salton Public Library over his head on the glass door.

Betty came running up, "Excuse me, sir, can you help us? Are you the librarian?"

The man smiled politely but with a mark of impatience. "I am one of them."

Betty turned on her brightest smile. "I'm Betty, and this is Truly and Frannie."

"Delighted."

"I'm sure you're really busy opening up, but we have a really specific question that requires an expert."

The man in the jacket paused, clearly flattered, and opened the doors for them.

"Well, I don't know if I'm an expert, but I'll try. What are you looking for?"

Betty was practically beaming. "We're doing a history report for summer school, and we wanted to study Salton— the original one."

Frannie piped up. "Yeah, the Town of Salton, the one that got drowned? When they put the dam in? We were hoping maybe you would know where to find a map of the old town, and where it is under the lake."

"Yeah," the man nodded. "We would probably have something like that. Let me just pull up the file."

"Thank you very much, Sir," Frannie said.

They hurried into the library. The librarian followed them and then pulled ahead when they realized they had no idea where they were going.

"The maps are this way," he said.

Out in the truck, in the back seat, Newp leaned back and folded his arms in front of him. He looked over at Hooky, who was in the front seat in his full bandaged up regalia. "Of all the things that we do for her."

Hooky tilted his wooden head. "I don't know if we're doing this for her. It sounds like we're doing it for all mankind. Again."

"Sure. Okay," Newp said. "Listen. What are you gonna do?"

Hooky looked back. "What do you mean?"

"I mean, what are you going to do when this is done? Are you gonna live out your life as a wooden man?"

"I hadn't really thought about it."

Newp looked at the ground, kicking at a loose pebble. "I heard Frannie talking about how maybe there was a way to get you a body again."

"I don't know anything about that. Who is they?"

"Frannie. Maybe she talked to Saul. Maybe they have some ideas."

The mannequin did not respond for a moment. "Let's just worry about what's in front of us," Hooky said.

Inside the library, the librarian brought them down a set of maps, which had enormous ends attached to long poles and arranged in a special holder. He laid them out on a great wooden table.

"This is the city of Salton as it originally stood," he said, and he looked up for a moment. "What was it you were looking for in particular?"

"We're looking for churches," Frannie said. "The essay is about the expansion of Christianity into the West."

The man consulted the map. He ran his hand down to a key in a square on the bottom right and then back up circling his hand around the boxes and lines of the whole city which took up the entire four-foot map. "It looks like you have three churches. You have the Catholic Church, which is up here in the northwest, they have the Lutherans over here." he tapped the map. "And right next to what is now the dam, down by the river, that's where you find the Baptists. Naturally."

"Naturally," Betty agreed. "Do you have a map that shows the lake?"

"Yes indeed," He said, and unrolled another sheet from the hanger, laying it atop the first map.

"Do you mind if I..." Frannie reached for the map and the librarian let her take it. She held it there looking at where they were and added a spot on the brochure map that said LIBRARY. "And it's that way to the lake," she mumbled.

Then she lifted up the map and the lake disappeared, and she saw the town that was. She looked at the old river and the Baptist Church, then lowered the map and saw the dam. She made a quick sketch, then held it up to Truly and Betty. "Think we got it?"

"We could use a diagram," Truly said. "Like the key on that map."

She nodded, "I think that Dr. Clemens was a Baptist."

"Which is here." The librarian reached and tapped the Baptist Church. "Is that somebody that you're writing about? Dr. Clemens?"

"Yeah, that's right. Do you know him?" Frannie handed the map to Betty, who took over sketching streets and buildings from the original map.

"He was a famous revivalist. His career ended when Salton was drowned. He used to have this trick of making it seem like a donkey's jawbone held the voice of a spirit, and it would talk to you. My mother went to see him. All complete nonsense Of course," the librarian said.

The girls all stared at each other.

"Thank you so much sir!" they cried, nearly in unison. After another hearty round of thanks, they left the map on the table, and he walked them out of the map room and all the way to the front door. "Good luck with your project, girls," said the librarian, as they walked away.

Behind him, something with glowing blue eyes retreated into the shadows of the stacks.

It was nearly ten by the time they were on the boat and in the water. Hooky gave Frannie a set of diving apparatus and lay out another set for Newp.

"And just what is it we're going to do?" asked Truly.

"Keep the boat running and your eyes open," said Hooky. "We might need to get out of here in a real hurry."

"I can drive," said Betty helpfully. "If you need me to."

"Then stay close and ready."

Newp came out of the wheelhouse and slipped on the oxygen tank— he had already doffed his street clothes in favor of trunks. Frannie debated, and then stripped down to her own underwear. Saving the world left little room for personal modesty at the best of times. "I've only been diving twice," she said, a little nervously. "I'm rusty on it."

"You'll be fine," said Newp coldly. "Just remember to breathe normally and not panic. And don't come up fast or you'll get the bends."

"Here's where we're after, Newp," said Betty, holding out the map. "You're looking for the Baptist Church. Good luck!"

Frannie nodded. "Let's go," said Hooky, diving in without another sound.

Frannie hit the water and dropped with the weight of the oxygen tank and steadied about twelve or fifteen feet down. She looked up as Newp came down next to her, breathing perfectly through the apparatus as though he were born to it. Newp looked up and she followed his eyes and saw that Hooky seemed to be struggling.

Hooky was floating very near the surface, and Frannie began to wonder if maybe he was too buoyant to be able to dive. But then after a moment, perhaps as the cavity of his chest filled with water, he was swimming down. Soon he reached them and pointed the way forward. They headed down into the dark, drowned town of Salton.

The first thing they saw as they dropped was the street running not far from the river. There were the remnants of wooden curbs and lampposts, and Frannie saw an old mailbox teaming with flickering red and goldfish, next to a great tree that had long ago died and still swayed with the water, the fish darting in and around gnarled limbs.

They began to swim down the street. Houses emerged out of the darkness on their left and right, some of them just skeletal remains, frameworks that still had doors that lay open and swayed with the soft current. Some of the houses were complete and Frannie briefly wished that she could take the time to swim in and explore.

The people of Salton had been given plenty of warning, and yet from the street it looked as though all of this may have taken them by surprise. She wondered if, were she to go into the houses, whether there would still be dishes on the tables.

Personally, Frannie was a stranger to the idea of having to flee anything. She had left Germany as a baby and had absolutely no memory of the experience. She had moved around with her family but there had never been a feeling of flight. There had never been a moment when a government came to her and said, take your goods and leave, because this is no longer your home. She passed another house with a tree that swayed in the water and looked at the peeling wooden wall of the house behind it. She saw a darkened window with muddy curtains. Every single piece of all of this had once been crafted by a person, had once been nailed up or painted or just admired by a person who said, this is my home. And then one day they were all forced to go.

She thought she saw frames on the wall through one of the windows and was almost desperate to swim in and find out what somebody not so long ago had pinned to their wall and saw fit to leave.

But there was no time for that right now. They had somewhere to get to. The team moved down a block and then another block until they reached the street of the Baptist Church. The three of them hung there in the water, looking towards the dam which appeared as an enormous wall at the end of the block. Before the dam, a simple white, wooden church was lit up by a shaft of bright sunlight. She saw the words Salton Baptist Church.

The wooden front door curled with peeling white paint. As they approached, she reached out to turn the brass knob of the door, and a great fish swam out of a window right next to her head. She felt her heart skip a beat and waved her arms, almost losing the regulator. Newp grabbed her arm and steadied her in the water. She wasn't able to smile with the regulator in her mouth, but she felt embarrassed and gave Newp the thumbs up.

She swam again towards the door but was unable to turn the knob. Even Hooky with his superhuman strength could not make the door budge.

It doesn't matter, she shrugged. They went to the busted window that the fish had come out of. Although flimsy wooden frames still remained, Hooky was able to make short work of them by karate chopping around the window with his wooden arm. It was a large front window, easy enough for each of them to swim through.

Frannie had never been inside a Baptist Church, but she had seen them in the movies and on TV. They were not so different from a synagogue, long rows of pews, and up at the front, a dais with a lectern and behind it a large cross. Not a crucifix, that was a Catholic thing.

This swam up the length of the building until they reached the lectern. It was about four feet tall, with a wide sloping top. Frannie could picture Thomas Clemens with his fingers on the wood as he spoke. She swam around behind the lectern, and to her surprise, it appeared to have a lid. She lifted the hinged top, heart pounding with anticipation. On a little shelf inside she found a waterlogged hymnal crawling with silverfish and a few coins. Nothing else. Below the shelf, the hollow lectern was open, with a curtain that hung before it. Frannie moved the tattered curtain aside, expecting another fish to dart out of here. But all that was inside it was mud and water. She searched all around the bottom of the open section, but it was empty.

Newp swam up next to her, pointing at the wooden base of the lectern. She gently lowered the whole thing to the ground. The base was open at the bottom and there was nothing there.

For a moment, the three of them hung there staring at it. What they were looking for was not here.

Finally, Hooky pointed at the ceiling of the church, towards the surface. They swam their way back up the nave of the church and out towards the door. Out to the rotted street.

They had been wrong. But Frannie had no idea how.

When they were out in the street, they began to rise, taking the time to stop every fifteen feet to make sure that they didn't injure themselves. Finally, they reached the surface and swam towards the boat. When they reached it, Frannie treaded water and pushed back her goggles and looked around at the others who swam nearby. She took the regulator out of her mouth and let it hang over her chest.

She looked at friends. "What did we get wrong?"

Newp shook his head, thinking. "What exactly did the preacher say again?"

"Sacraments," she said. "He talked about where the sacraments were kept. What's a sacrament?"

"What?" Hooky asked from next to the boat. She could hear his voice rumbling up from his chest and out through the mouth.

"What's a sacrament?"

"The Eucharist and the wine. Communion? Didn't you ever go to Sunday school?"

"Hebrew school," said Newp.

It was Truly's turn to pipe up. "We just call it communion. Catholics call it the sacrament."

"So why would he, if he was Baptist?"

"It means he changed his faith," Hooky said.

"I don't think we marked the Catholic church on the map." Betty said, concerned.

"It'll be close to the center of town," said Hooky. "At least, mine was."

"Let's start exploring," said Frannie, putting her goggles back on.

She put the map away and they swam back down. Once again they were moving along the streets, and this time the great wall of the dam was more visible to Frannie and unnerved her more. It gave her the feeling of this entire town being walled off, even though of course there was oxygen above them.

Finally, they reached the Catholic Church which stood taller than the Baptist Church, with long narrow stained-glass windows, some of them still intact.

Whereas the front door had been closed at the Baptist Church, here, a large, dark, wooden door was already cracked slightly. Hooky strained to push it open and then they were able to swim through looking down the expanse of tile, a multitude of dark pews and at the end, an altar. A great crucifix hung behind, overlooking them all.

There were shapes around the lectern and Frannie wasn't sure what they were until they turned around and all of their eyes glowed blue.

The altar was swarming with mannequins.

CHAPTER 30

TONI SUTCLIFFE WAS NOWHERE IN evidence— but the mannequins were there, surely doing her bidding, and they had already set to taking the lectern apart. One of them picked up the top half and pulled it apart by sticking his hands inside of it and stretching wide. Frannie saw a glint of metal tumble down to the marble floor.

That was it. She looked at Hooky and Newp. She made a shape of a triangle with her fingers and pointed to her chest. I'll get it. Then she pointed at Hooky. You protect me.

As she and Hooky swam towards the altar, one of the mannequins reached down, sliding his fingers through the double piece of metal, and picking it up. Frannie swam straight for it.

As the mannequin looked up, it seemed to become aware of her and moved its jaws, and Frannie could almost hear the clack as she grabbed at the metal piece.

But another mannequin came in beside her, shoving her violently to the side, so that she lost her grip as she twisted around. She tumbled backwards, her diving tanks slamming into the pews. The regulator came out of her

240

mouth, and she scrambled for a moment in a panic until she got it back in and could breathe once more.

Newp was fighting one of the mannequins, and as he tumbled with it, Frannie thought that he resembled Tarzan spinning with a crocodile in an old movie. Spinning out of control. They were about to crash into the altar, its splintered wood jutting up like shark's teeth in the water. Newp kicked it away, but the mannequin returned, lunging towards him, grabbing him around the throat, falling together, crashing through a stained-glass window and out of the church.

Frannie kicked and swam towards the mannequin with the Delta piece, who was moving back towards the door of the church. As she approached, she spun so that the oxygen tanks on her back smashed into the mannequin. He sprawled out, floating in the water and dropped the metal piece once more.

This time, she dove for it and snatched it up. She turned to face the door and found it blocked by yet another pair of glowing blue eyes and clacking jaws.

But of course, the world was above them, and so she went straight up.

The ceiling of the church was plaster and practically sludge. She reached it and kicked, and chunks of the plaster fell all around her. She clawed her way into the attic, using the Delta to hammer and push material aside. Up she drifted toward the roof when suddenly one of the mannequins was below her, grasping at her feet. She kicked out, reaching up, expecting to tear away the roof as easily as she had torn away the ceiling.

The roof held. She pushed and pushed. The mannequin was on her now, squeezing its wooden hands into her ribs. She felt the metal piece in one hand and began battering at the roof with it.

The pain was unbearable as it pressed into her ribs, but she found a seam in the roof and pushed. It felt like rotten rubber, the roof tiles bending. She grabbed onto a rafter and flipped in the air, punching with her muscular legs, and tore a hole as a big board went free. She saw shimmering water above her and swam through.

The problem occurred to her far too late. She would have to stop and wait to adjust or get the bends and potentially drown.

The mannequin did not.

She held tightly to the Delta, feeling it hum and shiver in her hands. It was heavy, and the point was sharp, but—

As suddenly and clearly as a bolt of lightning sets the sky alight, she heard Saul's voice in her head. "What does the Delta do?"

She kicked up as high as she dared without stopping before she held out the Delta in both hands. She pointed it at the mannequin beneath her, praying that she wasn't just giving it a chance to drown her.

Go, spirit, and rejoin the cosmic. I release you.

She couldn't read the expression in the eyes— it could have been shock, or relief, or her own wishful thinking. But slowly, the blue light faded away, and the mannequin began to sink lifelessly to the bottom, its wooden jaw silent and its hand forever reached upward toward her.

Frannie looked around, hoping to see more mannequins, but none appeared. In the weird, muffled world of the water she could sense the sound of struggle in the church. Were Newp and Hooky all right? She didn't know. She needed to get the Delta to the boat. Then she could go back to look for the boys.

She squared her shoulders and turned her face to the sun. The noon glare made sparks fly in the darkness when she closed her eyes, but she began the steady climb toward the surface. She could see the bottom of the boat, casting its deep shadow into the lake, and aimed her body for the back and the ladder. As she neared, a blurry figure reached out an arm, and she swam up to grab it. The arm pulled as she stepped onto the bottom rung of the ship's ladder, and she felt herself lifted right into a set of feminine arms. She pulled off her foggy mask to discover an unconscious Truly, a terrified Betty, a pair of blazing-eyed mannequins, and a gun in the free hand of Toni Sutcliffe.

She reached out her arm. "Give it to me," Toni said as though this were all so tiresome. For a moment Frannie thought about dropping it back into the lake when Toni seemed to read her mind and shook her head. "Let it drop, and your friends are never coming back up," she said.

Frannie set her jaw and dropped the Delta piece into Toni Sutcliffe's outstretched hand.

Hooky and Newp reached the surface in time to watch the boat go tearing away from them. A hundred yards away, a small dinghy with an outboard motor was anchored, bobbing softly in the waves. "Sutcliffe," said Newp, recognizing the disappearing figure of the blonde at the helm. "And she's got the girls."

"And the Delta."

They swam until they reached the tiny boat. Newp was pretty exhausted by the time they got there. He looked haggard as he peeled off the diving equipment. Hooky began to pull up the anchor as Newp revved the engine.

"So, what do we do now?"

"Now she has all the pieces," Hooky said. "That means she'll want to use them in some way, in some kind of ritual."

"Do you think she'll need to prepare for that?" Newp asked.

"I think she's been preparing for it her whole life. We just have to find her."

They sat in silence as the boat puttered along. Newp looked miserably at the passing scenery, silently kicking himself for putting the girls in danger, when he turned to Hooky.

"I have an idea where she is," Newp said.

"Then that's where we'll go," Hooky said.

Their faces, one a painted smile, one haunted and grim, turned toward Salton Bay Marina. They had to get to the truck. Now it was a race.

CHAPTER 31

TONI TURNED FRANNIE'S STAFF OVER in her hands as they made the return trip to Laguna. One of the mannequins drove, and Betty had hauled Truly into her lap on the floor of the box truck as Toni sat on the floor beside them, knees tucked up, inspecting the staff. Frannie sat opposite, shivering and glaring. She had believed Toni. She had trusted Toni. And how here they were, all because she had been an utter fool.

"So, what are you waiting for? Aren't you going to kill us?"

Toni looked up from the staff, and then leaned her chin in her hand, balancing her elbow on her knee. "I don't believe in killing. You know that. You saw me in the Blank."

"You killed those people you put in the mannequins."

A startled laugh erupted from the older woman. "Is that what you think? Oh no, no. No one is dead. The body does just fine on its own without a soul in it, for quite some time. No, they're all safe and sound. I'm just borrowing their souls until I don't need them anymore. Which, thanks to you, will be much sooner."

"You killed those kids on the beach. I heard his soul screaming."

"Oh, the one you released? The minute you did that his soul zipped right back into his body. Scared the living daylights out of me when he came charging out of the guest room demanding to be taken to the police. It took quite a bit of work to get him back under control. He's certainly not been as useful in his normal body as he was as a mannequin. But he'll be fine in a few days."

Frannie felt her grasp on the situation slipping. No one was dead? Then why all the subterfuge? What about the Phantoms? What about Hooky?

"Let me guess— why did I go to all this trouble when I could have just told you the truth?"

Toni sighed and turned the staff in her hands again. "Because your Uncle is more right than you know. The most precious and rare commodity in the Hidden World is trust. You can't trust other magics, or other magicians. You can't trust the shadowy organizations, the cloak and dagger of it all. The only thing you can trust and believe in is yourself, and those closest to you. And I want you to know— I deeply regret being the one to break your trust, Frannie, I really do. If it had just been you and the other kids, perhaps things would have been different. Perhaps we could have worked together. But Saul…"

Toni slid a finger down a set of curses, and Frannie felt her blood turn hot.

"Poor Saul. I can't imagine how badly he's been treated by the Blankguards, to strike out on his own like this. Or that he thinks Monsignor Matthias is any kind of threat anymore. He's just a lovely, toothless old hound sitting at the Vatican's feet like an ancient dog in the sun. No, I couldn't trust Saul, but my word, was it easy to use you. This was all so much faster with all your help. As much as I would have liked to just accept your help and leave you in peace, when you all decided to destroy the Delta, well…I'm afraid that does force my hand a bit."

Frannie glanced at the leather satchel next to Toni. She could feel the pieces vibrating, like two opposing magnets desperate to come together.

"I don't think it'll surprise you that I think you can shove your apology and take it straight to hell."

"No, it doesn't."

"So, what, then? What are you going to do to us."

Toni swung the staff idly, testing its weight.

"As long as you don't cause a fuss, nothing. Well, mostly nothing. I will need to borrow Truly for…a very long time, I'm afraid. But she'll still be here, I've been refinishing the nicest of the female mannequins for her vessel. I like the articulated fingers Kurt put on Hooky, I'm sure he'll be able to do something similar for Truly. She'll even be able to still play piano."

Betty started to sob and hugged Truly tighter. "You horrible witch. Don't you touch her! Don't you even think to touch her, I'll never let you! She's mine and I'm hers, do you hear me?"

A mannequin shuffled forward threateningly, and Betty glared at it.

"I'm sorry, my dear, but I'll be needing her body. Her soul you are welcome to keep. And isn't that what we really fall in love with in the end, a person's soul? Like you and Hooky."

The barb hit home, and Frannie felt her eyes tearing up with rage and frustration. "It's okay, Betty," she said. "We're not going to let her do anything to Truly."

"You'll find it difficult to stop me if I decide to trap your soul in a floor lamp or a desk chair," Toni replied. "So, for now I think it very, very wise for you to consider your situation, and sit tight. I have no desire to hurt you. But Michael…the wolf has very specific desires where hurting you is concerned. Do I make myself clear, Frannie?"

She didn't answer. The defeat in her heart was already settling on her like the cold of her wet clothes settled on her skin. No curse she could throw would be quick or powerful enough to stop three mannequins and Toni's gun in this small space. No, she couldn't curse them. She barely had the energy to sit upright. Despite herself, the exhaustion of a days and night's events closed in on her, and she drifted into a restless sleep.

Frannie wasn't sure how much time had passed— the box truck had been dim at best, and most of the ambient light came from the blue glow of the mannequin's eyes. She knew it had been past noon when they left, but the summer sun was deceptive; often the day felt early when the hour grew late, and it was harder to estimate the shifts in hours. She was surprised that when the back door to the box truck finally opened, dusk had fallen. She was even more surprised at who was standing at the back of the truck, waiting to help unload the captured crew.

Michael Landry held out his hand to help her down, and her heart plummeted.

She declined with a sniff but gave up and helped him to get the still unconscious Truly out of the truck. He swept Truly up in his arms, and Frannie helped Betty down as the mannequins gathered around them wordlessly. Toni was nowhere in sight.

"Come on," said Michael, somberly. "She's got everything ready, it's time to go."

"Go where?" demanded Betty, sourly.

But Frannie already knew. She nudged Betty and nodded upward.

They were standing at the back entrance of the Hotel Riviera.

They were led up the back stairs to the penthouse suite. It would have been a large, airy space, built in the tropic style with lots of wood and tile and white walls— except for the large sigil drawn in, sand laid out on the tiled floor. Other oddities littered the room; masks, statues, bits of scroll and spears. What was most disturbing however were the bodies. Bodies of the missing Phantoms, a young couple that Frannie guessed had to be the couple from the beach, and a literal pile of mannequins in the far corner. At the center of the sand design was an open, oval space. Michael stepped carefully so as not to disturb any of the sand and laid Truly in the center. He paused, then looked back at Betty and Frannie.

"I'm sorry. I don't have a choice. You saw what happened on the beach. What I— what the wolf did. I can't be that anymore."

Frannie frowned. "I thought you didn't remember anything that happens when you turn into a wolf?"

"I didn't. Until you hit me with your stick, and then...and then I remembered everything."

Her blood ran cold. Zol er krenken un gedenken. Let him suffer and remember. Her curse.

"It's a curse."

"Yeah. It is."

She straightened. "It's what you deserve, helping her. Do you have any idea what she's planning to do to Truly?!"

Michael hung his head, and then shook like a dog, as though trying to get rid of the guilt.

"The same thing I'm about to do that poor bastard."

He nodded toward the body of a Phantom. It was the young man whose neck had been snapped by the wolf.

"But...he's dead!" cried Betty, horrified.

Michael shook his head. "He was dead. A little. And no one came to claim him, no family, nobody. He's available real-estate."

Frannie snorted. "You're going to trade a cursed body for a dead one."

A female voice interrupted.

"I already took care of that. He's perfectly viable. It's amazing what you can do when you mix medicine and magic. Rigor mortis didn't even set in before I had that heart working again."

Toni strode into the room then, every hair in place and looking none the worse for wear. In one hand she held Frannie's staff, and in the other, a small platter on which lay the two pieces of the Delta. They vibrated quietly, causing a soft, tinny noise like an antenna pulled taut, and then let go, whipping through the air. She set the platter on a large wooden desk, that seemed to be serving as a makeshift altar. Above it hung the wooden tiki mask that Frannie recognized from Toni's university office. Her fears were confirmed as a deep voice emanated from the carved wooden mouth.

"Soon what is sundered shall be made whole."

"It is true, my love," said Toni to the statue. She turned to face the younger people head on, a beautiful blonde woman in a room full of bodies, real and crafted. "We have so much to work with. Frannie, you and Betty will stay right where you are, do you understand? I don't want to hurt you. And I won't hurt Truly. Do you see that mannequin there, on the stand?"

A beautiful female mannequin, polished to a high shine, stood propped on a stand. It was draped in a deep blue dress that shimmered with sequins like silver stars in the night sky.

"That's for her. It's the least I could do after that young ruffian sliced up her dress. We'll begin the ritual now, Michael, if you'd be so kind."

He shivered at her command but stepped toward the altar.

Saul Cohn hated hospitals. He hated the look, the feel, the smell. He hated the clean surfaces and the crisp, uncomfortable sheets that he knew for a fact people had died in. He hated the squeaky floors and the squeaky young candy stripers and the squeaky wheels of the gurneys rolling in and out. And above all else, Saul Cohn hated being told what to do.

It was a trait that ran true in their family.

"Sit," Kurt said. "You're making me nervous, and the doctor said to rest. You only woke up five minutes ago, you putz."

"I won't sit. So, I had a heart attack. Okay, so what. I eat less schmear and I go for more walks. We left the kids in danger; we need to get back to the café."

"They're not kids, they can handle themselves, and Hooky is with them."

"Toni Sutcliffe is a dangerous practitioner. And if she is by herself, then she's even more dangerous than we thought. We can't sit here."

"Absolutely we can and will."

Saul looked at Kurt, at his exhausted, sleepless face, his salt and pepper stubble. He saw underneath the worry, the deep and endless ocean of love he had sailed for so long and yet so short a time. He walked over to Kurt, and kneeling, took the artist's face in his hands.

"I wish I had met you sooner. I wish I had known you longer. I wish we were sailing on our beautiful boat. I wish...I wish I had never looked in the Blank, I wish I didn't have this knowledge, but I do. I love you, Kurt. I do. But... a wise Rebbe, Nachman of Breslov, he said...'if you will not be a better person tomorrow than you are today, what need have you of a tomorrow?'"

Kurt covered Saul's hands with his own. His eyes were dry and steady, and Saul saw the farewell in them before he even finished.

"I know what's waiting for me. And I know that today, I will be the best person I have ever been."

"You could stay," said Kurt, his voice struggling for the mild, dry tone he always used whenever he thought Saul was about to do something profoundly stupid. Saul knew that Kurt wouldn't cry, not here, not now. It broke his heart to know that his lover would do his crying alone.

"But then what need would I have of a tomorrow?"

Kurt let out the breath he had been holding. He'd done what grieving he could while Saul was unconscious. Now the moment was here, and he had to face it.

"I'll drive."

Michael hefted the body of the Phantom onto his shoulder and dropped it next to Truly. He walked over and picked up the evening gown mannequin and added it to the now crowded circle. Toni appeared to be consulting a scroll, marking little notes with an anachronistic golf pencil in the margins. She looked up at his handiwork.

"They need to be touching, and they need to touch the sand. Link their arms and make sure they're touching the sand."

"Thieves," said Frannie, suddenly, hoarsely. "Thieves and murderers. I don't care if you haven't killed anyone, you're about take people's lives away. I don't see how that's different."

From the corner of her eye, Frannie noticed Betty sliding slowly toward a large potted plant in the corner, near the door. Good, she thought. Get out of here honey. She cleared her throat and decided to play for time. "You're not even a wolf after all, just Sutcliffe's lapdog. Murderers."

Michael turned, clearly stung, but Toni ignored her. "He's a lowlife thug who was going to kill you and your friends. I'm a good guy who is trapped in a curse. Who deserves it more, Frannie? Huh? I don't make the choices. The wolf does, and I have to live with them. But this piece of shit, Eric, he chooses to hurt people. He thinks it's fun. So, we're going to trade."

Frannie felt like she had been slapped. He wasn't wrong. She glanced at the other Phantom bodies, and then at the body of Eric. He had tried to kill Truly. If she hadn't been wearing her sequined dress, he might have succeeded. Toni had the power to remove that dark and twisted soul, to put it in a vase or a candlestick or a book, to trap it like a fly in amber. Leaving behind a perfectly good body. A perfectly good body for a perfectly good soul.

A body for Hooky. A second chance.

"You understand, don't you? It'll still be me. One less dangerous slimeball on the planet, one less werewolf on the loose, one more good man out in the world living a second chance. A chance I can spend with you."

Michael stepped toward her then, closing the distance with blinding, uncanny speed, and swept her up in a kiss before she knew what was happening.

It was dark and sweet and hot, like the luau fruit cooked in the embers. She was in the river of stars again, when she felt the press of the fangs against her lips, sharp and bitter with drawn blood. Michael threw himself away from her, crossing the room to Toni's side in two strides, and whirled to face Frannie. His eyes had returned to the dark glow of yellow amber, and his fangs bisected his lips. "We're going to trade, so I can kiss you without killing you," he said, and shuddered.

She wanted to cry. "I want to help you," she said. "Michael, I want to help you, if you just want to swap bodies with Eric, that's fine, I understand that, you're right. But leave Truly out of this, she's innocent!"

He shook his shaggy head miserably, looking at Toni, still engrossed in the scroll. "I had to make a deal, Frannie. Please understand, this is the price I have to pay."

Truly stirred slightly, drawing their gaze. That was the fate in store for Truly's soul. Trapped in a mannequin body. She shook her head. It wasn't right. Nothing they said could make that theft all right. It was a step too far. To neutralize the evil, that was one thing, but this...

Frannie locked her eyes on Michael's— she couldn't risk looking away and betraying Betty's movements. She hoped Betty had made it closer to the door. Slowly, she raised the back of her hand, and wiped the kiss from her lips.

"If I wanted a dog to slobber on me, I would have kept the one we found on the beach."

Michael snarled, and Toni's hand became a restraining one. "Just wait. You lovebirds can quarrel in a minute."

Frannie smirked and crossed her arms over her pounding heart. She hadn't heard the door go. What did Betty think she was doing? Where was she? Frannie wished she could risk even a single glance, but she knew she couldn't. She had to keep their attention on her. Toni turned to the tiki mask.

"Did you pick the one you liked, dear?"

The dark amber voice dropped heavily from the mask.

"The dark-haired one will do until we find something more suitable."

Toni nodded, and Michael, throwing a furious glance at Frannie, walked over to pick Eric up and add him to the circle. Frannie risked a glance, and her heart skipped a beat. Where the hell was Betty? There was no sign of her flannel clad friend anywhere. She heard a 'thud' as Eric's body joined the others. They were running out of time.

Toni laid Eric's switchblade in a small pile of sand. There were three such piles, Frannie saw, at the curve of the design closest to Toni. Toni noticed Frannie's interest and smiled. "I thought it would be an appropriate vessel for him. Can't have that kind of character traipsing around Laguna now can we. All right, Michael, stand there," she said, pointing to a pile of sand on her left. Carefully she lifted down the tiki mask and settled it on top of the final pile of sand. "There. Shall we?"

The mannequins all stood, except for the pile in the corner, and made a little semicircle around Frannie and the swirling pattern of sand. Where is Betty? They were going to notice she was missing any minute!

Betty did not consider herself to be much good at anything beyond her singing. She'd had passable grades in school (though her highest marks were always for penmanship), she was an average cook, and, she hoped, a good sister and daughter. She had long since decided she was a fair to middling person in the world. What Betty did not realize about herself was a particular talent she subconsciously used to great effect.

Betty was observant. She delighted in details. She knew before her friends did what it was they were about to reach for, she always knew where everything in every room was, and a great deal of the success of the band came from her ability to read a room.

So, from the moment she could pull her mind away from the trouble they were in, Betty had been watching. What she had seen in the hallway just beyond Michael's left shoulder had finally given her hope. Halfway down it, affixed to the wall, was a bright red metal box.

A fire alarm.

Betty watched Frannie, and Michael, and Toni. It was hard not to look at Frannie— she drew the eye like a light drew moths. It was easy to see that Michael was besotted with her, and that Toni was preoccupied. If she moved very slowly, very carefully, they would be too busy looking at Frannie.

Let this work, she prayed silently. I have to save Truly. Please let this work.

She didn't turn as she moved. She didn't look back. She fixed her eyes on the red box like a lifeline, rolling her bare feet along the tile floor from heel through the arch to the toe, making no sound. Ten more steps. Five. Three.

She reached out a hand to the cool, heavy bar of the alarm, and pulled it gently downwards.

When nothing happened, she almost sobbed in fear. Panicked, she shoved the handle up and pulled it down again, hard.

With the ringing of the klaxon, all hell broke loose.

"I knew it," cried Newp, leaping from the truck. The klaxon of the fire alarm rang in the summer air, radiating out from the Hotel Riviera. "There's nowhere else she could have thrown the mannequins from. Come on!"

Hooky and Newp raced from the truck into the Hotel, just in time to see Kurt and Saul pull up in the Studebaker.

"You should be in the hospital!" called Newp.

"You should be so lucky!" Saul replied, getting out to join them. Kurt parked and got out, tossing Saul his small staves.

"Going up?" he said dryly.

Without another word, the four began to run up the stairs.

Toni lifted her hands, the two pieces of the Delta beginning to glow. Taking her chance, Frannie ground the ball of her right foot into the ground and pushed forward, making the longest leap she could toward her staff. There was a brilliant blast of light, from the Delta as the two pieces came together, and the sand lit with St. Elmo's fire. The blue electricity crackled and snapped between the bodies and objects on the floor, like something out of the old Frankenstein movies. Two more steps and she would have her staff in her hand.

The fire klaxon rang. She stumbled, startled, her foot touching the flaming sand. She could feel something pushing, straining, trying to work its way into her like a needle into an arm. She gasped and kicked it away, grabbing for her staff. She grabbed it triumphantly and stood to face the mannequins.

Already Eric was starting to rise, looking in amazement at his hands, running them over his chest. He laughed deeply in the voice of the mask, and looking over at Frannie, laughed again. He pointed, and the mannequins moved on her, five blazing pairs of blue eyes locked on her. She twirled her staff and began to chant the unbinding spell, but her resolve was failing. How much energy would she have left to fight Toni, after taking out five mannequins?

She gripped the staff tighter. If this was it, it was going to be everything she had and more.

The door to the room burst open, and after that there was no time to think.

Saul waded into the room like a bald warrior king, swinging his short staves from side to side. Mannequins tumbled like bowling pins right and left, as Newp, Kurt and Hooky leapt into the fray. Michael's body crumpled to the ground as the Phantom boy began to stand, looking groggy and disoriented. Truly was next. There was no more time.

With a cry of frustration, Frannie swung upward with the staff, knocking the Delta out of Toni's upstretched hands, before bringing it back down again on the woman's outstretched forearms. There was a sickening, crunching sound, like stepping on beetles. The blue fire died away, and Toni screamed, her arms hanging limp.

"You stupid little bitch! You stupid little bitch!"

From behind her, a mannequin grabbed the staff and wrenched it away. Frannie turned as it swung her own staff at her and cracked her across the jaw, and her vision blurred with the pain as she hit the ground. Toni flung herself at the Delta, grasping at it with her barely responding hands, as Eric's newly claimed body bent and picked up Truly's limp one. Somewhere behind them there was a crack and a scream as a mannequin grabbed Kurt's arm and wrenched him up by it. Newp and Betty were cornered by two mannequins, Newp covering his sister with his body as they beat at him. All about Frannie were the sounds of combat and chaos, and vague shapes of people she loved and the trapped souls in wooden bodies.

She couldn't see through the pain, so she focused on what she could hear.

"I've got the girl," said the tiki mask voice. "Come on, lets—"

A large shape seemed to float past Frannie's vision. A large shape that moved with a predatory deliberateness. A large shape with something that flashed silver in its hand.

God should bless him with three people: one should grab him, the second should stab him and the third should hide him.

SMACK, the staff came down on her again, knocking the air from her lungs. Frannie couldn't have screamed if she had wanted to. Her vision started to clear as the long silver switchblade found a home in what had once been Eric's side. His white suit began to stain darkly red.

Suddenly Hooky's face filled her vision and hauled her up. She could hear Toni screaming and babbling, turned to see Michael in his new body drop the knife and grab a groggy Truly before she hit the ground. At Frannie's feet, a mannequin head landed, its jaws clacking maniacally. Hooky stood her on her feet and handed her the staff. "I'll get them out. Do your hero thing, Angel."

She shook her head to clear it. Hooky scooped up Truly and was headed for the door. Michael bowled through the two mannequins, pushing Newp and Betty away toward the door. Betty supported her bruised and bloodied brother to the exit, where Saul was beating the two remaining mannequins away from Kurt with his golden glowing short staves. In the light, he looked like some kind of marble statue come to life, seeking vengeance against its creators. Toni held the bloody switchblade in her hands, sobbing audibly. "Kill them!" she cried to the mannequins. "Kill them all!"

There was only one thing Frannie could think to do. She swept her staff across the backs of the mannequins, crying the stone curse. They slowed and knelt, almost as though they were melting into the floor. She muscled past them and touched her staff to Saul's staves. She would unbind it, all of it, undo everything that Toni Sutcliffe had wrought in her grief and greed. She closed her eyes and began it.

"I call on the Tetragrammaton," she chanted, feeling the power rise within her. "I call on EMET, I tell you the truth, that all is vanity. I call on Guoral, the path of Fate, and on the power of Mihv'ar, our choice."

She could hear Saul chanting faintly behind her, lending her his power, chanting through the Tetragrammaton. She closed her eyes against the blinding golden glow of the staff and staves. It would have to be enough; the mannequins would rise again soon.

"Chofesh," she cried, releasing the power in a wide arc, sending her staff through the air to strike each mannequin in turn. They stood, shaking heads and clacking jaws in confusion. She had released the spell binding them to Toni— there hadn't been enough time to grow the spell to banish everything. She swore silently, feeling the drain on her body and soul. She was so tired. Would this never end?

"Frannie!" yelled Kurt, and Frannie turned to see the Phantom girl swinging the switchblade toward her throat. Saul batted the weapon away and it went spinning across the floor, under the desk. Michael dove as the girl did, both of them disappearing under the large wooden furniture. They screamed and scuffled, the whicker of the slicing knife cutting through the air.

"Get them up!" cried Frannie at the mannequins. One of them blinked, and then with one hand upended the desk, revealing two huddled figures— the Phantom Girl curled around the switchblade and one half of the Delta, and the Phantom Michael, one shoulder drenched in blood, clutching the other.

With a desperate look around, the Phantom Toni pointed the Delta at the female mannequin. "Return to the cosmic spirit, I release you!"

There was a soft sighing sound, and the mannequin dropped to the floor, it's eyes nothing more than lifeless brushstrokes of paint.

"It's my body now," said Phantom Toni, holding the knife and the Delta in shaking hands. "Give me the piece, Michael. You got your new body, now give me the piece."

"No," said Phantom Michael. He glanced at their old bodies, prone on the floor. "You promised you wouldn't cross the line when we started this. You swore no one would get hurt. You told me the only body you would take was one that didn't matter, someone no one would miss. Well, Truly matters. You know who no one will miss? Toni Sutcliffe."

With a scream of rage, she drove the knife toward Michael once again, who turned and threw his half of the Delta to Frannie.

She snatched it out of the air, and wrapping herself around Toni's back, forced the two pieces together.

Together they floated in the river of stars.

CHAPTER 32

OUR TIME WAS STOLEN.

They floated silently, facing each other, each with a hand on the Delta. Frannie knew the stars were there and didn't feel the need to look at them—the shine that intrigued her was the knife in Toni's hand.

She appeared as herself, here, not as the body she had stolen. The knife glimmered in the starlight.

That's your husband, isn't it, she said. She didn't need Toni's answer—she could feel the soul inside the weapon. That was probably all there was of it here, much as the pages of the blanks were only a backdrop when you were in them. Toni turned her gaze to Frannie to reply.

I will have him back. Why should these children get to waste their lives, when ours were good? We did such good. I will take back what was mine.

Toni's soul flickered a bit as it floated, with anger or fatigue Frannie couldn't tell. The river carried on, stars passed them in slow currents of time and space.

No, said Frannie, slowly raising her arm through the resistance of the river. You've taken enough.

She reached her other hand for the Delta. It shone in the space between them, fraught with power and potential. It was heavy, so heavy, but she had to wrest control of it from Toni.

My will is stronger, child, said Toni, increasing her grip on the Delta. Frannie felt it pull back away from her, slowly, like thick cold honey pulling away from a spoon. Frannie continued to reach, feeling her right hand grow weary, and gritted her teeth. She pressed forward against the current, willing her left hand closer and closer to the Delta. Suddenly, she smiled.

Your will is strong. But your will is split. You won't let go of the knife. You can't let go of your husband. But I can let go of everything.

And she did. Frannie let go of thought, of feeling, of emotion. She let go of everything that wasn't reaching for the Delta, grasping it, pulling it from Toni's clutches. She felt Toni's fingers lose their grip, one by one, as the other woman yelled faint curses at her in frustration. Her left hand closed around the Delta. She pried it from Toni's grip.

They were back in the room full of sand and blood. Frannie held the Delta, her eyes matching its gentle rosy glow. Michael, Kurt, Saul and the mannequins turned to look at Toni. She straightened and pointed the knife at Frannie's face.

"I will have what is mine. And I will have revenge."

With that, she turned and fled into the night.

Michael started to give chase, and Frannie stopped him.

"You can't. We can't. No one is in any condition to chase her."

She closed her hands around the Delta and breathed slowly out.

She was in the river of stars again, standing in a constellation. She had never before thought to wonder what the stars were, and now she knew. She cradled the Delta to her heart and made a swirling motion with her hand. The stars aligned before her, free of their bodies. One, two, three, four five—

Too many. There are too many souls. I pulled everyone's soul out of their body.

She would have to put them back. Kurt was easy, she plucked the familiar feeling amethyst star out of the sky and nestled it gently back into his body. The two mannequins were more difficult— it was hard to parse which soul belonged to which body. She discovered it was a matter of resistance when she tried to push a springy peridot green star into the remaining young woman's body. It wouldn't go and pushed back against her attempts. She moved the star to the young man, and it slid easily back into his being.

Michael's topaz soul, and Saul's sky blue one remained. Four bodies littered the floor.

It's not your body, she said. It's wrong.

I know, he said. You don't have to justify anything. I killed him— the wolf killed him. But when my body dies, the wolf will too. His soul is gone— he's just a body now. Will you curse me again with the wolf? I'll just kill more people— I won't have a choice. Please, Frannie— give me the chance to have a choice.

She couldn't win. He wasn't wrong. It wasn't right. But he wasn't wrong.

I will never see you again, she said. *There will be bodies in this room when the police come. It will be Michael Landry that did this. That's what we will tell them, and that's what they'll believe. You will disappear to make your choices. Do you understand?*

He did. The effort of forcing the topaz soul into the Phantom boy's body was exhausting. She could feel her physical self shaking, growing weak. At last, there was an easing, and the soul and body merged. Toni must be powerful indeed, Frannie thought, to have done all she did with the Delta in the short time she had it.

Wearily, Frannie reached for Saul's sky-blue soul. She held it gingerly— something about it felt fragile, and she mistrusted it. She turned to put it back in his body.

It would not go.

She tried again, harder this time. She felt the star start to burn under her fingertips. The soul would not return to the body.

Saul, come on! She cried. Take it, you have to take it! What's happening, what's wrong?

He's dead, dummkopf. It was his fate to die here. Guoral.

The too-familiar voice echoed in the void.

...Emmett?

You called on me, und zo who do you think, it is the Easter bunny?

The voice of Emmett the Golem, dark with sardonic hues, made a slow circle about her.

Emmett, help me! Help me get Saul's soul back into his body, please, PLEASE Emmett!

The voice sighed heavily.

Mortals do not learn. Control is an illusion.

All is vanity, I know, Emmett. PLEASE.

She knows, she says! Yet she puts souls where they don't belong, casts curses where they should not fall.

The voice scoffed, and she felt herself growing weaker, dimmer. She clutched the blue star, the pain of its fire keeping her present. After a moment, the voice returned.

There are consequences, you know. Not small ones. No skinned knees anymore. Now there is life, and not life.

She knew she was crying. She could feel the tears on her own face. Her grip on the Delta was slipping, as was her grip on consciousness.

please

There was a pause. She could feel it considering.

It was his fate to die.

But maybe nowhere is it written... that he must stay dead.

The fire faded from her hand, and she wept.

He died. He did his job. You have done too much.

She was falling away, falling far away from the voice of the Golem.

All the knowledge of eternity have I.
She was winking out like an ember.
But still, I do not know what to do with you.
Everything was silence.

CHAPTER 33

THE LAGUNA LOCAL

Guest Professor Comatose After Break-In

Local Gang Responsible— Report

In a scene officers could only describe as 'ghastly' and 'disturbing,' Professor Toni Sutcliffe— guest lecturer in the University Summer Series— was found unresponsive but alive after a gang broke into her penthouse suite at the Riviera Hotel Saturday night. Several other bodies were located at the scene, deceased. Identities of the deceased and their role in the break-in have not yet been disclosed to the Laguna Local. Detective Matthew 'Mutt' Winters refused to comment. Prof. Sutcliffe has been moved to St. Andrews Memorial Hospital near the University for observation. There is no clear prognosis for her recovery at this time.

Hooky folded the paper and tucked it into the small cabinet Kurt had built into his chest, closing the door and fastening the latch. Visiting hours would be over soon. He decided he liked hospitals. No one gave him a sideways glance, wrapped as he was in bandages, and several pretty young candy stripers had offered him coffee and the odd chocolate. He was sad to refuse—he missed the taste of coffee—but the feeling of being welcome somewhere that people bustled around was at least as comforting as any cup of joe would have been. He watched the people go by contentedly, as the clock drew down to 6 P.M.

"And you remembered to reach out to Samara to restock the Danishes, yes?" said Saul thinly, taking another shallow sip of tepid water. Mein Gott but he hated hospitals.

"The Danish case is fine, if the Danes themselves came in and demanded Danishes we could feed a lot of Danishes to Danes," Frannie chirped. The humor was brittle at best, but it was all she could do.

"Good, good," murmured Saul, putting the cup down.

They had chatted this way for half an hour, dancing slowly around the elephant in the room, like clowns at a circus trying to out-do each other. A glance at the clock warned them both that time for the day was running out.

"The doctor says you're looking swell," she said, tucking the counterpane under his arms. "Maybe another two weeks and we can spring you from this joint, eh?"

"It'll be under a week, I promise you, or I'll go mad for real."

"We'll see how you're doing."

There it was, the opening he was waiting for.

"When are you going to tell me how you're doing?"

Frannie flinched. Three days had not been enough time to put herself back together after the events of the past week. Three weeks might not be enough time. Who knows if she would be over it in three years.

"I'm fine. Newp and the girls mostly run the café, I'm not allowed to help much beyond wiping the odd malt glass yet. Kurt's orders. He's quite something, now that he's in charge."

Saul nodded. He knew exactly what she meant. He almost felt bad for Newp.

"And the Delta?"

"One half is locked in a dybbuk box in the back left corner of the freezer."

"Classic. And the other?"

"Kurt made a little lockable cabinet for Hooky where that hole in his chest was. He stores stuff in it. The other half is in there, so it's always moving. Sutcliffe is still out there."

He grinned "Brilliant. That'll do. For now."

"Kurt already called Magda."

Saul groaned, and Frannie leapt up, ready to hit the call button. He waved her back down limply.

"Damn it. He's not wrong. It's just an aggravation. Maybe I'll just stay here in the hospital until she's gone..."

A smile ghosted around Frannie's face. "That bad, huh?"

"You'll understand later, I'm sure."

The clock ticked. The weight on her heart grew heavier.

"Uncle Saul? Remember when you said cursing maybe worked on normal people, but it was black magic?"

"Yes, I do recall."

"I cu-cursed—" she struggled and cleared her throat. "I cursed Eric, that night, at the café. I think...I think I'm the reason he's dead."

"What? What did you curse him with?"

She told him, and he paled a bit, but nodded.

"Nab him, stab him, slab him, is that what you think?"

She nodded silently, tears rolling down her face.

"I'm sorry, sweetheart. Maybe it's possible you did do that. But it's also possible you didn't, and that was his fate all along. You're never going to know, so you gotta make a peace with that as best you can."

"Emmett said there are consequences now, life and death."

"He's right, there are. That's what it means to be a grown up. That's why I've done my best not to mature too much, who needs the responsibility?"

"Saul, I'm serious."

"So am I. I wanted to protect you from all this—and that was selfish, I know. This is heavy stuff kiddo. I thought it was too heavy for you. What I should have been doing is training you up for it. Forgive a foolish old man, please?"

She nodded tearfully. The clock began to chime the hour, and an officious voice on the intercom announced that visiting hours were coming to a close.

"Anything else?"

"I showed Toni a Blank. I know you told me not to, and I'm so sorry, and it—"

"It Burned the Book?"

She blinked. "Y-yeah."

He nodded. "Same thing happened when I looked in the Blank. She decided her path long ago, and where it would take her. The Blank had no potential to show her, so it burned. My path led me to my untimely demise, as you witnessed earlier."

She was confused. "But here you are. Alive."

Saul shrugged and grinned as a nurse came to shoo Frannie out.

"Call it a sequel!"

Hooky was waiting on a bench at the end of the hall when Frannie joined him. He had said his hellos and well wishes to Saul earlier, and then excused himself when it was clear his presence was impeding the important conversations. They walked slowly—it was easy to pretend that Hooky was a patient and Frannie was his minder. She stopped them for a moment next to the room of Toni Sutcliffe, who was in a deep coma that had everyone baffled. She took a deep breath and let it out shakily.

"Is there something you wanted to show me, Angel?"

"This is a common ward," Frannie said.

"You seem to know your way around here."

"Yeah, I'm going to start helping out around the hospital while I figure out nursing school. I've decided."

Hooky nodded and made to keep walking. She stopped him.

Frannie went on, "There was something that Toni said about all the good that she did in the South Pacific. I think before she went bad, she was really on to something. So... There's an army ROTC program for recent graduates. I can start nurse training here, and then when I graduate, I join up... And I patch people up."

Hooky nodded. "I knew a lot of nurses."

"I'll bet you did."

The wooden man laughed. "It wasn't like that. I mean, it wasn't always like that. You'll give 'em all a run for their money, though."

They walked a bit further, her grip tightening on his arm as they did. She stopped by a different glass window, a different room. Frannie gestured with her head towards the patient inside. A young man of about twenty years old lay in a hospital bed. He was very thin, with sunken eyes and an oxygen mask on his face. Curly, dark brown hair lay over his forehead.

Catscratch.

"This is Reggie Tomlin," Frannie said. "We call him Catscratch. He is—was—a Legionnaire. They think he's brain dead. They think he'll never wake up."

"Frannie..."

"No, let me finish." Frannie patted the air with her hands. "Hooky, you can do a lot of good. And you know that I could do this. Toni was wrong, she did it the wrong way, but this...Catscratch went down a hero. And you're a hero. Together you could keep fighting. You could have a body and he would get to have the rest of his life, in a way."

"No, Frannie," Hooky said, grabbing her arm. "That guy in there has potential. Stealing potentiality, that's the thing that the Book Man did. Stealing what people could become. They only think he'll never wake up, but there's potential that he will."

She shook her head seriously. "He won't. Or at least, he might not in time. Catscratch—" her voice broke, but she soldiered on. "Catscratch is alone. No family. What's the hospital going to do, keep him forever? Someone is going to make a decision about what to...do with him. We can save him from that."

She looked up at him, eyes pleading. "Will you think about it?"

"I won't."

"Just tell me you will. Don't answer me right now. I just want you to think about it." He started to walk away, and she put her hand back on his arm. "Hooky, please."

"I love you, Angel. I do. In whatever way that means anything between people. But just the fact that you asked me that tells me I'm making the right decision."

"What decision? Hooky, what decision?"

He wrapped her briefly in a hug, and then tousled her hair. "I'll tell you in the morning, I promise. Come on, I've got food to cook, and you've got plates to sling. Hopefully the café is quiet tonight, Kurt gets real sassy when it's busy."

The night went quietly by. Newp manned the bar, and he and Frannie held an uneasy truce between them. She had to resist flinching every time she saw him, as nearly every inch of his face and neck and shoulders were mottled with grey-yellow-green bruises. Kurt, arm in a cast and sling, shouted orders and harried the girls along like a mother hen. Only Betty and Truly seemed content, holding hands beneath the counter when the work was slow, and leaning on each other's shoulder for comfort. She envied them.

The next morning, she woke up early because she heard the doorbell ring. She went down and her mother was already there bustling towards the front door.

"Who could be ringing the doorbell at 6:00 AM," Sally said scowling a little. She bent down, picking up a card that was laying there. She turned around and handed it to Frannie.

Frannie read the card and immediately got on her bike and headed for the beach.

Angel—

You won't want to hear this, but you need to. You and Sutcliffe have a lot in common. You say this all started because she wanted to save people—so do you. She's smart, and resourceful, and powerful—so are you.

She will never stop.

Neither will you.

So, I have to go. You don't need to worry about me. I'm taking the Delta half—it'll be a lot harder for her to hit a thinking, moving, never-sleeping target. Think of it like a heart for the Tin Man. And who knows, maybe I'll get to do some good.

Gotta go. Waves to catch. You should catch some too.

I'll see you later.

—Hooky

The sun was barely up and shining on the waves. Go-Go's shaping stand wasn't up yet, but Hooky's hut lay open to the morning breeze, the cloth door flapping in the wind. She looked into it. Everything was there except for the photograph of Gracie Allen. Frannie turned around and ran towards the surf.

That was when she saw him.

Kurt's sailboat was moving out to sea; at the mast a wooden man, sailing into the west.

CASTLE BRIDGE MEDIA RECOMMENDS...

If you liked *Dark of the Curl*, you might also enjoy reading the following titles from Castle Bridge Media available on Amazon or by order at your favorite book store:

Austinites
By In Churl Yo

Bloodsucker City
By Jim Towns

THE CASTLE OF HORROR
ANTHOLOGY SERIES
Volume 1
Volume 2: Holiday Horrors
Volume 3: Scary Summer Stories
Volume 4: Women Running From Houses
Volume 5: Thinly Veiled: The 70s
Volume 6: Femme Fatales*
Volume 7: Love Gone Wrong
Volume 8: Thinly Veiled: The 80s
Edited By Jason Henderson and
In Churl Yo
*Edited By P.J. Hoover

Castle of Horror Podcast
Book of Great Horror:
Our Favorites, Top Tens
and Bizarre Pleasures
Edited By Jason Henderson

Dream State
By Martin Ott

FuturePast Sci-Fi Anthology
Edited by In Churl Yo

Isonation
By In Churl Yo

MID-LIFE CRISIS THRILLERS
18 Miles From Town
By Jason Henderson

THE PATH
The Blue-Spangled Blue
By David Bowles
The Deepest Green
By David Bowles

SURF MYSTIC
Night of the Book Man
By Peyton Douglas

Nightwalkers: Gothic Horror Movies
By Bruce Lanier Wright

Yesterday's Tomorrows:
The Golden Age of Science Fiction
Movie Posters
By Bruce Lanier Wright

Please remember to leave us your reviews on Amazon and Goodreads!

THANK YOU FOR SUPPORTING INDEPENDENT PUBLISHERS AND AUTHORS!
castlebridgemedia.com

www.ingramcontent.com/pod-product-compliance
Lightning Source LLC
Chambersburg PA
CBHW020310200626
46814CB00006BA/2184